THE ILLUMINATIONS

ALSO BY ANDREW O'HAGAN

The Illuminations

ANDREW O'HAGAN

FARRAR, STRAUS AND GIROUX

NEW YORK

O'Hagan

Farrar, Straus and Giroux
18 West 18th Street, New York 10011

Library of Congress Control Number: 2014957896
ISBN: 978-0-374-17456-9

Farrar, Straus and Giroux books may be purchased for educational, business, or promotional use. For information on bulk purchases, please contact the Macmillan Corporate and Premium Sales Department at 1-800-221-7945, extension 5442, or write to specialmarkets@macmillan.com.

www.fsgbooks.com
www.twitter.com/fsgbooks • www.facebook.com/fsgbooks

1   3   5   7   9   10   8   6   4   2

TO KARL MILLER

'Photography takes an instant out of time, altering life by holding it still.'

DOROTHEA LANGE

Author's Note

The author thanks Abdul Aziz Froutan and colleagues in Afghanistan, as well as members of the Royal Irish Regiment, who have been answering his questions since he began *The Illuminations* in 2010. Thanks also to Yaddo, and to Mary O'Connor and the keepers of the Joseph Mulholland Archive at McMaster University in Hamilton, Ontario, where he studied the papers of the photographer Margaret Watkins.

I

NEIGHBOURS

Snow was falling past the window and in her sleep she pictured a small girl and her father in a railway carriage. The train passed into Ayrshire and the girl looked at nothing over the fields, losing herself in a sense of winter and the smell of soap on her father's hands. *It's cold, Mog.* He carried a light for her all his life and proved she was easy to love. Maureen opened her eyes and found that sixty years had gone by in an instant. Snowflakes poured from the street lamp like sparks from a bonfire. The night was empty and there wasn't a sound in the flat except for the echo of yesterday's talk shows.

This weather would put years on you. The sentence ran through her mind and then she wiped her eyes. Things are slow at that hour and you can easily miss a knock at the door or someone calling your name. Her memory had taken her to another place, where snow blew around a vanished train, and now she was home in her own warm bed and already tense for the day's share of things sent to try her. Her thoughts came out at night like mice and the old scratching woke her up.

How hard can it be to stop what you're doing for five minutes and dial your mother's number? I could be lying dead, thought Maureen. You give them the best years of your life and then you get the sob stories, the hard-done-to stuff, as if you hadn't given them everything under the sun.

She moved the pillows up. They have short memories. No she didn't take them to art galleries and no she didn't sit down with the homework. She was too busy putting a meal on the table. Short memories, she thought again, looking to the window. Someday she would write something down on paper from her heart, just to tell the truth. Her father often said it was good to write a letter because it's something people can keep. They can look at it again and think about what they did. And they can write back and say sorry because they think the world of you.

It wasn't even five in the morning. She reached for the clock and knocked over a pile of audiobooks. 'Some people have too many friends to be a good friend to anyone,' she said. Then the sound registered, a knock at the door. She swung her legs and waited to hear it again, then she was up, putting on a cardigan and turning on the lamps. Maureen told herself the roads would be bad unless the lorries were out with the salt. She couldn't find her carpet slippers and she kept the door-chain on.

'It's you, Anne.'

Anne was her neighbour, eighty-two, and a bad sleeper. She had taken to wandering the corridors at night. Her neighbours often saw her shadow passing their glass doors, but they were used to upsets. It was a sheltered housing complex and none of the residents was young. The flats had front doors onto the street but the other doors, glass ones, led to a common area made up of a breakfast room, a reception, a launderette.

'It's me, Maureen. I'm so sorry.'

Maureen undid the chain. Anne was fully dressed, biting her lip. The ferns behind her made it look as if she had just walked in from the woods. But Anne always looked like she'd seen the world. She had beautiful skin. And her skirts were always made of the best.

'Good God,' Maureen said. 'You're like somebody dressed for a summer dance. Come away in.'

'I won't come in.'

'What's wrong?'

'Can I borrow your tin opener?'

Anne was holding a tin of Heinz tomato soup. It didn't do to argue with her at a time like this, so Maureen went off to find her slippers. When she came back Anne was in the middle of saying something about how she loved Blackpool and how the Illuminations were the best thing about it, the night when they turned on all the lights. She wanted to see it again. She put her arms across her chest and tapped rapidly at her own shoulder. Maureen had seen that before.

'Come on, then,' she said.

Anne's flat was like a palace. Maureen loved the story it told, not that she knew it, but a person with taste always has a story. Once they were inside, Anne walked to the microwave and turned round. 'The rabbit wants his dinner,' she said. 'He's not had a thing all day.'

'Who?'

'The rabbit.'

Anne nodded towards the breakfast bar. The rabbit was ceramic, about six inches tall with green eyes and crumbs of bread at its feet. Maureen noticed the snow falling past the window in the living-room. The rabbit looked creepy. 'Now, Anne,' she said, 'we need to make sure we're not telling stories.'

'I know it's daft,' Anne said. 'But it's okay. He's only sitting and it's cold outside.'

'But, Anne . . .'

'He's awful hungry.'

Anne's mind opened onto itself. She thought of water for a second and the warm baths she used to draw. *Children don't like it too warm. The same as a photographic solution in fact, one hundred and twenty-five degrees Fahrenheit. That's what you want. Let the chemicals dissolve in the listed order and make sure it's not too hot or the solution can't take it and the image will be blurred.*

Maureen looked into the rabbit's eyes.

'This is his favourite,' Anne said. 'Soup is all he ever wants for his dinner.' Then she wiped the tin with a damp cloth and handed it to Maureen. 'Some of these things have a ring you can pull, but this one doesn't for some reason.'

BLACKPOOL

In a photograph pinned above the kettle, the face of George Formby was peeking round a door. 'Turned out nice again!' it said in ink under his name, a curly signature. He was smiling for the whole of Britain. The electricity sockets were covered over with Elastoplast, and the rings on the cooker were out of bounds, too, taped over with a saltire of white plastic tape. Maureen thought it was like the stuff the police put up around the murder scene in those crime dramas. No hot kettles or rings. It was Jackie the warden's decision, and it was made, Maureen knew, in consultation with Social Services. They were sorry but Anne just couldn't operate these electrical goods because she might burn herself. Maureen warmed the soup and Anne stood back ready to say something. 'I'd like to take him to Blackpool, by the sea, by the sea, by the beautiful sea,' she said, half-singing. 'I always thought I would end up there.'

Anne was fine most days, but she was changing. The rules at Lochranza Court stated clearly that any resident incapable of working a kettle would have to be moved to a nursing home. Nobody wanted that. Every few months it happened to one of the residents, but Anne needed her friends. 'That's right, Maureen,' said Jackie. Anne added somehow to the dignity of the place, with her past and her pictures and all her nice cushions. So the warden was in cahoots with Maureen, at sixty-eight the youngest resident in the complex. They pretended it was still fine for Anne to be in the flat by herself, but she wasn't able to use the kitchen. The microwave was okay.

Maureen was looking at the rabbit again.

'Once upon a time, I used to go to restaurants,' Anne said. 'Fancy ones. In New York. Now it's "ping" this and "ping" that. The cooker doesn't work. And the rabbit doesn't like his soup cold.'

'How do you know that, Anne?'

'Well, it's me that lives with him.'

Anne used to read lots of books. Somebody said she was a well-known photographer years ago and Maureen could believe it. You knew by the way Anne arranged her lamps – and by the lamps themselves, the beautiful shades – that she had travelled. She had the kind of rugs you can't buy in Saltcoats. You just don't see rugs like that. And what a lovely radio she had by the sofa next to all those paperweights showing Blackpool in the old days. When Maureen visited the flat next door she always went round looking at the faces of the people in the framed photographs. She loved seeing them caught in the middle of their interesting lives. That was a thing. People who didn't know Maureen immediately had her respect, as if not knowing her was part of their achievement.

[7]

Anne talked about him with the kind of deference that keeps its own counsel against the living. There was nobody wiser than Harry. And he did look like a man in charge, peering from holiday snaps taken on the Isle of Arran. They weren't snaps, actually, but carefully taken photographs, developed, printed and framed with love, and they tended to involve the sky or the sea or a beautiful mixture of both. The one hanging over the telephone table showed the Pladda lighthouse at the end of a field of bluebells, and by her bed she had Harry sitting near a loch. He was smoking a pipe and looking down at a model aeroplane in his hands. His smile was a private note to Anne. They might have been hiding out from the world.

'I owe everything to him,' she once said.

'Is that right?'

'My history begins with Harry.' She looked happy to say it.

'That can't be true,' Maureen said. 'What about everything else? Your childhood and your career?'

'It began again with him. That's how it felt.'

Maureen didn't know what she was looking at in the photographs but she was certain they showed contentment. She herself had never been with a man with that kind of patience. The longer she looked at the photographs the more she could tell Harry was a generous person who had wanted to bring out Anne's intelligence. Maureen had seen things like that on television and it was lovely to think about. She looked out the window and imagined the coast was filled with Harry.

He had never lived in Saltcoats. It seemed he had died in the 1970s, but the details were sketchy and Maureen felt it would test

Anne's patience to ask for more information. It didn't matter. It was just nice to know there were men like that in the world. 'This one's my favourite.' Maureen picked up a black-and-white portrait from the 1950s. It showed a man in a short-sleeved shirt sitting at a bar with a bottle of beer in front of him and an empty camera case. A monkey was eating nuts out of his hand. 'Exotic,' Maureen said. The man was young in the picture and so was the Queen in a poster tacked to the wall behind him.

'That's my Harry at his best,' Anne said. 'He was serving with the army in Singapore.'

'But that's an English bottle of beer.'

'It's Singapore, Mrs Ward.'

Maureen knew when to let things go. A full bowl of soup sat between them and Anne stared at it as if she was remembering something important. 'Don't drive tonight,' she said. And when Maureen told her she didn't have a car Anne just looked blank and said, 'That's true.'

It was around New Year that Maureen had first noticed Anne getting mixed up about dates. At Lochranza Court they often saw the onset of dementia, but with Anne it was different because she appeared to be trying to climb out of herself before it was too late. Whatever vessel Anne had sailed in all her life, it began to drift and that was the start of it all. She rolled into a darkness where everything old was suddenly new, and when she returned to the surface her life's materials were bobbing up around her. 'We all have flotsam, Mum,' said Esther on the phone. (Esther was a therapist.) 'No matter how we weight it and sink it to the bottom, it comes loose. And that's what's happening to your nice lady next door.'

Maureen poured the soup away and her neighbour sauntered over to stare at the bright red splashes in the sink. Anne spoke about a book she and her grandson once read. He was doing it at university and she bought a copy. She couldn't remember the book's name but the man in the story was Sergeant Troy and he wore a nice red coat. Maureen washed the bowl and was quietly amazed.

Anne sat on the sofa. She looked at the window, her hands neatly clasped in her lap. 'The rabbit was out there in the cold,' she said. 'He was by himself in the middle of the road.'

'When?'

'At Christmas. The snow was falling. Nice, if you like snow. But rabbits don't.'

'Don't they?'

'No. Not a bit. Or the dark. They don't like the dark. They like to be out playing with the other boys.' Anne said she'd been standing at the window not doing anything, just looking into the road, and she saw the rabbit come from the dark at the top of the shore. 'It came from the bandstand where the Punch and Judy thing used to be.'

'Just there, beside the beach?'

'That's right,' she said. 'And it just hopped up the road. I was watching it. And you know what, Maureen? It stopped and looked at me. Just looked. Then it kept going. Disappeared.'

'Just like that?'

'Just like that through the snow.'

Maureen had finished washing up and she leaned on the breakfast bar with both hands. 'Don't think about it,' she said. 'You had better get some sleep or you'll be shattered tomorrow.'

'But he's all right now. He likes it here.'

Maureen got her friend into bed and closed the blinds. Anne wanted the rabbit on the wicker chair but Maureen said no and got an unhappy look. 'You're not in charge,' Anne said, leaning back. She stared into the corner at a pair of old suitcases and recalled the day one of the cases was sitting on the station platform at Preston. It was a long time ago. It was raining. She stood that afternoon and looked back at the Park Hotel, where she'd just had tea with Harry and he'd told her about his other life. He drove back to Manchester and she waited for the train to Blackpool, her heart racing, the suitcase filled with negligees and film spools.

I've got the flat for good, Harry. And all the beakers are there and the safelights. All the solutions. Paper. Everything we need. It will do as a darkroom but a place to stay as well. It will just be ours. We can spend the night, in the summer.

'Go to sleep, Anne,' Maureen said.

'You're not the boss.'

Before closing the door, Maureen looked at a picture of a handsome young man in uniform that hung above the light-switch. 'That's Luke,' Anne said, her eyes shining.

'He's a fine boy.'

'He's a captain in the British army.'

SALTCOATS

Maureen went out every day to buy milk. On her way to the SPAR she passed the empty boating pond and looked over to Arran; it was nice to be out in the fresh air; the island was clear and romantic, like one of those pictures you could buy for over the sofa. The mountains were covered in snow and the top of Goat-fell looked dangerous, as if the man in the Milk Tray advert was about to come down on his skis. She used to like that man in the black polo-neck who raced down mountains and dived off cliffs to bring the lady a box of chocolates. In the summer, Arran was a totally different place because the hills were brown and cheery and if the sky was blue it seemed the whole island was close enough to touch.

Maureen considered herself the warden's deputy. It wasn't a real job or anything like that but she could help the older ones with their laundry. She watered the plants and went for the milk, tasks that gave her a feeling of usefulness she had missed. When Ian, Esther and Alex were children she seldom had a minute to herself. If she wasn't ironing shirts she was filling in school forms or making beds, or cooking. But people looked after their kids in those days. You put in the work and enjoyed their young years. Not like nowadays when everybody's harassed and the mothers line up at the school gates in their giant jeeps. Her three walked to school. But by the time Esther was fifteen it was all over with the parenting. Finished. And one by one they left the house with their LPs and their T-shirts. That's what happens, Maureen thought. That's how it is. You kill yourself looking after them and then they get up and leave you.

She never imagined she'd end up in a place like Lochranza Court, but it had been six years and she was used to it. Her house in Stobbs Crescent had got too big and then a couple of druggies smashed the patio doors one night and stole her television. She was terrified. In the morning there was broken glass all over the carpet and her ornaments were scattered around the garden and the gate was nearly off its hinges. Maureen remembered looking at all this and seeing that her old life was spoiled. After a few weeks, Esther drove over from Edinburgh to try bringing a bit of calm to the situation. She could see the point of a new house but not an old people's home.

'It's not a home,' Alex said. There was booze on his breath. 'Get a grip, Esther, it's not a home. It's retirement housing.'

'That's right,' Ian said. Esther knew the matter was settled when Ian backed the plan. (Ian worked with computers, as Maureen often liked to remind them. By this she meant he was always likely to be right. 'And he keeps up his annual member- ship at the gym.')

'It's sheltered housing accommodation,' Ian said. 'She'll have a door onto the street, like a normal person. But the other door goes into the complex, where all the people can have breakfast together. There's a warden. It's safe. And there's a tropical plants area.'

'People die in there,' Esther said. 'Every day. And she's only sixty-two.'

'What's dying?' Alex said. 'People die every day all the time.'

Ian made a face like he couldn't understand what was wrong with people. 'What?'

'Everybody dies.'

'Not if they look after themselves, they don't.'

'It's a home,' Esther said. 'I've got patients, Ian, and I've seen what happens when they give up. They dwindle. And Mum's prone to depression. She's been closing down her life since we were teenagers. She's gone from marital crisis to infirmity with- out a break in between, and that makes me sad, Ian, because I'd always hoped for a bit of optimism. A bit of hope. Just once to see our mother happy.'

'You know everything,' Ian said. 'Keep that shit for your patients, Esther. She's not asking for gold. She wants to be safe at night and this place is the answer.'

Maureen never heard the details of this argument, but Alex later gave her a few clues and it upset her to think of them not getting on. She didn't want the boys being too hard on Esther just because she was different. Esther had a lot on her mind and she sometimes blamed people, that was her problem, and you have to remember, Maureen noted, that Esther wasn't too happy in her own life, not nearly as happy as she liked to think, and she sometimes took it out on other people. It was only natural. When you had a big job like Esther's, people could expect too much. That's right. Esther was her own worst enemy.

On her way back from the SPAR, hugging the milk, Maureen saw the street lights switching off. In winter it was often dark when she went out and getting light as she returned. She liked the sudden change of atmosphere and the sense of a new day beginning. Only when she went to cross the road to Lochranza Court did Maureen spot the fire-engine and notice that smoke was escaping from an open window. Jackie the warden was standing out in the car park with a clipboard, the elderly residents gathered around in their dressing-gowns.

'Jesus, Mary and Joseph, what's the matter?' Maureen said, putting the milk down on a bench.

'It's Mr MacDonald in 29,' Jackie said. 'Burnt the toast again.'

'Oh dear,' Maureen said.

'Evacuation.'

'Heaven help us,' said Mrs Souter from flat 24. 'Is this what they call an evacuation?'

'It has different meanings,' Jackie said.

Anne was sitting on the bench. There was a suitcase at her feet and a smile on her face. 'It's not that bad,' she said, looking at the sea. 'Beautiful lines over there, don't you think?' Maureen had wandered back to pick up the milk she'd left on the bench. 'It's all nice when you stop and frame it,' Anne went on, 'the people and the horizon and everything. If we wait long enough we'll see the *Waverley* sailing past.'

NATURAL LIGHT

One day Anne asked for an outing and Maureen took it upon herself to see that the trip went well. It was a constant battle in Maureen's head, the wonder of central heating versus the benefit of fresh air, but she was happy to do all the zipping and buttoning required for a walk into town. Ian dropped in on his way to work to change a light-bulb in his mother's airing cupboard. 'What are you up to today?' he asked. 'Going down Shenanigans for a few pints with the biddies?'

'That'll be right,' Maureen said. 'It's too cold to go out. Plus there's nowhere to go.'

'Really? You could go to the pictures. If I wasn't working I'd go to the pictures every day.'

'It's too dear,' she said. 'Plus you have to go to Kilmarnock and all the films are about sex or blowing people up.'

'Awesome,' he said.

'Plus, I am working. That living-room won't vacuum itself and the plants out there are begging for water. Somebody's got to do it and it might as well be me.'

She needed him to think her enjoyments were few and far

between. But after Ian left she went in to help Anne choose a dress and a coat and sensible shoes that would grip. Anne talked about the clothes that once belonged to her aunts who had lived in Glasgow: 'Atholl Gardens. Number 73. I'm talking about a place with fourteen rooms,' Anne said. 'You don't get houses like that nowadays.'

'Was it nice?' asked Maureen.

'I'm talking rheumatism. Varicose veins. And chests of drawers full to overflowing with corsets and what have you.'

'You should wear a cardigan under your coat.'

'There were six floors. The moths had a great time and God knows how many coats they ate.'

'Put your scarf on.'

'A scarf's like a friend, isn't it?'

Maureen smoothed Anne's hair. 'I was always telling them to get rid of stuff,' Anne added. 'But they wouldn't, Maureen. They couldn't bear to get rid of so much as a pair of stockings.'

'Is that right?'

'My father was never out of the church. That was before Glasgow, mind you. In Canada. He was looking for God, up there in the church. My mother didn't keep well. She had the disease that makes you shake. She stayed in her bed and I think she died in that bed.'

'In Canada?'

'That's right. I was young then.'

The rabbit sat on the sofa with a tea towel tied around him and Anne stopped to look over.

'I think we'll leave him behind today,' Maureen said. Anne offered no argument but said again that she had been a child in Canada, something about ice on the road to Dundas.

Anne sometimes looked at things and you felt she was developing a picture in her mind's eye. 'That was the old bathing pond,' she said, measuring the light as they walked into town. 'And I think rock 'n' roll groups used to play there in their suits – the Marine Theatre.'

'Groups? I don't think so.'

'All the girls would scream,' Anne said. After a few more steps, they stopped. 'Don't let me miss the post again today.'

'What?'

'The post. I always send a cheque. Never miss it. They'll be waiting for a cheque in Blackpool.'

This was a mystery to Maureen. She'd heard Anne speak before about people in Blackpool who were waiting for money. She mentioned it on the phone to Anne's daughter, Alice, who just sighed and said she didn't want anything to do with it. It was clearly a part of Anne's life that was off-limits or stuck in the past, but the dementia was bringing it out and Maureen wanted to know more, in case she could help.

'Who, Anne? Who's waiting for a cheque?'

'A nice man and his wife.'

'And who are they?'

'Never mind,' Anne said. 'I'll do it myself.' They walked on and Maureen told herself not to take it personally. It was part of the illness. She could only do what she could do. Anne had her own wee things to contend with and didn't really need the post office.

Alice lived up the coast and Maureen knew it had been a risk to phone her that morning. But she thought Alice might like to drive down and take over after lunch. It was a stressful situation because Anne undervalued her daughter, as Maureen heard said on television, and the daughter had self-esteem issues and the family was dysfunctional. But two wrongs don't make a right and what doesn't kill you makes you stronger. Maureen sometimes heard herself sounding like a wise person on a talk show and it made her feel modern that she understood people's problems. 'I think it's healing the way you always tried to keep in step with your grandson,' she said.

'In step?'

'Yes, with Luke. Before he went into the army.'

'Books,' Anne said. 'He studied literature and it was lovely stuff.'

'You read all those books?'

'Oh, yes. We used to buy them at Dillon's. And we'd discuss them when he came over to visit me.'

'It's a surprise when a boy like that chooses the army.'

'I thought he'd be a somethingologist,' Anne said, 'but men don't always get to be what they want to be.'

On their way down Sidney Street, Maureen told Anne it would do her good to see her daughter. 'She just wants to put me in a home,' Anne said. 'She just wants to get the keys to the flat.'

'That's not true, Anne. They wouldn't give her the keys. Our place isn't for young people.'

Maureen thought it was a true saying: You can choose your friends but you can't choose your family. Anne looped her arm through hers and they stopped in at the newsagent so that Maureen could buy some mints. The magazine rack was full of faces that Maureen knew off the telly and Anne stared past the men's magazines to a shelf stacked to the ceiling with Airfix boxes.

The Candy Bar wasn't busy. Maureen was all smiles, leading Anne by the arm through a group of empty tables. 'We're waiting for a part in *Charlie's Angels*,' she said to the waitress, 'so mind and keep the strawberry tarts away from us today. We're watching the figure.' Maureen peeled off her friend's coat and put the scarf inside the sleeve. She sniffed the scarf before tucking it in, liking the perfume, the essence of Anne. Then she went round to her own side and placed her purse on the table.

'This is my treat. Ian left me a wee tenner this morning so we'll let him buy us our tea.'

Anne was looking at the light coming off the teaspoons. It was a familiar process for her, looking at objects and the way the light picked them out and changed them. Her mind fell back to when she first met him. He was giving a talk about documentary photography and capturing life on the street. He spoke at the Masons' Hall not far from the tower and his cheeks were flushed as he stood on the stage.

You were a lovely speaker. You had the audience in the palm of your hand for the best part of two hours.

They went for a drink at the Washington Arms that night and he began to tell her a story about himself, a story that never ended. Even after he died the story continued and became something she added to herself. She liked to think of him walking on the promenade with his back to where he was going, looking at her, talking with his hands.

A man called Cotton worked at the Air Ministry. That's right. He got planes off the ground, Spitfires and Blenheims. Your eyes burned naming them. You were never a bad man, Harry. Not really. The planes did photographic intelligence at a height of 30,000 feet. They were the first, the first of their kind you said and I'm saying watch where you're going. You nearly tripped. It seems there was fog and snow over Germany . . .

'Anne, that's the salt, hen. Not the sugar.' Maureen was smiling as if to say that it didn't matter. Anne had ripped the salt sachet instead of the sugar and poured it into her tea.

'It's nae bother,' the girl said and she took the mug away and came back with a fresh one.

'We stopped for ice-cream,' Anne said, remembering Harry. She could see his scarf blowing in the wind. 'There was a jukebox inside and it played the new music.'

Maureen stirred her coffee and then turned her attention to something new. She spoke with a changed expression. 'I'm worried about my three. It's these children they have. They run riot.'

'Grandkids is the good bit,' Anne said. 'You can love them but you don't have to take all the blame.'

'And that Kirsty one. Ian's wife. She hired an au pair. An *au pair*, just to look after the child while she goes to the hairdresser. *The hairdresser*. I mean, is it me, Anne? Is it me that's half-daft? Weak. They got that from their father: they can't stand up to these women.'

'Are you divorced, Maureen?'

'Oh, years ago. He's dead, to me anyhow. Lives in Stirling with someone. I don't want to know. They can't pull the wool over my eyes.'

'You like being upset, don't you?' Anne said. The question came innocently and Maureen thought it was part of her illness.

'Families,' she replied. 'They take it out of you. If I won the lottery I think I'd just go and lose myself in Spain. To hell with the lot of them. They could come and find me.'

'Harry flew planes during the war,' Anne said. 'His were called Lysanders.'

'Is that right?'

'They flew in secret out of a place in Devon. All hush-hush. That's how he learned his trade, going into Germany and France during the night to take pictures of factories and docks. They got medals because every night they put their lives at risk, eh? That was Harry.'

'That's something to be proud of, Anne.'

'I think it was hard for those men to live with what they'd done. Keeping it secret all the time.' Anne said it softly.

'Are you all right, Anne?'

She drew a deep breath and made a motion with her hand. 'There used to be a lovely gypsy in Blackpool who could tell your future.'

It was amazing to talk to Anne. She had all these pieces in her life that didn't really fit together, and when she was talkative she said things that made you think her life had been quite complete. Yet everybody has their problems. Maureen didn't know what the trouble in Anne's family was all about but she knew instinctively how to treat it as important. Alice came into the cafe looking nervous, looking televised, unwinding her beautiful scarf as she walked to the table. She'll be on one of her diets and won't want any cake, thought Maureen.

VIDEO GAMES

Alice's doctor in Troon had said something lasting. He said the thing with dementia was that it trapped the sufferer in vagueness and spoiled the offspring's hopes for a satisfying closure, especially if the relationship had been difficult. Alice had lived with a mother who thought her daughter lacked something, and now, aged fifty, Alice wondered if she couldn't mount one last attempt to change her mind.

The problem was that Alice slightly agreed with her mother's view of her. Anne possessed a little mystery and a good imagination, while Alice had always been a little demon of reality. Even as a teenager Alice could see those traits in herself: first to correct, last to believe, and always resistant when asked to imagine the impossible. She wanted proof that something was valuable, needed evidence beyond the word of some artist, and for years she prided herself on this distrust, as if it was a gift to be so hard to fool. Nowadays, when she looked in the mirror and pouted and shook her hair, she sometimes got a glimpse of the person other people saw, a certain sourness, a gleam of small-mindedness. Alice knew she was better than her demeanour, but it was hard to prove.

She was saying how she'd recently gone to Luke's place in Glasgow. He had one of those modern flats near Central Station, the kind with underground parking, bushes and an intercom. He wasn't there that often because of serving abroad or being down at the barracks in England, but he'd been up for what Alice called 'the Christmas period'. 'He didn't come down to Ayrshire,' she said to her mother, 'unless he came over to see you without telling me.' She shrugged and smiled, looked at Maureen. 'It's always a possibility,' she added.

She went on to say it was more likely he'd been up boozing in the city with his squaddie pals and then returned to Helmand without anyone noticing. Maureen nodded. She felt that was the kind of thing men did, they came and went, never realising how much they were hurting people. Such a sensible-looking young man, too, in his tunic and green beret. 'It hasn't changed in years, that flat,' Alice was saying. 'You should see the mess. He gave me a key but if he thinks I'm going up there to clean for him, he's got another think coming.'

Anne was irritated. She drank her tea. An old sentence ran in her mind whenever Alice was giving one of her speeches. 'She knows the price of everything and the value of nothing.' Luke was like her and not dull or small like his mother. He was someone who loved pictures, shells, and all sorts of things. He loved to fly away. She could recall seeing the start of an artistic temperament in the boy and being delighted. It had spelled out a closeness between them. He once dropped in from school to tell her that Lysander was not only the name of a fighter plane but a Spartan warrior, and it remained with her, the way he smiled, the way he ran into the living-room with his big open eyes.

'He's a cut above the usual kid, my grandson,' she said.

'He might be a cut above,' Alice said, 'but you should see the state of that flat of his.'

Alice didn't go into it, didn't say that when she'd opened the door to her son's flat, she suddenly felt safe. His mail was piled in the hall and she gathered it all up. She put it on the kitchen top next to some empty beer bottles and a book called *Kim*. She went round dusting and she loved loading the dishwasher and making the bed. She boiled the kettle and she enjoyed choosing a cup and placing it on a saucer. She loved cleaning an ashtray and taking it out onto the narrow balcony and smoking a cigarette, looking over to the glass roof of the railway station. Luke was in a desert at that very moment and he was probably shooting a rifle or riding in a tank and she was here, waiting. It wasn't the life she wanted for him. And she was sure that was one of the reasons he wanted it for himself.

'Such a nice flat, but what a mess.' This was what she chose to say to the women. 'It's the same every time I go up. Not just a mess, but a man-mess. I can understand socks and all that. But it's the bottles of beer and the cables – oh my God, the cables.'

When she walked around the flat that day, Alice had worried that maybe her son didn't really know how to live. He was one of those people whose sitting room is full of travel stuff and suit-cases, duty-free bags, washing kits, as if he didn't really live any-where and just wanted to be in transit. Those people are sort of homeless, she thought. They don't know how to belong or how to be at peace with themselves. They live out of bags; they eat on the run. And there's no dignity or order in that kind of life. To not know where the clean towels are kept or that you have cutlery in the drawer; it's no good, she thought, it's a half-life.

'What are the cables for?' Maureen asked.

'Video games,' Alice said. 'Just everywhere. Those handsets, you know. Cables like you wouldn't believe and all these DVDs out of their cases. I think he just gets into Glasgow and goes to the flat and smokes that stuff. The ashtrays are full of it. Hash. And he plays those games, the ones that have soldiers on the cover.'

'Leave Luke alone,' Anne said suddenly. 'He's old enough to look after himself.'

'He's twenty-nine.'

'That's old enough.'

When Anne looked up, ready to scrutinise her daughter, she noticed Alice had some kind of light stuff under her eyes. It's one of those make-up pens that are supposed to take years off your age, thought Anne. One of those concealers you can buy. She'd seen them in magazines and thought it was silly to touch up your pictures.

The younger women made allowances. Maureen inclined her head the way the interviewers did on *The One Show* and created a little moment between her and Alice. 'It must be very frightening for you,' she said, 'knowing Luke's out in that horrible place.'

'You get used to it,' Alice said. 'I went through it all with his father. You just pray the same thing won't happen to him.'

'Did he die, Alice, your man?'

Anne got in quickly. 'His name was Sean Campbell.' She put her hands on the table and began smoothing them.

'That's right, Mum.'

'I'm not daft,' Anne said. 'I know who Sean is.'

Alice pursed her lips. She felt better for not jumping down her mother's throat. Then she lowered her voice in the manner of a considered and patient person. 'My husband Sean was killed in Northern Ireland,' she said. 'He was serving with the Western Fusiliers, the same regiment that Luke is with now, and they were on patrol in Belfast, you know. And there was this place, the Divis Flats, where a bomb went off. There was a primary school just there and it was playtime but the kids weren't out and the bomb went off and it killed Sean.'

'Holy Mother of God,' Maureen said.

'That's right.'

Anne heard what they were saying but she didn't want to hear it and thought instead about the cafes she used to go to with Harry. Oh, the lovely places. She also thought about bombers and things from history that existed for her now as evidence of someone she used to be. When the women at the table paused she looked up. 'Was that 1940?'

'Sorry, Mum?' Alice said.

'The Sean thing.'

'It was 1987,' Alice said. 'Luke was only five.'

'Then she met *somebody else*,' Anne said. She liked to talk about Alice as if she wasn't there. 'Another man.'

'That's not fair, Mum. I didn't go out of the house. Not for ten years, I didn't go out. Luke was at school.'

'You were living in Glasgow?' asked Maureen.

'Glasgow, yes. We lived in Kent Road. It was a wee flat Sean and I bought when we got married.'

'You got a pension, though,' Anne said. She was staring at the crumbs on her plate. 'Somebody always gets the pension.'

'I was a widow with a small boy,' Alice said. 'A widow. My husband was dead and it was —'

'Husband.'

'Yes, Mum. My *husband*, Sean.' She turned back to Maureen and was keen to finish the story. 'I didn't meet Gordon until Luke was settled at university.'

'At Strathclyde?'

'That's right. Luke went to the University of Strathclyde. And the next thing we knew he had applied for army entrance and he passed the exams down south and went to Sandhurst.'

'When was that, Alice?'

'It was 2001. I remember he went in September 2001 because it was just after the thing in New York.'

'It was planes,' Anne said.

'That's right,' said Maureen. 'It was on TV.'

'The Royal Western Fusiliers,' Alice continued. 'You pick the regiment you want during officer training. Sean liked being with the Scots and the Irish, boys from there or the North of England.

[26]

And so does Luke. I can tell you it's not what I wanted for my Luke.'

'The North Pier,' Anne said.

They just ignored her. It was now part of the routine, to assume Anne was now and then speaking to herself.

'Those planes went over Jane Street,' Anne said, lost in her own thoughts. 'That's where I used to live in New York.'

'Mum says she lived in New York,' Alice said. 'When she was a young woman. Before me.'

'Jane Street,' Anne said. 'I took pictures. I took them for J. Walter Thompson. Colgate.'

'Everything was before me,' Alice said. At times she felt that her mother might suffocate her with the past. Yet she went silent, admiring the mix of periods, wondering if her mother's neighbour really had any notion of the places that Anne had been to in her busy life. Sometimes Alice would just be sitting like this and she'd suddenly realise she was in pain, without really knowing where it came from.

JANE STREET

It was a rainy night when Maureen heard tapping through the wall and knew Anne must be up to something. 'It's all slush outside,' she said as she opened the door to Anne's flat. She had used the skeleton key and made a bit of a noise so as not to frighten her when she came in. 'It's all slush. Are you there, dear? Are you all right?'

Anne was sitting in a dining chair. The room was lit with a single lamp. She had a hammer across her knees, a pool of tacks in her lap. 'My mother didn't keep well,' Anne said, turning as Maureen came in. 'She was an awful one for headaches.'

'You came to live with the aunties?'

'That's right. I came to Glasgow to look after them. Aunt Anna. Aunt Grace. Four of them.'

'You came from New York?'

'When I was a young woman,' Anne said, 'I took nice pictures. At night you could see the lights on in every building.'

'That must have been nice.'

'Yes. Before I met Harry.'

'And when exactly did Harry die, Anne?'

She took one of the tacks from her lap and tapped it into the wall in front of her, then she turned. 'The hot summer,' she said. 'All the children were outside in their bikinis and what have you. Squeezy bottles filled with water. Running about in the sun soaking one another.'

'And what happened to your photography?'

'I don't know.'

'All that talent of yours?'

'I don't remember.'

She sat back in the chair and looked at the shadow she'd created with tacks on the living-room wall. The rabbit was on the carpet but it seemed neglected and Anne didn't mention it.

'I brought you some scent,' Maureen said. 'A wee bottle that was sitting in a drawer next door. I won't use it.'

'You always put on too much perfume.'

Maureen could be hurt by some of the things the old people said but she knew they didn't mean it.

'But I don't wear this one,' she said. 'Esther brought it from France but it's too strong for me. I used to like strong ones.' She took it over to Anne and unscrewed the top so Anne could have a sniff.

'France, did you say?'

'Aye.'

'I don't know about France,' Anne said. 'More like the kind of thing they wear in Manchester.'

The winter had given Maureen lessons in patience and they were lessons she felt she probably needed. She and Alice had a conversation on the telephone and agreed that Luke's going off to Afghanistan had seen the beginning of a change in Anne. It was odd. All this Harry stuff and talk about Blackpool. All this about war-planes, about Canada and New York and the old aunts. Anne was fading away and becoming known at the same time and Maureen was there to see it happening. It was fast at first and then slow. That morning Anne was looking at the picture of Luke on the wall of her bedroom and said, 'These are the men I know.'

When Maureen was installing the new perfume in Anne's bathroom she happened to notice two more suitcases and several boxes on top of the linen cupboard. They must have gone with Anne from house to house. Using the towel-rail for assistance, she stood on the toilet seat and reached up to put her hand into one of the boxes. Right at the top, Maureen found a photograph that appeared silvery in the bathroom light. It showed a kitchen sink with old taps and a pair of breakfast bowls waiting to be washed and a milk bottle filled with soapy water. The sink and its contents shone like nothing on earth and Maureen held it out in front of her, trying to imagine the young woman who could make a picture like that.

'Good Lord, Anne,' she said, returning to the living-room. 'I had no idea you kept even more of these old suitcases. They have labels on them, those beautiful old labels you used to get. It says: *Anne Quirk, 12 Jane Street, New York*. That must be you.'

'That was me.'

Maureen's own mother had been self-sufficient at the end and didn't want help, but Anne was different and full of surprises, like the miracle of that photograph, thought Maureen. She helped Anne into bed. She spread the covers and leaned in to put off the lamp.

'I need to send a cheque or a postal order,' Anne said.

'Everything's all right.' Maureen tucked her in and felt glad that she and Anne were the great pals of Lochranza Court. It was lovely to know a person who doesn't want to judge you all the time.

'But it needs to be sent to Blackpool,' Anne said. 'They have two daughters and one's called Sheila.'

'Who are these people, Anne? Can I help you?'

'They're my friends. She's the landlady.'

She enjoyed looking at Maureen's face, how it became lively when things were upsetting, how she always had something to say. Maybe Maureen was a shopkeeper, the way she came to her room with soup and milk. And maybe she could help her send the money to Blackpool.

Don't forget the Scotch tape, Harry. And if I were you I would get some cotton wool. Bert phoned and said there's an editor who wants the youth of today. That's what they're looking for. I was out half the night at the cafes and these pictures, Harry, you'll like one or two, I'm sure you will. These teenagers. You wouldn't believe them. On Saturday I'm photographing a group at the Fleetwood Marine.

Maureen stroked her hand. 'Away to sleep,' she said. 'There'll be another day tomorrow, if God spares us.'

[30]

'Harry said he would come.'

'Away to sleep.'

Maureen wandered back to her own flat. It must be good to know that your husband was something in the world and that he loved you. Must give you a good feeling, Harry saying your name as he flew over the fields and saying your name when he lay down beside you at night.

2

2M2H

Early one morning in the summer of that year a troop carrier roared past a melon stall on the road to Maiwand. Inside the vehicle the boys were ribbing each other, the boys of A Section, a pair of fire teams in the 1st Royal Western Fusiliers. It wasn't strictly an Irish regiment but it had always attracted boys with a sense of Ireland behind them, a number of songs or a father who swore by an old decision.

The cab shook and you could taste the dust. The lads were jammed in the middle of the convoy. Captain Luke Campbell was in charge of the section and he sat in the Vector with his rifle flat across his knees. He was talking about the Afghan servicemen they were meant to be looking after during the mission. 'The nobs can blab all they like,' Luke said. 'There are ANA troops I'd choose over half the Paras.'

'Too right,' Private Dooley said.

'No messin',' Flannigan said. 'I'd take the ragamuffins every time over the Plonkers.'

Luke screwed up his face. 'But we're not training the Plonkers, much as they fucken need it. We're training the Fundies. Keep it clear in your heads: we're the Operational Mentor Liaison Team.'

'We're their Sandhurst,' Dooley said.

'Whatever, Doosh.'

They rode along and the air got hotter. Private Lennox had

been up top for two hours with sand smacking him in the face and he was melting when he came down. They passed another stall. The boys' tongues were hanging out for a cold drink but the boss said they couldn't stop because every local fucker was probably a roadside bomb. 'Best fucken army training in the world,' he said, 'and you crows are still unconvinced that water is better for you than cans of Fanta.' Private Flannigan of fire team Delta saw on the gauge that it was fifty degrees inside the Vector and he clocked that Lennox had nearly passed out when he dropped down. The boys from Charlie team pulled off his armour and fanned him and pumped him full of water. Flannigan cleaned his face with a wet wipe and grinned. 'You're fucken burning up, our kid.'

Private Dooley removed the boy's helmet. 'I'll just hop off the bus and get him a Ribena,' he said.

'Shut up, Dooley,' Flannigan said. 'It's the South Armagh of Afghanistan out there, nothing but Terry Taliban waiting behind the wall to chop your balls off and send them back to your mammy.'

'Bring it on, bitch,' said Private Dooley, a big, smiling boy of eighteen with fleshy lips and a bent ear. Nothing surprised him. They all cheered and Lennox sat up. 'He's back!' Dooley said.

'You were fucken babblin', man. The heat got to you.'

'What's the difference?' Flannigan said. 'That's the way he always talks. A thick gypsy from Belfast, eh?'

'Shut your face,' Lennox said; then Flannigan reached inside his tunic and took out a Lambert & Butler, passing the cigarette to Lennox as the vehicle jolted and went on. It had been Lennox's first tour the year before and Flannigan looked after him when they were pinned down together during a battle on the Pharmacy Road in Sangin. The boys in this section were close and they all knew it. And the soldiers in the rest of the platoon, travelling behind, they knew it, too. The boys in A Section had their own language and said whatever they wanted.

'What you got a thigh-holster for, man?' asked Flannigan. He was from Liverpool and never got tired of mocking.

Dooley looked like he'd barely started to shave. His green eyes were bright and he used a lot of words, some of them wrong.

'Shut yer face,' he said. 'This gear is highly appropriated.'

'You mean "appropriate",' Luke said. 'Get some more water inside you, Lennox. You're dehydrated.'

Lennox's red face was shining with sweat. 'Have you seen Dooley's thigh-holster, sir?'

'You were out for the count a minute ago,' Luke said. 'Spark out. Couldn't take the pace.'

The boys laughed and Luke smiled and turned away. 'You just keep saving up for your big fat gypsy wedding,' he said to Dooley.

'Harsh,' Dooley said. Then Luke studied the map. The boys loved it when the captain joined in: it made them feel lucky, grown-up, selected. 'I've been thinking of inventing a new thing for the wedding,' Dooley added. 'Worst man. Like the opposite of best man. I was thinking of asking Lennox: he's definitely first choice. He could make a speech proving he's the biggest gobshite ever to leave the Falls Road.'

'Your talk makes me proud of my regiment,' Luke said.

'Thank you, sir. *Veritas vos liberabit*.'

'Oh, Jesus.'

'Regimental motto,' Flannigan said.

'Onwards the 1st Royal Western,' Dooley said to himself, looking down at their boots smeared in dirt. 'The truth will set you free.'

Luke was always telling Major Scullion that his boys were the salt of the British army. Especially 5 Platoon. They were full of shite, he said, and they talked non-stop, but when it came to fighting, these men were the bomb. Luke was a full ten years older than most of the platoon and had spent a lot of time with them at Camp Bastion and in Salisbury. The boys recognised Luke was a bit of a thinker but he wasn't the careerist kind of officer. They never said it to his face, but they knew, they all knew, that his father had been a captain in the regiment and had died in Northern Ireland.

Sergeant Sean Docherty was driving the vehicle behind, carrying a group of men from the Afghan National Army. Docherty was quiet, thought Luke, a self-made officer who missed his wife and steadily avoided most of the banter around him. Luke was always conscious of the men, checking their positions, ensuring they were ready, and for him they constituted an unconscious world of faith and necessity. You go to sleep knowing these men might be the last thing between you and the shit. They stand up for you. They think your thoughts. They need what you need. He loved the banter and the way the banter brought the boys together. But he felt worried on the road to Maiwand that they were jumpy in advance of the mission. They weren't coping well with the heat and their brains were soft from months spent doing nothing, killing some imagined enemy onscreen, posting rubbish on YouTube, or lying under mosquito nets thinking hard about the car they'd buy if they ever got home.

The convoy stopped on Highway 1 and some of the ordnance blokes got out to check for roadside bombs. 'That's fine,' Luke said to the three soldiers in the Vector, 'you can get down. We've got half an hour. Try not to shit your pants. Eat the oranges but not too many. This is Terry bandit country and we're camping right in the middle of their spawn-point here, waiting for them to drop on us.'

'2M2H?' Dooley said.

'No, Doosh. Not too much to handle. Don't be a prick. I just don't fancy my crack platoon getting wiped while sitting on their skinny wee arses eating tropical fruit. Keep your peepers open and do what the captain says, there's a good lad.'

'Roger that.'

The Royal Engineers had work to do on some of the convoy's vehicles and the search for roadside bombs took longer than they thought, so they were stuck. Luke radioed to Sean in the vehicle behind, telling him to ask the ANA soldiers who knew the terrain if they had any clues about where the bombs might be. 'They should do,' said Sean's crackling voice. 'They probably planted half of them.'

LIGHTWEIGHT

Sitting against the trucks, shirts round their necks, the boys had smokes going. It was way too hot. 'If you don't know the difference between Death Metal and Thrash Metal,' Lennox said, 'you may as well just get out your fucken assault weapon and start blowing your tiny brains all over the fucken desert.'

'He reasoned,' Luke said.

'I mean it, bitches. I can't believe I'm turtling here in the sand with a bunch of fucken newbs with a low-ping connection to the universe – Dooley, Flange, look at the nick of them – and it's Game On in this shithole and these fucken 'tards think that "The

Punishment Due" by Megadeth is an example of Thrash Metal. Cop on, bell-ends. Go up the front there and sell that shit to the Gobblers.'

'What's the Gobblers?' Dooley asked.

'The Grenadier Guards,' Luke said.

'Awesome. It's all Royal Engineers up there,' Dooley said.

'The Chunkies,' Lennox said. 'A corps of Bennies up there with a single fucken standard grade and a metal ruler between them, pumping up tyres and thinking they're God.'

'Fuck them all, man. We got the battle honours.'

'Fucken right,' Flannigan said, leaning on the cabin door and closing his eyes. 'But we're the ones sitting here for hours going red pigs . . .'

'Hot, man.'

'Like boiling,' Flannigan said. 'And the cocknoshes up there, man, the fucken Chunkies, giving it fuck-o-nometry with some cunting Rupert from Bastion nodding all impressed like and we're sitting up here getting Kit-Kat arse in the sun.'

'Some officers are dicks and they'll always be dicks,' Lennox said. 'Not you, Captain.'

'Steady,' Luke said.

'Jesus,' Dooley whispered. 'I wish something would happen. I want to be all over this map. I want a whole lot of kills and then I don't give a fuck what happens. They can take me home.' His voice had gone down a level with the heat and he swigged water from a plastic bottle and then threw the bottle into the road among the rocks.

'I don't care what anybody says,' Lennox said. 'Megadeth is not Thrash Metal. It's Death Metal, so it is.'

'The guitars are gunning, man. It's Thrash.'

'Bollocks, it is.'

'They practically invented Thrash. Them and Metallica.' Lennox began poking himself in the chest. 'I'm telling you, man. I was into them before any other kid at St Gerard's.'

'Cop on, Lennox, you daft bitch. Get real. You were about two when *Countdown to Extinction* came out.'

Lennox pondered this. 'I was definitely listening to *Youthanasia* when I was in primary school, so I was.'

So the conversation went, all day, half the night, between joints and scran, boredom and mortars. The time to start worrying on a mission, Luke always said, is when the boys are being too nice to one another. And in a firefight, you only panic when the boys go silent.

He smiled and walked off the road. He could see the wavering line of the horizon and everything in the distance looked like a form of sunstroke. There was a mud house by an irrigation ditch, a smell of shit and rotten hay, a man in a pink turban strolling with his goats. Out there, the ragged mountains appeared like a video still, not reality but a screen-grab. The whole scene looked parched and ruined. A clear picture came into Luke's mind of a fresher landscape, Loch Lomond in the black-and-white summer of an old photograph at his grandmother's. He could almost taste a pint of lager, and taste Anne's art. He didn't think that any of his Helmand images would end up in a frame.

There was heat inside the heat. Sweat ran down the back of his neck and between his shoulder blades. Luke hated the hours it took to dig out land-mines and the wait for incoming fire. Scullion said the mission would be the biggest logistical task of the war. Two hundred vehicles and a shitload of grunts desperate as fuck to get out there and banjo the Taliban. Luke felt weak. Just as there was heat inside the heat, there was weakness inside his weakness. Everything is dense with itself out there; everything is thick with its own crazed lack of known limits. Things could escalate. You could sense it in your nerves and feel it on your skin.

Jesus, the boys were mad for action. They were mad for wild-eyed bogeymen covered in rags, for teams of degenerates to appear on the horizon wearing beards and mucky sandals, pouring through the heat wave with their sabres held high. By late August the men in the platoon were chin-strapped and breathing through their arses. They needed a story to tell and they needed pictures. They longed for something they would hate the moment it arrived. But they wanted it and their want appeared to seep into the deadly hot distances that surrounded them.

'Jesus,' Luke said. They'd given up on the famous victory long ago and now they gave a toss for nothing but the regiment. To everybody it was a cluster fuck where nobody wins.

'Mad out here,' he said quietly.

Luke walked a dozen yards away from the convoy. The horizon was a bundle of grey and brown garments, a heap of old linen, surely not stones and mountains. The distance seemed to come and go in the heat, it appeared to liquefy before him and he felt lost on the empty map with the troops and vehicles ranged at his back. At Bastion he'd told the boys to write their last letters. A quick note just in case. Two seconds. They wrote them while waiting for their turn on Xbox.

It began early on that first day. It began with the melting horizon and the threat of forces lying outside his vision. He felt the Kajaki operation was cursed and he wanted to be out of there. He felt the pressure of his younger self, the one who missed his father, the boy in touch with beautiful ideas. Back then, Luke often walked through Kelvingrove Park in Glasgow to spend the day with his gran. Anne was a woman who lived quietly and knew how to disappear into her own experience. He could still see her standing near the window with a magnifying glass and an old catalogue, sitting him down to explain things. Even when speaking to a boy she spoke as a person not only ready to invest in you but ready to bear the costs to the end. In Helmand, he already understood that Anne was now ill, and, thinking of her, he realised her quest had long since become part of who he was himself. It was inside him. He didn't yet know what her quest was, but he had never forgotten that by going round galleries with him and talking about books, Anne had given him the world not as it was but as it might be. He could see himself as a boy on her sofa with a large seashell clamped to his ear. He felt he needed her more than ever, he wanted her close, the person who once revealed to him a world beyond the obvious. He recalled the time she took him to Dunure Harbour. He was twelve years old and they stood holding hands on the jetty, the wind pushing them back as they took great gulps of air. 'Breathe, Luke!' she said. 'You can't argue with that! Fresh wind off the sea. Oh my. I wish I could catch it with the camera.'

It all felt different now, the ethos, the habits, the taste he and his fellow soldiers had developed for a high kill ratio. Out there, staring into the mountains, it occurred to him that he had travelled far from his old resources, far from Anne Quirk and her mysterious belief that truth and silence can conquer everything. Was she even real in herself? he asked. Or was she just another of life's compelling hopes? He remembered her bringing books back from the library and then disappearing down to England for weeks at a time. His mother wouldn't tell him anything about Anne's story and the books stood, in his mind, for everything missing. 'You're the first officer I've met in years', Major Scullion had told him, 'who knows that Browning is not just a small-arms weapon.'

Luke and the major were now miles from the shared conscience that had once elevated their friendship. Something was wrong. 'Jesus,' he said again. 'This war is dirty as fuck. There's nothing good here. And we the police are coming to our end.' He blew out his breath and watched his thoughts vaporise against a wall of daylight. Some crazy box of frogs out here, he thought, goats and fuck knows what, Fat Alberts flying overhead dropping cannon on the wrong people.

MAJOR SCULLION

Some men say they love it. They love the flamingos that once nested in the alkali lakes of Ghazni. Major Scullion could speak a little Pashtun: he was that kind of man, a perpetual scholar of green river valleys, an inspector of old travel books. And now he was a veteran of long hot days spent eating pomegranates in the Afghan mire. Like many people who love walking, Charles Scullion was a professor of his own singularity, yet he preferred to speak of himself as a dot in a majestic landscape. He liked the clichés, the phrase 'harsh beauty'. In his mind he had reformed all images of blood so that now he only saw Kipling's vistas of white carnations. The major came with recent memories of Sierra Leone and Kosovo, but it was Afghanistan he loved more than home, and he spoke of the Caspian tiger the way others spoke of the nightclubs in Temple Bar.

'What's in the horror-bag?' said a tall kid from Edinburgh

who'd been in the jeep with Docherty and the Afghan soldiers. They had high hopes for the canteen at Maiwand and the queue was long. Luke's head was miles away. He turned after a moment and saw the kid.

'Eh?'

'What's the snap, Captain?'

'Curry, I think.

Private Flannigan scraped past with a full tray in his hands. He winked at Luke, who just shook his head and gave him the finger. The canteen was buzzing, the soldiers ate quickly. Luke went over to a corner mess with Major Scullion and listened, not for the first time, while the major gave a lecture about medieval barbarism. Luke knew it was unreal. What was behind all this talk of the British attempt, whether in Bosnia or Kandahar, to obliterate ignorance with firepower? With the smell of boil-in-the-bag curry coming over the partition, Scullion reminded Luke of the defeat once suffered by the British at Maiwand. 'Your fucking Jockey ancestors were forming a football team in Glasgow around that time,' he said. 'God bless them. They were bog Irish like my own, with hardly a kilo of potatoes between the lot of them. And what do you think was happening over here in that year of Our Lord, 1880?'

'Death and destruction, I presume.'

'Correct! A British brigade was massacred by 25,000 Afghan savages. A thousand of our lads. And here we are, making ready to bring water to the same ungrateful pigs in their madrasas, still teaching their young how to blow up British soldiers who are out here to help them.'

'They're mainly in Pakistan, the kind of madrasas you're speaking about.'

'Wherever. It's all the same.'

'In any case I would cut that speech, sir,' said Luke. 'For the briefing. This is a two-day mission requiring tolerance.'

Scullion was in the mood for firing off questions. Luke had seen it before and knew it was coming. 'You've seen this country from the air a number of times?' he said.

'Of course.'

'What does it look like to you?'

'Dunno, sir. Empty. Bleak.'

'No, Campbell. It looks like bundles of brown blankets slung over history. And that is what it is.'

'You've said that before.'

Scullion stood up and took a few steps and drew his finger down some bullet holes in the window frame. A few hundred yards off he could see whorls of razor wire with plastic bags snagged on the blades. The bags didn't flutter, they were still, it was hot.

'Did you have a nice time at university?' Scullion asked.

'Just normal, I suppose.'

'And what did you learn?'

'I learned how to climb. I was in the climbing club.'

'What else?'

'I learned how to drink snakebite and blackcurrant. And I learned that nationalism is a false promise.'

'Well worth the visit,' Scullion said. 'I met my wife at Trinity. We used to lie in bed listening to Duke Ellington. Frost on the trees. Early 1980s. The cleaner in the halls of residence used to bring us a lit Carroll's cigarette and a cup of tea in the morning.'

'That's the life.'

'It was, Luke. It was the life.'

'You're upset, sir.'

'You know something . . .' He sat down and his shoulders sank. It wasn't ordinary for a man like Scullion to let his shoulders go. He coughed. Luke knew he had recently split up with his wife. 'A bad marriage can smash a person's life for years. You haven't really lived until you've been fucked over by a person who claimed to love you. Some people have it in the bag by the time they're twenty. But most of us get it at forty or forty-five, the lunatic surge, desperate to take you down. They force you out of your own house and claim you left them. Madeleine was so hormonal and dark I think it actually wiped her memory. She can't remember what she did. The hostility. I never faced a bigger battle.'

'Come on, sir,' said Luke. 'You fought in Bosnia.'

'Dead on. I'd faced dictators before but none of them controlled access to my dog.'

'She never hated you, Charlie.'

'No, she didn't. Her negatives were just too deeply cooked into the casserole.' He smirked and sat down again. 'But she didn't love me either. She used me, man. She used me as an alibi against the accusation she was messing up her life.'

'No way, sir.'

'Oh, yes. She saw me coming along and she thought, "He'll do. He's respectable. He'll take the sting out of it for a while." It was her father and mother that did it. They were liars, too. By an early age she was totally fucking destroyed as an ethical being. She could speak endlessly about love but her actions were without it. And that's evil, Luke. That's badness for you, right there.'

'Charlie . . .'

'They never see it, those people. They never see what they're doing because they're too busy doing it. And when you finally find them out it's part of their brilliant act to deny it, to pretend they are the victim and then convince themselves of it. That's the brilliance, Luke. They lie and lie, those people, and never face up to who they are or what they did. And then they move on to the next person and it's mansions on top of ruins. Thank Christ there are no children to pass this stuff on to.'

'Let's think about the briefing.'

'Every day there are fresh outrages . . .'

'It's not worth thinking about.'

'Oh, but it is, Luke. You have to keep good accounts with yourself. Because one day the inspectors come round, the inspectors in your head. The moral cops. And you have to be able to show them what you did. You've got to show them that you tried to do the right thing.'

'People can grow apart, sir. It's nobody's fault.'

'I wish we weren't here, Luke. I wish we were sitting down at home with a couple of drinks talking about good poetry. Housman or whatever or Ezra Pound. Just to sit down with a bottle of Talisker.'

'The plan, sir. We need to talk about the plan.'

'I left her with everything and set her free. She could honour me for that, but she doesn't.'

'Doesn't she?'

'No, man. She acts like life is just the sum total of what you can get away with.'

'Right.'

'And on a bad day I do think that's quite evil.'

'It's not evil if you can't help it.'

He was probably the toughest guy Luke had ever known, yet

simple things were clearly hard for him as he got older. He was a veteran of many battles but life at home was casting doubt over his authority. Luke wasn't sure the major had got it right about how to live: the uncomplicated things, the comforts. He was probably a nightmare to live with. Their friendship used to be like a winter coat to Luke. In the regiment, Scullion had always had a reputation as a brave soldier, but Luke wondered if that was even true anymore. He wasn't sure. To him the major looked scarred and self-indulgent, unreliable, and whatever had been tough in him was in danger of going softly malignant. Maybe it was Luke. Maybe the war made him question everything.

'You think it's simple?' Scullion said. 'Domestic life is harsher than Stalingrad. You've got a long way to go, Captain. How old are you, thirty or something?' Scullion laughed and slapped Luke's back and then drank his cold tea in one go. Luke saw that the major's hand was shaking as he lifted the plastic cup. 'The bottom dropped out,' Scullion added. 'I had no ambition. I thought she was out to fucking kill me. And all she had in her arsenal was my feeling for her.'

'Come on, Major. Take these.' Luke passed him two sedatives from his wallet. 'See you out there in twenty minutes.'

'I would like you and the others to forgive me for anything cruel I've ever done,' Scullion said. 'Just stuff that I might have said or times when I lost my temper. Like the wee things that stick around and before you know it the person thinks you've stopped listening to them. I want you to know I never meant to be cruel about anything. It was only life and sometimes you're not yourself.' The smell of baked curry and stewed tea was mixed in the air with unsaid things.

'Army curry,' Luke said, nudging his plate.

'You have to taste the real McCoy. You have to go to Calcutta.'

'Don't sweat it, Major,' Luke said. 'We're going to get this job done and then we're out of here.' Scullion gripped his shoulder and Luke imagined he was talking to all the boys.

'It's a great operation this, Captain Campbell. A brilliant thing to be doing. I just feel upset.'

'Come on, sir. We're the Western Fusiliers.'

'I'm the son of a barman, Luke. Believe me. The sons of barmen have taken over the world.'

OQAB TSUKA

Private Dooley was rolling a cigarette at the back of the hall, a breeze-block community centre in Maiwand. The hall was packed and after a while Luke sat in the row beside him. In front a staff sergeant with the new Royal Caledonians was gassing about Scullion and the regiment. 'And this major's a total fucking mentalist,' he said.

'What's mental about him?' asked the lance corporal beside him.

'Brutal cunt, Mark. He's about forty-eight. He fought in every fucking battle you can think of since the Falklands. Bosnia, the lot. I'm talking about Northern Ireland, Sierra Leone.'

People change, thought Luke. The world changes. Maybe he's just not the person he was anymore. Maybe he's sick. He thought carefully as he listened to the Scottish men. Just as likely it's me that's sick. It's me that can't stand the pace. The major is probably as committed as he ever was and it's me that's changed my mind. Every soldier has his ups and downs, don't they? Every soldier. Maybe Scullion's just going through a bad patch in his personal life, like he said, and it's nothing more, except in your own head, Luke.

'Iraq? He fought in Iraq?' asked Mark.

'Obviously. He was a big man in Basra. Is that when you joined up?'

'Aye. In 2003.'

'Right. Well: Scullion. Jesus fuck. He would lift a bazooka to swat a fly.'

'Cool,' Mark said. 'You've got to have your team.' Luke thought there was something familiar about the young lance corporal, but he didn't say anything and just listened.

'Aye, well. Scullion certainly knows his team. And he gave the IRA a right shoeing as well. A brutal cunt is what they say. Republicans, Republican Guard: he wiped half of them before they could even get their sandshoes on. Did the whole thing on expensive whisky and a raging fucken hard-on for modern warfare. Knows everything. Goes into battle with a book in his hand. A brain-box. Like Tim Collins, man. I'm talking supersoldier and I'm not kidding on. Goes hard. Could melt a platoon without trying. Half of the pikeys in here would surrender to his fucken verbals alone.'

'Easy, boys,' Luke said from behind.

'What the fuck . . .'

'Shut yer cake-hole. Captain Campbell here. Yer in mixed company, boys.' The lance corporal turned when he heard the Scottish accent, but then he put his eyes front.

'You tell them, sir,' said Private Lennox, squeezing into the back row and stealing the captain's roll-up from behind his ear. 'Fucken Aquafresh sitting there. A tube wi' three stripes.' Dooley said it loud enough for the staff sergeant to hear.

'That's enough,' Luke said. They all enjoyed a bit of inter-regimental strife, but he wanted to get back in focus.

There was a lot of noise in the hall and every soldier was hungry to get past the mountains and do some damage. Dooley, Flannigan and Lennox kept close to the captain, but he wasn't paying much attention to them. He was busy waiting for Scullion to come through the door, looking for signs that the major was under control.

When Scullion came in Luke saw Rashid behind him. Jamal Rashid was a good soldier in the Afghan army, a captain in fact, and he had emerged during training at Camp Bastion as a future military leader and an effective speaker of English. He had an eyepatch and it made him seem very distinguished to Scullion. The Afghan captain was a one-man justification for the surge: 'Look,' they said, 'look at him; in ten years' time the country will be filled with Rashids.'

He was always with Scullion that summer and it sometimes appeared that Scullion's last great push was to show Rashid the old arts. Only Luke knew how tough that must have been. Scullion had scars in places nobody would ever see and he wasn't sleeping. He was falling apart. Looking from the back row, the captain remembered a night two years before, a night he spent with the major and a bottle of Bushmills. Scullion had spoken of a terrible thing that had happened in Bosnia. A squaddie had his face torn off by a sniper in Vitez in 1993, right next to the major, who had been friends with the young man. But all that stuff had taken its toll. Luke remembered how the major loved the old ballads and said his mother had sung them at lock-ins in Mullingar.

Scullion had persuaded himself, just about, that creating electricity and irrigating the warlords' poppy fields was a better idea than blasting the population from its caves. In his heart, Scullion felt the Afghans had been destroyed by corruption, by keeping faith with sociopaths and fascists. He agreed with those who spoke of an international caliphate, an order of terror, and, in his militant dreams, he believed such murderers might eventually be bombed into civilisation. This was the war. Scullion felt that bomb strikes and ground troops were the only way because these people didn't respect talks. What they liked was to cut people's heads off live on the Internet. What they liked was to cut out the enemy's liver and eat it. He often said this, but he said many things and now he was trying irrigation.

It had taken a while to reach Trinity College, a while to reach Edmund Burke, then Gower Street in London, University College and afternoon walks round the British Museum. It took a while for him to learn that kneecappings and beheadings might be beaten by good will and enlightenment, but Charles Scullion was still arguing with himself. In his heart he was old school. Since Christmas in Helmand he had held the coalition line on peace-building while thinking constantly of the trigger. When Luke examined his face he saw the eyes of a little counter-assassin from Westmeath. They were fogged with humanitarianism and strict orders, but they were still the eyes of a man who knew what to do in a dark alleyway.

Smoke, trepidation, farts. The air-conditioning could do its best but the room was unpleasant. Luke nodded at the major as he lifted the pointer. He was probably going to be okay because he'd got whatever it was out of his system and Luke imagined the Xanax must have dipped his headlamps. He appeared to be breathing normally and thinking straight, his silver hair combed into a neat parting and his eyes blue. Scullion placed a volume of Matthew Arnold's poems on the table.

Rashid was the only ANA soldier in the room. With the eyepatch and the blue uniform he stood out. 'Okay, fellas,' Scullion said. 'You all have your jobs. Many of you will be cheered to learn that some senior officers, including yours truly, will be on the ground for this mission.' He was leaning on the pointer with his sleeves rolled up. Luke reminded himself of an old truth about briefings: they are never brief. Yet Scullion could bring the weather in on time. 'I will be travelling with a section of the Royal Western Fusiliers deployed here in a mentoring capacity. But you all have a mentoring role in this operation: be sure to show our local colleagues how to behave.' Scullion seemed to absorb a cold look from Rashid. 'And learn from them, too,' he added. The hall shifted from one foot to the other and Rashid wiped his good eye.

'Recent events in this theatre notwithstanding,' Scullion said, 'I believe our mission is absolutely clear. This will be a major development project for the Afghan people. Five dozen officers have worked for six months preparing the way. We bring clean water, we also bring culture. Now listen. This is Operation Eagle's Summit. By necessity and by grand design, our job is to facilitate the onset of prosperity among the peasants. Putting aside our previous efforts to bomb them to kingdom come, we now rectify all political errors by giving them light and water. The operation's code name is T2. Remember that. You are part of a convoy led by 13 Air Assault delivering a third turbine to the great dam at Kajaki. HET trucks will carry the blessed item in seven parts weighing thirty tons each. Assuredly, these vital organs will pump new blood to the valley. We're talking fifty-one megawatts of new power. Got that? A great sufficiency of electrical power and enough water flowing through to irrigate 650,000 acres of arid land. Tune your PRRs to channel one for minute-by-minute instructions.'

The troops felt inspired. It was not the job they wanted but they were susceptible to the major's speech. Inspiration is a con, thought Luke. It always has been a con. People who want blood will always encourage each other with talk of life-giving water. 'The main convoy is set to avoid Route 611,' Scullion said. 'For that place be riddled with insurgents. They have been smashing us for months. Many of you enjoyed this routine in Helmand, being locked down, but this operation can't fail. The logistics boys have established a route through the desert: Route Harriet. There are more than a hundred vehicles in the convoy. Canadian troops have delivered the parts here this morning from Kandahar. The Western Fusiliers have a role in the command group as part of 13 Air Assault Brigade. We will have attack helicopters providing overwatch, and, as well as the Canadians, we have the Dutch rolling with us and Yanks in the distance.'

A lieutenant in 3 Platoon raised his hand during questions. Luke knew him from the base: he was clever, modern, speeding up the ranks, a counter-insurgency nutter from County Louth. Nobody liked him. He took notes. He looked like a future boss. Luke listened to the guy and imagined he'd been designed by computers at the Dundalk Institute of Technology to get right up Scullion's nose. 'We wanted to destroy the dam in 2001,' he said. 'Now the Taliban wants to destroy it. So this op is real progress, trying to build things, not destroy them. It's like government-in-a-box.'

'Just man your guns,' Scullion said, almost sneering at the boy. Luke could see the major's contradictions coming gently to the boil. 'We've got a hundred miles of bandit country to cross out there. And the area to the south of the dam, the area called Kajaki Sofla, is crawling. We're going to have a fight down there, soldier, so keep your powder dry.'

'But building partnerships,' the soldier said. 'The aim is to secure and serve the population. Understanding local circumstances. In the long run – just like we did in Iraq – we want to stop Afghanistan from being a sanctuary for transnational extremists. Right?'

'We'll see. If we can make it past their IEDs we can start to talk about partnership.'

Luke stood up. 'Logistics?' he said.

'We'll be dispersed along the convoy,' said Scullion. 'And part of 3 Platoon will go on Highway 633 to join a decoy convoy to throw them off. Our group, Captain Campbell, will be part of the main formation over the mountains to the dam. Your big job is mentoring. Show our ANA colleagues how it's done. I want you at the front and I want you all eyes. We want safe passage to the dam for delivery tomorrow p.m.'

The soldiers filed out and Luke came to the front and was joined there by Rashid. 'We need more, sir,' said Luke. 'We're setting out. That's clear. But what are the details? Who's doing what?' Scullion lowered his voice and he picked the book off the table and smiled at the emptying hall.

'Zero pyrotechnics,' Scullion said. 'We're rolling along and protecting the delivery of the turbine. Cool? No fucking drama, Campbell, and no fucking gang-bang and no big deal. Just roll along the road and keep your boys in or alongside the vehicles, ready to shoot any fucken Terry daft enough to run at the iron horse as it passes by. Got that?'

'Should there be any separation of duties?'

'The decisions are coming from above on this, Luke. Let's just get through the mountains. It's a taxi run. There's beer on the other side. Just stick to your group and keep the signaller listening.'

At that, the keen young lieutenant from Louth came back into the hall to shake the major's hand. Scullion had languages, but he didn't have this soldier's way of talking.

'You boys are the decoy' is all he said.

'We can spread the word as we pass through the villages,' the lieutenant said with enthusiasm. 'We've got terps. We can say that this is all for the good of the community.'

'I wouldn't bother,' Scullion said. 'Just roll up the fucking road like a good boy. Your job is not to dish out philosophy, okay? It's to look like you're delivering a fierce bit of kit to a dam.'

'Yes, sir.'

'It's electricity. It's power. And I don't give a fuck for the rest of that shit you're spouting.'

'Really?'

Luke stepped back to let Scullion lose his temper. He knew it was about more than the boy.

'Yes, fucking really. Ask Rashid here. Let the American generals say what they like, Lieutenant. The people in these villages would sooner we were delivering fucking Mars bars. And even more than that: they'd sooner we'd let them deliver our no-use fucking arses to Allah. They have no great sympathy for our sympathy, and believe me, Lieutenant, they would sooner strap a bomb to their firstborn child and throw him at you as thank you for your efforts in bringing them democracy.'

'This is true, sir,' said Rashid. 'The people here do not know this American democracy you talk about.'

'We're doing a good thing,' the lieutenant said.

'How do you stick him?' shouted Scullion, looking at the boys standing by the door of the hall. The major smirked and returned his gaze to the young man in front of him. 'It's all good. We're the excellent fucken citizen that helps the poor old lady across

[57]

the road. No more, no less. So just keep your men in the convoy and they'll be back in Shadows Nightclub drinking pints of piss-water in the time it takes you to spell counter-insurgency, sure they will. You with me, Nosey?'

'This is truth the major speaks,' Rashid said. 'Oqab Tsuka, which means Operation Eagle's Summit, the beginning of the new Kajaki. The people will have justice.'

'No, Rashid,' Scullion said. 'They'll have electricity. That's all.' The ANA captain turned and Luke saw him muttering something as he wiped the board.

THE CROSSING POINT

The convoy had travelled a few miles north when Luke looked down and told the boys to cut the chat. The engine was quiet; other vehicles rumbled and heaved to a stop. A bird screamed up in the trees that stood along the banks of a canal.

The signals guy was called Bosh-Bosh. He had waved three fingers at the captain and now they were at a stop. But Luke knew: he'd been watching from up top and saw the guys at the crossing point hurriedly changing into their police uniforms when they spotted the first vehicles. Luke jumped down and signalled for Sean in the WMIK behind to come out. Then he shouted back to his own Vector for one of the boys. 'Dooley, come down here. These guys are dodgy. Sling us my helmet.'

'Right, sir.'

'Where's the terp?'

'With the Leper,' Dooley said. The captain pulled on his helmet and tapped his radio mouthpiece. 'And Sean-Sean,' he said.

'Bring the terp down here. Walking up to the checkpoint. Over.'

Soon they were all there and Dooley and the captain had their rifles up as they walked forward. 'Shouldn't we check the ground?' Sean asked. They called him the Leper, the Leprechaun, or Sean-Sean. He was the sergeant and he got respect from the boys without trying. To Scullion, Sergeant Docherty was too private and too calm: by that stage of the game the major needed friends who raised the volume and showed their weaknesses, and Docherty was the quiet man of the platoon.

'Let's go forward, man,' said Dooley. 'These fuckers are crooks but they're not daft enough to mine their own doorstep.' The heat went with them, every step of the way. It was baking out there, and a soft, choking dust lay over the chunked-up road. Steam was rising from some of the vehicles and heads appeared down the line, curious for news.

The Afghan National Police guys at the crossing looked suspicious, but to Luke they always looked that way. Dooley was at his side chattering in his big Cork accent about the mess of the checkpoint and the fact that nobody was ready for what was coming. He couldn't believe the state of them with their blue uniforms half-on and filthy. 'Fucken idiots,' he said. 'Did no one tell you there was a kilometre-long fucken convoy driving through here? Eh? What are ye, a bunch of red-arsed motherfuckers? Totally disorganisational. Waiting for Saint Patrick's Day or what?'

Luke motioned with his rifle for the policemen in the booth to move aside. One of the policemen had a boot on one foot and a sandal on the other. The guy's lip was scarred. 'Fucken shape of him,' Luke said to Dooley, 'one flip-flop and one ammo boot.'

'Cocknosh,' Dooley said.

Dooley then began shouting at the men as if only increased volume would help them understand. 'What the fuck are you doing changing into civvies?' They were babbling and the interpreter was translating at speed but Luke put up a hand and turned back to Dooley.

'Of course, they didn't know we were coming,' he said. 'Nobody would tell them. Why would anybody tell them anything?' A plastic basin of stew and dates was on the desk, a heap of okra. Next to that a slab of uncooked meat and two old Russian pistols. Under the desk there was a red-striped cement bag of dried marijuana.

One of the policemen waved his hands and pointed to the basin and said, '*Karoot Maust*.'

'He offers you food,' the interpreter said.

'Nobody would tell them anything,' repeated Luke.

'Nobody?' Dooley said. 'But they're ANP.'

'Afghan Non-Players,' muttered Luke. 'These stoners are Tippex commandos for the fucken Taliban.' He tapped his radio again and made contact with Major Scullion, who was with Rashid and the ANA kandak further down the line. They sent an ANA sergeant to the checkpoint who immediately began slapping the two guys.

'We are shamed,' he said.

'Forget it,' Luke said. 'Just get them out the fucken way.' He had gone through the drawers and thrown several rolls of money up on the desk. 'They are bandits. And worse, I imagine. We saw them changing into uniform as the vehicles approached.'

'We're from the 1st Royal Western,' Dooley said, 'and we'll bang your fucken brains out.' He then walked backwards with the cement bag swinging in his free hand. He threw the bag into the captain's vehicle. Private Lennox looked out with a huge grin on his face. 'See what just fell from the choccy tree,' he shouted down to Dooley.

THE WATCHES

It was slow all the way but eventually they were in the desert. The mountains in the distance were blue, and when the sun began to drop, pink clouds shrouded the tops of the trees. There must be places even here, Flannigan thought, where life isn't just a horror show. Private Lennox was still going on about the checkpoint and why the whole country was a mess. 'It's all just thieving bastards, so it is, and them that's not thieving bastards are trying to bomb the fuck out of you.'

'Well, you should feel right at home,' Flannigan said. 'You love a bit of thieving, you and the rest of the fucken tinks you grew up with in the Emerald Toilet.'

'Don't speak bad against the Irish,' Dooley said.

'Aye. You joined the regiment, mate,' Lennox said. 'And why's that? 'Cause yer daddy once got his wee arse spanked in Portadown?'

'No, you plank. Because I quite fancied spending my afternoons in foreign places beating up on no-hopers like you, Lennox.'

'That's violence, that,' Lennox said.

Pampas grass. Sweet tea and sandbags. Brown-eyed children smiling by the road. It all seemed so real to Luke. The carnations on tall stalks were straining past the sun and an old lady came up to a stationary WMIK with a helmet full of figs. She tapped the wheel of the vehicle and he saw the helmet was stamped

Twentynine Palms, CA. She was selling the figs and her smile seemed more like a knot. The convoy moved on and crept slowly into the mountains towards Ghorak – helicopters over the peaks – and before it got dark the vehicles halted on a plateau. 'Come on, you chozzies,' Dooley said. 'Grab your shit. We're stopping.'

'How long?' Flannigan asked.

'This'll be it for the night. It's slow going. They need to keep fixing the tracks and looking for bombs in the road.'

The captain turned down his radio. He just sat in the corner of the vehicle and watched the boys pulling stuff out of their packs. It was the low-level hum of his life: the constant banter, the laughter, the mock offence, the lingo. 'Have you seen Flannigan's watch, sir?'

'Nope. I don't care about watches.'

'It's cheap rubbish. Take your Casio G-Shock. Classic. Totally awesome. It's been that way since 1983.'

'Dooley!'

'An electro-luminescent panel causes the entire face to glow for easy reading.' The boys were laughing and making to leave the Vector, and Luke began chucking their bags after them.

'I mean it, Dooley,' he shouted. 'Get the fuck out the van or I'll mess you up.' Luke slammed the door and smiled to himself and then a mortar burst in the valley.

'*Kaboom*,' he said.

SANDHURST

Luke lay down and flicked off his helmet. It was good to feel the static falling away, the ops talk and Scullion. It was nice to be free of the jeering and the news from up and down the line. He stretched his legs out and pulled a folder from his backpack, a black folder from Strathclyde that had once held his Honours dissertation. Now it held photos and letters that came to the camp from home. He opened it and took out a flattened bag of wet wipes and a packet of sherbet. (From his grandmother, Anne, posted by the woman next door.) He held up a photograph and used a Maglite from the floor of the Vector to help him see. Anne was young in the picture and she looked like the happiest person alive. He searched her eyes and saw evidence of Harry's presence, the grandfather he had never met, just a glow in her eye, always there in portraits taken by him.

Dear Luke,

    This is a wee note to say hello from your gran and we really hope you're doing well over there. We see it on the news all the time but you probably see it differently when you're there. Nothing to report over here except the sun is finally out thank God and life in Saltcoats always takes a turn for the better in the nice weather. Gran says to thank you for sending the right address for parcels and don't forget she says to take pictures if the light is good. Gran's been getting a bit forgetful but she's not bad son and coping well since the winter time. Remember there's plenty of us in here to help with anything she needs doing. Anyway son that's us running out of things to say so please take good care. Everybody sends their love to you.

    All the best,
    Gran and Maureen

He could imagine her face at the window. He wondered if any of the boys had a grandmother like his, a woman with knowledge and secrets and a gentle habit of helping you up your game. He wasn't a very typical officer, he knew that and so did everyone else, but it had somehow played to his advantage to be different in the regiment. They knew he was a reader but thought he was made of heroic stuff because of his dad. It had been Anne who took up the slack, inspiration-wise, when his dad died, and he supposed he went to see her as part of working himself out. In those days he was always ready to get lost in other people's ideas, and Gran was a fountain of individuality if ever there was one. There was endless chat about how life used to be, with details missing. The slow-motion world of hinted-at summers and new lipstick and the Pleasure Beach. She spoke to him about Blackpool as if it was New York or Toronto, where she'd also been, and where she'd also taken photographs that were lost along the way.

He lay back and saw the parade ground at Sandhurst. And then he saw his mother, Alice, in a sky-blue hat with tears in her eyes, her new husband Gordon beside her as they gathered their camera straps and her billowing skirt, the day he passed out from officers' training. Gran arrived in a taxi that came all the way from Gatwick Airport. He was grateful she'd come and Alice had smiled thinly when he said, after the ceremony, that he wanted to take his gran for a walk down to the chapel. 'We'll go and find your ironing board and put it in the car,' said Alice, always practical. 'There's no point leaving it for someone else to take.'

The chapel appeared to move, but it wasn't the chapel, it was the trees that moved and once the rain came down the trees got darker and Anne pointed it out, the way the trees darkened in the rain. She took his arm and was proud of his uniform as they walked up the path. 'God, Granny, the world's going mad and you're noticing the trees.'

'Well, that's life,' she said. 'If you weren't looking you missed it. That's all I know.'

They walked the length of the chapel and sat to one side under a ragged flag rescued from a battlefield, set high up on the wall in a gilt frame. They were quiet in the pews and that was easy. After a while Anne put her hand over his hand and gave him advice. 'Be true,' she said, 'if not to yourself, then to something more interesting than yourself.'

'I chose the Royal Western Fusiliers.'

'All men are sentimental,' she said. 'Women get the reputation, but we just cry at the radio. Men are sentimental about institutions. You know: buildings. The old bricks, the old mottos. Harry was the same.'

'We're going to rid the world . . .'

'Don't say it,' she said.

'But Gran.'

'The task is to see.'

'Not for a soldier. There's a lot to be done.'

'We don't *rid the world*, dear. We create it.'

'We make it safe,' he said. She just nodded at that and the high windows showed their pattern on the pews. Before they went back to join the others she took a present out of her bag. He still had the paperback somewhere, a book entitled *Theory of Colours*.

'The colour red doesn't actually exist,' she said. 'It only exists as an idea in your head. Always remember that. You create it yourself when your imagination meets the light.'

His attention flickered as he lay in the Vector. Looking at the letter, he heard another thud down in the valley. The summer remembers nothing of the winter and nature is a kind of amnesia. He stretched out further and kicked off his boots, considering whether memory is just one of our little sicknesses. It was the sort of topic he used to discuss with Scullion in their happier days. His grandmother had stood up in the chapel at Sandhurst and tapped his cheek.

'Send me one of your mugshots,' she said.

And that's the one she put up on her wall. He saw it the last time he was home on leave, when he went to see Anne in secret. At the time nobody was talking about dementia or anything like that, but he noticed a change. Her mind was wandering as they spoke, and, by the end of his visit, she seemed miles away. She sat in her favourite chair by the window and said the lights on the sea were very festive. Luke imagined she was joking but then he saw the concentration on her face. She said she could feel the cold coming on but this was the sort of Christmas she had always wanted, just me and her and two glasses of sherry.

It was the beginning of something and he knew it. He stayed the whole evening and they spoke about old times. She reminded him of an exhibition they'd seen together, famous photographs of tenement houses and poor children in the Saltmarket. 'The exposure wasn't right,' she said, 'and the children are blurred for life.'

'That's an odd phrase,' Luke said.

He had gone his own way, but an interest in 'seeing things', as Anne called it, was what had made them close. At her flat in Glasgow, when he was young, she set up what she called his 'little conchological cabinet' – a term out of Charles Dickens, she told him – which was where he kept shells he'd found and bits of broken plate from the sea. The glass cabinet described their shared interest in the gathering of facts, their attempt to know life not only by our mistakes but by artistic ordering. When Anne returned from her travels in England she would often bring a new shell or a fancy nugget of Victorian crockery. And she always brought sherbet or a stick of rock from one of the sweet shops. 'Remember, Gran,' he said to her last time he was home, the time with the sherry, 'remember that group of starfish we put in the conchological cabinet?'

'I liked the stars,' she said. 'And one time Jayne Mansfield came to turn on the lights in Blackpool.'

He took her hand by the window. She looked down as if their joined hands formed an element with a life of its own. 'No, boss,' he said, laughing. It was the first time he knew she must be getting ill. 'I'm talking about something in the shape of stars. I mean these creatures that are shaped like stars in the sky and I found them on the beach, remember?'

There was puzzlement on her face for a second and then she smiled as if all the confusion had now cleared from her mind. 'I know what you're saying,' she said. 'I'm not daft. It's about the shape of things.'

'Yes,' he said. 'You trained my eye.'

'I know the cabinet you're talking about. We made it together.'

'You guided me.'

She smiled and drank the sherry down. Then she peered into the window glass and said, 'I lost you.'

'It was all art, you said. The cabinet.'

'Giving shape.'

'Knowing what's behind appearances,' Luke said. 'That's the photographer's gift and you have that and it's a wonderful thing.'

She pecked like a chicken and gave a kiss to the air. 'We knew the right thing to do with the shells and that's why we're pals, why we've always been pals,' she said.

'And plates,' Luke had said. 'You brought those bits of broken plate with the tiny blue patterns and the plates had been washed in the sea for a hundred years or . . . just fragments. Tiny bits. But I used to imagine them as whole plates laid on a Victorian table with a family sitting down together.'

They looked at each other. He knew he'd be off to Helmand in a few days and wondered if she'd ever be the same again. She raised a finger as if he had finally struck a chord. 'I could take a picture of that dinner you're talking about and you could help me,' she said.

'I'd love to. Will we do that? Will we get out your cameras and make a brilliant picture?'

Luke lay in the heat of the Vector and wondered why his mother and his grandmother had never clicked. His gran had made too much of the men in their lives, and so had he, and he began to see it as a form of harassment that had affected his mother. Yet he and Anne were friends. He lay back mulling it over and tipped into the kind of sleep where ideas feel like revelations until they slip so easily away.

THE RIDGE

Private Flannigan always set out his tent like a perfectionist. Mosquito net, maggot bag, folded corners: a big lumberjack of a guy pressing down his little corners. He was a born soldier. 'What's happening?' he said when Luke appeared in the camp rubbing his hair. The captain was carrying a book and he leaned on an old stone wall.

'Nothing much.'

'Did you get the head down?'

'A few zeds, aye.' Luke began to smile when he saw the delicate way Flannigan was handling his kit. 'Hey Flange,' he said. 'Is this you preparing your evening *toilette*?'

'Bite me,' Flannigan said. There was evening primrose in the cracks of the wall and Sergeant Docherty was scraping off a sample for his collection. He was also finishing off an argument, just as Luke came in. 'They thought they were going to get Belgium in two years,' he said. 'Turns out they might get Bangladesh in thirty.' The boys took the piss out of Docherty for being a square-bear and being pussy-whipped, but in secret they admired him, at twenty-six, for what he knew.

'Oh, look,' Major Scullion said. He was sitting on a petrol drum. 'It's the fucken sleeping beauty. Want a brew, Captain?'

'No, I'm fine. Thanks.'

Scullion had the menacing look. And he never made anybody tea. 'While you've been lying in your wank-pit, Captain Campbell,' he said, 'the boys and I have been arranging a party. A very private party, you understand. Private Lennox here, of the small stature, the ludicrous complexion and the ginger nut, has procured for the purpose of our evening entertainment a bag of the old Afghan sweet stuff.'

'Dead on,' Lennox said. 'Proper clackie, so it is.' He kicked the cement bag full of weed over the ground to Luke.

Another of the men in the platoon, a Paisley boy, chuckled like a monkey and peered with his mates over the top of a neighbouring tent. 'Fuck sake, sir,' he said, 'you don't even need cigarette papers. Just spark up the end of that bag and ye'll be toking a Superking.'

'Be quiet, McKenna,' Luke said.

'Yeah. Shut it, McCrack-Whore. The captain here's just getting his shit together after a small constitutional.'

'That's a walk, Doosh, not a sleep,' Flannigan said.

'Who cares? The captain will be joining the party in jig time. So fuck off, McCrack, and get on with unrolling your farter. And fuck off, Flange, with your *Oxford English Dictionary*.'

They were talking about food. It was usually girls or cars or watches or gaming, but tonight: food. Dooley's girlfriend sent him packets of Super Noodles and a box of Dairy Milk and it made him glad he was marrying her because she knew the score. 'Remember American Night?' Lennox said. He was talking about the Thursday cookouts at Camp Shorabak when the Americans would pitch a scoff-house between the tents. 'Gatorade. Chicken wings,' Lennox said.

'Beef jerky,' Luke said.

'That was proper plush,' said Lennox. 'You've never seen so many fucken rashers. American Night. I fucken love America. They'd have like Hershey bars and M&Ms to kill. Mounds of them. I'm talking chicken and beef motherfucker and those MREs falling off the truck, Meals-Ready-to-Eat. They were super-plush.'

'And films,' Dooley said.

'That's right. Lethal with the films. I love America. Stuff that isn't even on at the cinema for like a year.'

'Ben & Jerry's ice-cream,' Flannigan said. 'Buckets of it. How do they even get that stuff over here?'

'It was the same in Iraq,' Dooley said.

After an hour it was dark except for lights in some of the vehicles. The reefer glowed orange as it went round but it was the moon that picked out the ridge and the low buildings along the track. Scullion said a few fires in the distance were oil drums burning in Ghorak, nothing sinister, just elders playing chess probably or Terry twisting wires and making their wee roadside contraptions. 'That's the thing,' Scullion was saying. 'You all think you know the terrain 'cause you've seen it playing video games.' Half his face lit up as he smoked the joint and sniggered. 'But don't give me points, man; give me a body count any day.'

'Same,' Lennox said. 'I came here to get my fucken gun on, not to sit watching hexi-telly.'

'Speaking of which.' Dooley bent down and lit the hexamine tablet on top of the low stove. Quickly it burned blue and the boys all gave a whistle and some of them asked for whoever it was to hurry up with the joint. 'You're all going blind,' Lance Corporal McKenna said as he walked into the camp. 'Between staring at the hexi-telly and playing with your dobbers, you gimps will soon be applying for invalidity.'

'We'll have to join the queue,' Flannigan said. 'Behind all the pikey horror-pigs in your family.'

Luke just watched them. Scullion was right. Younger soldiers often thought they knew the battleground; they saw graphics, screens, solid cover and fuck-off guns you could swap. It wasn't all they saw but it was part of their understanding. They saw cheats and levels, badass motherfuckers, kill death ratios, and the kinds of marksmen who jump up after they're dead. Luke knew they all struggled, from time to time, to find the British army as interesting as its international gaming equivalent. They had run important missions with their best mate from school and called in air support, over their headsets, from some kid in Pasadena they'd never met, some kid like them in a box-room. They'd beaten the Russian mafia with the help of club kids from Reykjavik and bodyboarders from Magnetic Island. They'd obliterated the *A-rabs*. They'd topped the board. They'd stayed up all night smoking weed and drinking huge bottles of Coke and ordering pizza before they cleared the civilian areas. The boys wanted action. They wanted something real that would become the highest level, the one they couldn't reach on their consoles back home.

'If they're gonna hit us, I wish they'd just hit us,' Lennox said.

'Maybe it saves lives,' Scullion said. 'The war in Ireland might have ended sooner if those wee Provo kids could've blown up chip shops onscreen.'

'No, sir,' Flannigan said. 'It's recruitment. I'm telling you. That's the big new thing about it. Gamers are ripe. They're fucken jumping to get out and stretch their legs. Every guy in this regiment has served time on *Call of Duty*. Every one. Am I right?'

'Even the educated ones?'

Luke smiled. 'We started it,' he said. He took the joint off Lennox and walked up to the wall. A smell of rose petals was coming from the field on the other side. He could make out the furrows and a yellow hosepipe. 'The MOD has a game now called *Start Thinking, Soldier*.'

'Yep. That's right. That's recruitment,' Flannigan said. 'Grab the little fuckers by the thumbs.'

'There's always been that sort of thing,' Scullion said. 'I loved *Top Gun*. I loved fucken *Full Metal Jacket*. John Wayne before that. Little boys with their eyes wide, wanting a gun. It's all recruitment.'

'It's different,' Flannigan said. 'If you've got PlayStation then you actually know how to drive a tank. Jesus. I'm not kidding. The manufacturers have changed the controls on the new Challenger to be more like a video console. It's exactly the same.'

'Fuck off!' Dooley said.

'Look inside one. It's a fact. Walk up the line now and look inside one, Doosh. I'm telling you.'

'It's true,' Scullion said, taking the joint. 'The CIA are putting in money nowadays to start up gaming companies.'

'They used to put it into brainy magazines,' Luke said. The major looked up and his smile was nostalgic.

'*Encounter*,' he said.

Sergeant Docherty had taken off his boots while staring at the hexi-telly. 'Your hoofs are fucken rank, buddy,' Lennox said. 'Jesus, Leper.'

Docherty ignored him. He was never going to endanger his peace of mind with too much talk, yet he caught the officers' attention after he calmly put down his boot and spat into the fire. 'You're talking about simulators,' he said. 'I think it's ironic that the people who flew those planes on 9/11 taught themselves on flight simulators in Florida.'

'Ooh. *Ironic*,' Lennox said.

Scullion nipped the end of his tongue with two fingers and offered a bleary laugh in the Leper's direction. 'Everything now is pre-experienced,' he said. The men weren't listening. Another burst of machine-gun fire went off in the valley and Docherty stood up holding one boot. Scullion then went off at him and nobody could work out why. 'I can't stand the way you fucken stink,' he said. 'The smell of you . . . it's unbearable.'

'What?' Docherty said.

'You, *personally*,' Scullion said. He was suddenly over at Docherty and right up in his face, swaying in front of him. 'You reek of sweat, the smell of you, what, it makes me fucking puke.'

'I wash, just like everybody else, Major. I use deodorant. What do you want me to do?'

'Nothing. You can't do anything. You smell vile and it drives me mad.' The sergeant just stared at him and then he went to arrange the night guard.

'Put your boots back on,' Luke said to the others. 'We're in a state of alert up here and I want everybody ready.'

'Papers?' Lennox said. He was talking to the group and fondling the cement bag and giggling. But the boys ignored him. They were too stoned and they just stared at the low blue flame. Time passed and Scullion stood up and came out with some complicated nonsense. They all wished the stars could lift them up or else come down to play.

'I'm fucken stoned out my gourd,' Dooley said.

'No messing,' Lennox said.

'Champion weed,' said Flannigan.

Luke just watched the soldiers and felt warm for the cold night, or cold for the warm night, lost in some little question about whether the world was round or made of putty. He smiled and felt his mouth go dry and then rootled in his pack for a stick of gum. Flannigan went over to the wall and took a piss, then zipped up and looked down the edge of the plateau and saw bursts of green tracer. 'They're having a crack down there,' he said. 'Eat fire, you bitches! Eat metal, you Terry scum!'

'Hey, wind it in. You'll wake the babies,' Scullion said, stretching out on a groundsheet and putting a bunched-up smock under his head. 'Five billion stars and we still can't find the knives and forks. Get them a bloody knife and fork and they're yours for life. People will believe in the transition if they feel their lives are getting better, and that starts up there.'

'The major's talking pish,' said Lance Corporal McKenna, coming into the camp. He had two Afghan soldiers with him. 'Talking pure pish. That'll be the top-notch Asian *cigarettees*,' McKenna added.

'Drop dead, McCrack-Whore.'

'Is that the price? Too dear. How about a Bounty bar and a packet of Turkish playing-cards?'

'Done.'

They smoked and looked.

'There's a lot of fire down there.'

'Who gives? If it's not coming towards you, you don't give a fuck,' McKenna said.

The Afghans spoke not a word and smoked as if the weed was like a fresh supply of oxygen. Their teeth were knackered and they looked sixty but were probably thirty. 'Dam is good at Kajaki,' said one of them after his brain fogged over and the high settled in and the mellow scene shaped up like a welcome.

'That's right. We don't give a fuck,' Dooley said.

Luke examined the red returning fire – red was Allied, green was Terry – and thought of those strings of lights you get at funfairs. He followed the dots and thought of Ayrshire nights when the amusement arcade became the brightest thing on the coast. Lennox put *Natural Born Chaos* by Soilwork on his iPod. Usually he just listened with one earphone, but he had mini-speakers in the camp and he jacked the sound up. The guitars went off and everybody smiled, the Afghans too, not like their normal faces but actual smiles breaking out, and Luke stared up and imagined the tracer fire was firing in time to Lennox's stupid music. Yes, Luke thought, it was nice to be here with the smell of roses coming over the wall and the men showing the Afghan squaddies how to play air guitar and some of them falling asleep in their boots. Luke lay back giggling when he heard Lennox talking about the girl who was going to marry Doosh. He was rolling out the abuse, saying you'd think Dooley couldn't pull the ring off a can of Red Bull but it turns out the girl's as fit as a butcher's dog.

LET THEM KNOW

The ambush came early that night. Docherty was up and talking to Bosh-Bosh, the signals operator, and sticking his fingers in a muesli pack when the radio went berserk. 'Incoming on the crane side. Sniper fire. Over!' McKenna had been on guard with the two Afghans, but the Afghans couldn't be found. Luke was half awake. He felt he'd almost known it was coming, as if the enemy had been getting closer all day. His boots were on and he grabbed his helmet and smock and was zipped up in seconds. He never thought about how to distinguish himself in battle; that's not what good officers think. They think about the men. And then they think about how to obliterate the threat.

Flannigan was tossing sandbags. 'Over there, over there,' he kept shouting. Lennox pulled the machine-gun off the wagon and soon they were directing fire into the trees behind the old wall.

'Lennox, get your fucken helmet on,' Luke said.

'Over there!' shouted Flannigan.

The snipers were few and quite far off but fear of snipers shrinks distance: they are on top of you. They are here. Luke's eyes narrowed as if they were telescopic and his hands grew jumpy and his instincts made an instant grid of the ground. 'Against the wall! Dooley, Lennox. Get the gun propped in that corner. Bosh?'

'Captain?' the signals man said.

'What they saying?'

'Incoming fire from below. Quite heavy. Here's your set.' Luke put his helmet on and fixed the earpiece and immediately heard the crackles and the news that several dozen insurgents were under the plateau trying to poke holes in the convoy. The men around him were still shouting and bawling and sending out a great deal of fire. That was the thing you always forgot later – the shouting, the noise, the great thunder of lads in your ears. Gunsmoke was spreading eerily over the land down there like mist on a childhood morning. Luke shivered to see it, the white smoke coming from the poplar trees.

'Air cover?' he said.

'Air cover coming in,' Bosh said. 'The Yanks are on it. Ops says stay up high: they're going to scoop the valley and fill it with cannon.' The men of 5 Platoon were firing and reloading and Luke heard barks of excitement as they shouldered the wall and poked their bang-sticks over the top. A single shot came whizzing over their heads and fucked into the side of a truck, which sent them wild. They were shouting and swearing and pushing at the wall. 'Over there! Fucking Terry cunt at eleven o'clock. Doosh, get down! Get fucken down! You can see his fucking rag, man. Flange. In the gap to the right. Go for it. Smash the fuck out of him!'

Docherty at some point came up behind Luke and told him he

thought the major was pretending to be asleep. He was inside one of the vehicles, crouched down.

'What? Are you messing with me?'

'He's in the Vector.'

'What you talking about? Get him out here: he needs to direct this shit and support the boys.'

'He threw up.'

'Are you fucken having me on, Leper?'

'No, sir. He's not well.'

In seconds the boys would notice. Luke knew they would notice and he feared their bottle might collapse if they heard the major was hanging back in the van during a fire-fight. Yet he knew something was wrong with Scullion and he'd felt it since they left Bastion. 'Holy fuck,' Luke said. 'Am I medicine man to the whole platoon?'

'Let's cover for him, boss,' Docherty said. 'It's a bad week for him and we can easily cover it.'

'What is it, his fucken period?'

'It's going to be fine here.'

'Is it? I don't know what bins you're looking through, Docherty. But mine tells me there's Terry crawling up our fucken arses.'

'It's fine, sir. We're covered.'

'Not yet we're not. Scullion's losing it. I'm telling you, Leper. He's out the fucken game. He's supposed to be over here commanding his soldiers. He's the CO. He asked to be out here: he could be back at headquarters eating fucken Pot Noodle, like a normal. But he wanted to be involved with my section and now his head is fucking erupting with crap. You're seriously telling me he's fucken sweating his bollocks off in the back of the Vector? To hell with the turbine. It's about the boys.'

Luke got on the radio. 'What I'm saying is we're in the open here and request urgent air cover to the north side of the ridge. We're just a group. Yes. We're a short section. The rest of our platoon is manning other vehicles.' He looked at Docherty and read his thoughts. He flicked the mouthpiece on the PRR down for a second and breathed deeply. 'But bearing up and holding our position. Over.'

Flannigan was ordered to set up a mortar battery and was now pounding the poplar grove, laughing his big Scouse laugh. 'That should keep their cakey arses quiet for a bit, lads,' he said. He looked round at Luke. 'Eh, Jimmy-Jimmy! Fucking hardly out of my gonk-bag, man. Hardly opened my fucken eyes and these badasses are burning our toast!'

'Hardly had time to grab my cock,' Dooley said.

'That might've held us back for a while,' Luke said, reloading. 'Waiting for you to find your cock.'

Dooley darted his eyes around the camp. A bullet banged into the metal drum and it spewed diesel but didn't explode. 'Get that out of the fucken way,' Luke shouted to some men at the back. 'You in 5 Platoon! Ross. Private Bawn. Move it! Get that fucken drum cleared before we have a fucken Guy Fawkes party out here.'

There was a pause. Kind of horrible, the pauses. Luke got back on the radio and tried for more information. His hair was drenched. 'Roger that,' he said and looked along the wall at the boys.

'Where's the major?' Dooley said.

'He's checking maps,' said the captain.

'You what?'

'I don't know. Maps.'

'What's he checking maps for? We know where we are. We're up here and they're down there.'

'Wind your neck in, Dooley. Just leave it.'

The two men looked at each other and Dooley nipped his bottom lip with his teeth. He got it. 'No problem,' he said, a blush perceptible in his manner if not on his face, which was coated in white dust. 'The major's always been deadly when it comes to the maps.'

'Just cover me,' Luke said. 'I'll go and pull over the rest of the platoon.' But before he moved an inch and before Dooley could turn back to the machine-gun and start pounding the trees, a pair of Apache helicopters found their way into the valley and hovered above the ridge. They were high up but gunning the hell out of the mountainside. Luke shouted at the men to cover their heads and get down. 'Let's get the club classics going!' he shouted. 'Good life. Good life. Good life. Good life. *Good life!*' He sang the song with his face down in the dirt and it was bedlam all around. The cannon was tearing up the grove and splitting the trees and Flannigan crouched under his equipment and laughed into the broken wall.

'*Good life!*' he returned.

'Any fucker in those trees isn't coming out again,' Dooley shouted.

'Not for Christmas,' Flannigan said. The men laughed at this and Lennox passed a cigarette down the line. They had to keep low and the guns didn't stop overhead and Luke started off the Band Aid song about Christmas. The weird thing they would all remember was the warm, empty cartridges falling from the sky on top of the camp, glancing off the vehicles. Docherty took a few and stuffed them in his pack. The boys smiled as if the fight was all they had ever wanted and the cartridges fell like golden hail as they shouted a song about feeding the world. 'Do they know it's Christmas-time at all?' It was like American Night at Camp Shorabak. The Yanks never stinted on anything and the boys knew they'd be happy to tear up the fields all morning if it meant having one more kill.

3

HOLIDAYS

Anne opened her eyes and saw the blue sky and the inviting tracks of a passing plane. She blinked, sat up and recalled an old song they used to sing about airline tickets to romantic places. It was warm and the sun played silver over the Firth of Clyde and shone on the windows of the foreign coaches as they made their way to Largs.

And still my heart has wings.

And yellow was the room where she loved him. Down from Glasgow she would wait there in Blackpool and sometimes he didn't arrive. He just didn't come, she said to herself, and she'd be sitting there with a shopping bag full of breakfast, the square slice, the plain loaf. And sometimes he changed his mind and he would turn up late, good grief, in the middle of the night, chucking stones at the window, and she'd throw down the key. He'd come up the stairs and she'd bury her face in his neck and say nothing. Oh, the relief. And never to mention the sadness or the fright she'd got. She could still smell his Old Spice and was so glad she had waited.

Nobody ever tells you the natural world has all the answers and keeps count of all the days. They don't tell you – you work it out. One minute you're getting on with your tasks, the jobs and the life and all your goals and one thing and another; then, just like that, you notice the smell of burning leaves as you walk past

[85]

the playing-fields. The seasons seem for a long time to ask nothing of you, but eventually you must brave their familiarity. Most of the time she felt distant from her old artistic self, but some days, especially in sunshine, the feeling came.

A cigarette that bears a lipstick's traces.

She was in a deck-chair outside reception. 'Blackpool', she said to the warden, 'was often hotter than Spain. I want to go back.'

'Was it hotter, Anne?'

'Oh, yes. Hotter than any place. I used to say to my Harry, "You could fry an egg on the pavement down there." He never believed me. But it was always hot at that time, in the seventies.'

'The 1970s.'

'That's right.'

'Our Audrey goes to Faliraki,' the warden said.

'What's that?'

'Greece. Same place every year. Same hotel. She says the drink's dirt cheap.'

'Oh. We didn't have those places.'

Mrs Auld from flat 25 came out to curse the weather. It was never right for Mrs Auld. 'They'd let you just go down the beach there and get burnt to a crisp.'

'Who's they?' the warden said.

'You know fine well. The government.'

'What's the government got to do with sun-cream?'

'Everything, Jackie,' said Mrs Auld. 'You mark my words. They keep it back, the government. They make it too dear for pensioners to buy. And we all burn to a crisp, so we do.'

'Oh, Dorothy!'

'I'm telling you. It's true. We've all got cancer because of these English prime ministers.'

'That's ridiculous. And half of them are Scottish.'

'Mark my words. I've got liver spots on the backs of my hands that I didn't have before.'

'Are you going on the bus thing?' asked Anne without opening her eyes or looking over.

'The bus run? I am that,' Dorothy said. 'I certainly am. The bus is taking us all to Gretna Green first thing in the morning. Just for the day. You should come, Anne.'

'No.'

'You'll miss yourself. A walk about and a nice fish supper. If we get the sun it'll be lovely.'

'Unless you get burnt to a crisp,' the warden said. She liked to tease the residents as much as possible and stop them from getting down in the mouth. There are never enough jokes to go round.

'Aye, well, don't you worry. I'll be shelling out for the good stuff,' Dorothy said. 'Ambre Solaire: that's me.'

'Oh, you're that hard done-to,' the warden said.

'My family think I'm trapped in here,' Dorothy said, offering a sudden new bend to the conversation. 'They feel sorry for me. They do. But I love it in here. I'm going to Gretna. I have days out and I have breakfast every day with the ladies. I don't mind telling you – it's a great place, this. It would never occur to my family that it was the years living with them that made me feel trapped. And now I'm free, so I am.'

Anne opened her eyes. 'More power to your elbow.'

'More sun-cream to your elbow,' the warden said.

The warden and Mrs Auld left Anne alone again and she closed her eyes to think about the speech. She wished she could write things down or look at the old contact sheets, just to help her remember. But that was against the rules of the Memory

[87]

Club. You weren't allowed notes. The point was not to run past the window but to stop and admit things.

THE MEMORY CLUB

They met every Friday and sometimes more, if a doctor was coming in to see them. Anne said it was the nicest day of the week because she liked stories and the way the residents got into conversations about what they all did when they were young. She tried to speak up and some of the old agony about appearing in public had gone. That Friday, it was her turn to lead them off and the district nurse said it might be good to go back to when she was small. There were always biscuits in the lounge for the Memory Club and Anne lifted one and dunked it into her tea without ceremony. 'A lot of the times when you do this the biscuit drops into the tea,' she said.

'I know,' the nurse said. 'It happens to the best of us, so it does.'

'Well I'm just saying I don't mind,' Anne said. 'You can fish it out with a spoon.'

'Oh, Anne!' said Mrs Auld. 'That's not memories!'

'I never said it was.'

'You did.'

'I never. I've not started talking yet.' The ladies sat in a circle of chairs with one old man, Alex, asleep in his. Alex used to be in charge of the Saltcoats Darts Club. The district nurse said he was a great singer in his day and had won trophies at national level.

'For singing?' Mrs Auld asked.

'No. For darts. But the club is mainly known for the social side and they have some good singers.'

'I've never heard him sing,' Mrs Auld said. 'I've heard him snore plenty, right enough.'

'Okay,' said the nurse, folding her hands in her lap. 'Today it's Mrs Quirk's turn to talk about her early days. And it's exciting actually because it involves foreign parts, I believe.'

'Africa!' Mrs Auld said.

'It's not,' Anne said.

'Yes!'

'I never went to Africa,' said Anne. She knew Mrs Auld wanted it to be her turn to lead off every week. She was a torn-faced woman, always moaning and then marrying another one.

'Just let Anne speak, Dorothy.'

Anne's problem was the Friday meeting always made her think of memory rather than remember. She thought sketchily or vividly of the artists she had loved and supposed that was kind of remembering, but it was what they said, actually, the material and the ideas, the fact that they took an interest in making things permanent, this was the kind of thing that flooded Anne's mind on a Friday. The connections were personal and she couldn't always express them. 'There was a woman called Louise,' she said. 'Don't ask me what else she was called. She made spiders.'

'Is this one of your artists?' the nurse asked.

'That's right,' Anne said. 'From France. Wonderful woman. And she made rooms and she built spiders.'

'Art's boring,' said Dorothy.

'Quiet now. Let Anne speak. Now, what do you remember about this person? Did you read about her maybe?'

'I remember lines. She said the old . . .'

'All right. That's a start.'

'The old thing . . .'

'Take your time.'

'Louise was her name. She said the oldest secrecy is being alone.'

'They talk in riddles,' Dorothy said.

'We're going to ignore that,' the nurse said. 'This is Anne's week and she can say what she wants.'

Dorothy picked up a custard cream off the saucer and leaned back in her chair. 'It's up to her,' she said. 'I don't know about artists. She's educated, I suppose. That's where all the trouble starts.'

'Quiet, please.'

Maureen came into the lounge holding the hand of the lady from number 19. She sat the old lady down. 'Shush,' she said. 'We're being very quiet. We're not here.'

'But you are here,' Anne said. She noticed Maureen was wearing her old wedding ring. She did that sometimes: Anne understood fine well and said to herself it was just Maureen's way of cheering herself up. She claimed not to care about the father of her children – it was so long ago – but people who like drama also like props. Dorothy kept running her hands over the Yamaha organ beside her. Her fingerwork showed you she could play a tune if the machine was turned on.

'Anne's talking about an artist she likes.'

'Lovely,' said Maureen, picking some lint off her skirt. 'Because she's a dark horse, that Anne. Believe you me. She knows all about that kind of thing because she lived in New York.'

'Don't help her,' the nurse said.

'I know where I used to live,' Anne said. 'And you're going to give us advice about how to stay warm and how we should never open the door unless the chain is on, aren't you?'

'No, I'm not, love. We're doing memory today.'

'Oh, yes.'

'You were talking about artistic people.'

Anne took a deep breath and then a sip of her tea. 'My Luke is in the army,' she said. 'In the war. He used to be a private but now he's more than that. He's always been good at noticing. When he was six years old and his goldfish died I told him we could bury it and he said . . . he said he didn't want it in the ground or down the toilet. He decided to put the goldfish in a bag and place it in the freezer.'

'Aw. That's nice,' said Heather, a quiet Christian lady who always attended.

'To keep it,' Anne said.

'Not much use,' said Dorothy. 'You can't eat a goldfish. You know what you have to do with a goldfish? You have to flush it away and get another one before they even see it's gone.'

Anne just looked at her. What a silly woman. And then she remembered what she was talking about.

'Do you get letters from Luke?' the nurse asked.

'I've got one in the room,' Anne said. 'It came this week from a camping place. He's not dead.'

'Not at all,' said Maureen. 'Luke is doing very well and he's liking it over there. Blue paper, he writes on. We read it together and then we wrote a reply, didn't we, Anne?'

'The woman was called Louise,' Anne said. 'She was French and her other name was like the Communists.'

'Oh, for God's sake!'

'Calm down, Dorothy.'

'She knows her stuff,' Maureen said.

'It's because she's been abroad,' said Dorothy. 'That's where it all starts.'

Anne continued. 'She said a woman should have her own journey . . . her own . . . thing . . . *un itinéraire unique*.'

'She's speaking foreign now,' Dorothy said. 'Did you see? That's it: she's speaking foreign.'

'I have lots of souvenirs,' Anne said. She made the remark and put down her cup and saucer, as if everything was now settled and for the best. She saw a little sprinkler throwing jets of water over the yucca plants in the botanical trench. She was aware of the warm light coming through the ceiling and knew it was good for the plants. Anne had the words that Friday afternoon and was happy to answer the nurse's questions.

'You were born in Canada but your parents were Scottish?'

'I'll tell you what I know,' Anne said. 'It was a big house in Hamilton called Clydevia.'

'Hamilton in Canada?'

'That's right.'

'And the house was named after the River Clyde?'

'That's right.'

'Were they posh people?'

Harry wasn't from posh people. He liked the workers. He grew up near a brush-making factory in King's Cross.

'What did you say?' asked Anne.

'I was asking if your people were posh.'

'They were religious. My father owned stores but he wouldn't open on Sundays. I remember us all brushing . . . those big red leaves you get in Canada. Trying to sweep them up. Trying to catch them. They whirled about the yard in the fall and we ran in circles.' The money had come from Glasgow cotton-spinners and she remembered the aunts coming over one time to help her mother, when she was ill. Anne always felt she owed it to the aunts to come and help them when their time came. 'I had to leave my career in New York,' Anne said, 'but I don't want to talk about it.'

'But that was later,' the nurse said. 'We were talking about your childhood.'

'They helped my mother.'

'And what about your daddy?'

He sent her typewritten notes whenever he went away on business, always signed: 'I love you, Daddy x.' She could see them today. He fixed up a small light-bulb in the doll's house by her bed so that she could leave it on while she was sleeping, the perfect house, the perfect house to dream by, and it would stand there no matter what happened in the world. The child and the adult too lived in sympathy with the landing light. Her mother went mad when the jerking took over, when nobody could help her anymore, and one day she simply disappeared from their lives. And so it was that whenever Anne pictured the house called Clydevia she was really picturing the doll's house. 'It was lit with a bulb,' she said again. 'And that's what my father did and I think that's enough for now.'

Maureen looked moved by what she'd heard. She felt close to Anne when it came to certain things and put a hand on her sleeve.

Often prints for hanging and exhibits require a generous amount of fixing up and retouching. To prevent markings from showing, you should follow a certain treatment. This method works best with dead matte paper without any sheen. That was Harry. He could spend hours retouching because that was his thing. You don't mind me saying that, love? I never told you about the doll's house because I wanted our house to be the first.

A young man wearing a boiler suit came into the lounge

carrying a pole and he winked at the nurse. 'Afternoon, ladies. I won't be a minute, I'm just checking the smoke alarm.'

'What's that?' Dorothy said.

'It's a big pole, missus.'

'Jeezo,' Maureen said. 'They've got all the technology nowadays.' The man got two beeps out of the alarm and seemed satisfied with that. Dorothy played a few silent notes on the organ and the elderly man continued sleeping in the chair.

'Then what happened?' asked Maureen.

I might be daft, but I'm not as daft as I look, Anne thought when Maureen asked for more. She knew that her daughter and Maureen were always talking on the phone. And they wouldn't be talking about Luke or any of the important things because that would be unlike Alice. They would just be gossiping about Anne's pension book and probably talking about the photographs Anne had in the darkroom.

'You need to go easier on Alice.'

Maureen had said that to Anne the day before. And that was a sign, thought Anne. That was definitely a sign. Alice had always wanted to turn Anne's neighbours against her. She'd tried to poison Luke's mind but he was off fighting, so he wouldn't be bothering with all that nonsense. Anne believed nowadays that her daughter's main goal was to put her in a nursing home. Alice blamed her for everything. 'I don't remember anything else,' she said to the nurse, thumping the arm of the chair. The nurse pretended she was startled, then spoke with her eyes down.

'Aw. I think you do, Anne. I think you remember artists you used to like. You spoke about them last time. Maureen was helping you, remember? Because she says you were a very talented photographer.' Anne found it hard sometimes to tell the difference between Luke and Harry. And she found it hard to separate pictures she had taken herself from ones she just loved. The young man in the boiler suit had finished what he was doing and he just sat down with them. Nobody seemed to mind because he was nice and he was young and Anne was an open book.

'I wanted our house to be the first,' she said.

'What house is that?'

Anne waited. It took a while. 'When I left Canada I was only seventeen. The place I went to was a summer camp for photographers. A nice place. Upstate New York. We all wore sailor suits and that kind of thing. One of the girls became very good. Her father had owned a store as well and she loved taking pictures of people. It was a famous place by a lake and we were happy there. That was our lives at the time. We didn't need men and we were young and it was easy to be happy. You woke up that way. And one of the teachers in the colony had taken a famous picture of horses pulling a carriage through the snow.'

MY LUKE

The young man with the pole stood up. 'I'm just listening to you,' he said to Anne. 'Is your name Mrs Quirk?'

'It is,' Maureen answered, leaning forward. 'Mrs Quirk. And you're the man from the council, aren't you?'

'Aye. My name's Russell. I'm here to check the smoke alarm.' It turned out his older brother had gone to the same university as Luke. 'My big brother did politics at Strathclyde,' he said, 'and he knew your grandson, Mrs Quirk.'

'Luke is in the army,' Anne said.

[95]

'Jesus,' the young man said. 'We had the radio on in the van and they were saying another soldier got killed.'

Maureen looked up. 'In Afghanistan?'

'Another one, aye,' the boy said. 'It was on West Sound. They say he came from around here.'

Maureen was looking at Anne but it wasn't clear if the young man's news had got through to her; then Maureen noticed a spot of colour on each of her friend's cheeks. 'My Luke's over there,' Anne said. 'He's called Luke Campbell but he's from Glasgow.'

The young man rubbed at his ear and stepped back. 'Well, obviously they're talking about somebody else.'

'Obviously,' Maureen said.

Anne's eyes went to the pinboard where some of the cards still remained from Easter. She felt tired suddenly and wished she could lie down on the bed she and Harry had bought that time in Blackpool.

THE EXTRAORDINARY LIFE OF HARRY BLAKE

The next day a child brought in a tortoise and it sat in Anne's lap at the breakfast table. She liked the feeling of its paws. 'He's all right,' she said when the boy tried to lift him off. 'I'll tell you something, dear. At one time I could've run right past this creature. Long ago, I was quick. You wouldn't have seen me for dust.'

After the toast and marmalade, Jack from flat 19 began talking about the blackout. Anne shuddered when he first used the word. He said it again: 'You know, the blackout. When they had to board up all the windows.'

'That's right,' Anne said. 'That was before I came to live in Glasgow with my aunts.'

'What year was that?'

'I couldn't tell you. There was a new war on. They said they wouldn't let the ships pass through.'

'Suez.'

Another of the men looked up. 'So that's 1956,' he said.

Anne's experience at the Memory Club had ignited her curiosity or irritated her, she couldn't decide. It was odd. There was just so much detail in a person's life and you did well to get rid of the half of it. If you were any good you protected yourself by holding on to this and forgetting that. And even the bits you keep are best kept in silence.

These foolish things remind me of you.

She used to say it to Luke when he was a boy. 'You've got to live a life proportionate to your nature,' she said. 'You've got to find out what that means and then stick to it.' She could still see the boy's eyes, ready to understand, even if he couldn't yet. That was Luke. 'Never worry a jot about what other people are going to say,' she said to him. When he later decided to join the army it was a shock to many people but she didn't hesitate to come after him and shake his hand. She remembered the time she got the plane and went all the way to England to see him graduate in his nice red sash and they walked round a church.

'My Harry flew Lysanders,' she said to the others at the breakfast table. 'I know that much. They were painted black to beat the radar. Nobody knew where the airstrip was.'

'It's nice nattering to you, Anne,' said Jack from number 19. 'Because you're educated.' Maureen came in with the news that Mr Obama was disliked by quite a lot of people. She said it as she cleared away the breakfast things, believing the TV news was private and that it was her choice to spread it about, after the toast. The others could always tell when Maureen had just been speaking to one of her children because the rims of her eyes were pink and she became efficient.

'This is more than one load for the dishwasher,' she said. It was obvious Maureen resented them all using a separate knife for the butter and the jam. Jack cast her a look as if to say, 'Who gives a toss about cutlery?' That calmed her down a bit and she sat down to listen, even though her hands were shaking.

'So was your Harry in the RAF?' Jack asked. When he asked that question it was Maureen who reacted first: she put down her cup and her eyes moistened again. At the same time, Anne looked a little flustered and flicked the edge of the tablecloth.

'Not just that,' she said.

When Maureen thought about Anne in the future, her mind would settle on this moment, when she saw Anne looking helpless about Harry and the Royal Air Force. It appeared to Jack that Anne simply couldn't remember what it was her husband did. But there was some kind of notebook on top of the ottoman in Anne's bedroom, and she asked Maureen, very precisely in that moment, if she would kindly bring a folded piece of paper from the front of the notebook. When Maureen returned with it, Jack had moved on from that part of the conversation. But Anne thanked Maureen and unfolded the paper, on which was typed a single-spaced biographical report. Harry must have typed it years ago. The paper had a heading across the top that said 'Manchester Polytechnic School of Photography'. Anne smiled, she had confidence in the evidence she was about to give, and her clear voice gave dignity to the stops and starts.

Harry Blake was born in 1920 at King's Cross in London. His father was a train driver and his mother worked in a brush factory off Caledonian Road. He went to school locally and then into the RAF. He flew Blenheims and Lysanders doing solo reconnaissance work in World War II, mainly photographic work as part of the RAF's special operations 161 Squadron. This was abysmal work flying a jet-black aircraft into enemy territory from RAF Winkleigh in Devon. Terrifying missions were also flown out of St Eval in Cornwall. Harry Blake would often photograph German installations using moonlight for navigation and many times he delivered agents to France, landing in fields lit with only three torches. After the war Mr Blake attended Guildford College – handily only a few miles from RAF Farnborough – where he helped found one of the first photographic schools in Britain. He was later decorated for his war service before taking up a teaching position in Manchester. He is credited with supporting a new generation of British documentary photographers.

Anne folded the piece of paper and placed it under her saucer. 'He was some man,' Jack said.

'He was certainly that,' Anne said. She looked over at Maureen as if daring her to say otherwise. 'That's what you call loyalty. Sticking with people. And loyalty's just the same as courage.'

'Well,' Jack said. 'You have plenty of words. I'll say that for you, Anne. You have more words in you this morning than Heather's had in sixty-odd years of marriage.'

Maureen frowned. 'Now, Jack. What was that Anne was saying about loyalty? Don't speak ill of Heather. You've got to stick by your family, haven't you?' Anne was staring into the plants. And after a few moments Maureen was off on one, rattling away before crashing her cup down on her saucer. 'Stick by them? Hell as like. You stick by them for years and what thanks do you get? Wouldn't give you daylight in a dark corner. Talk about selfish: you could be lying dead.'

Maureen was upset because one of her kids hadn't sent her a birthday card. Esther was always busy and it was good to be busy but it hurt Maureen to think that her own daughter couldn't stop and buy a card. Maureen was a slave to Hallmark and she'd never met a flowery card she didn't like. It was the way her family expressed emotion, sending cards with nice words printed inside, and Esther had no right just ignoring it. No right at all. After all the things Maureen had done for her and all the sacrifices.

Anne's mind was somewhere else, dreaming about the Beatles. They walked down the promenade in their silver suits and the girls came after them and the light was perfect that day. Jack turned over his newspaper and gave a low whistle. 'That Abramovich thinks he can buy up the world,' he said. 'And it's always the Russians that cause the trouble. Look at Afghanistan. It was the Russians that started all that. Brezhnev. Remember him? Brezhnev and his tanks upsetting all those people and now we've got to go in there and sort it all out. It's a scandal.'

'They would send word, wouldn't they?' Anne said. 'If anything had happened to my Luke?'

'Of course they would,' Jack said. He folded the newspaper while staring into space and then turned to Anne. 'It's amazing to think about your husband and your grandson both being war heroes. They say talent often skips a generation.'

'Not in this case,' Maureen said. She was finally glad to have a new subject and felt wise about family. 'To be fair. Luke's father was a soldier in Northern Ireland and he died.'

'Is that right?' Jack said, turning to Anne. 'You never mention him.'

'It's my family she's talking about,' Anne said. She was obviously put out by Maureen taking over and parcelling out facts. 'Our Luke's a soldier,' she said, 'but really he's a bit of a thinker, more like my Harry than like his father, who was a nice fellow but had none of that.'

'Your grandson's a clever one?'

'That's right. He could always give tongue to an idea.'

'Really?'

'Oh, yes. He can see what happens behind a photograph.'

'That's nice,' Jack said.

'Oh, it's everything,' Anne said.

JUNGLE

Anne liked to use the laundry room because it was spacious and it had a big drier and she felt she was going on an outing when she went along the corridor with her washing basket and her powder. It was important, Anne used to say, to feel that you had your independence. You could close your back door or you could join the others, it was up to you. Nobody forced you to spend time in the common area if you were having a bad day or couldn't remember the names. Some days are like that. Some days you are just muddled and every day is different.

It was a long walk down the corridor and the lights would come on at night because of the sensor. She sat in the reception area. She placed her things on the ground and just looked at the plants. The gardener from the council had made a sunken forest with a border of breeze blocks. A forest of yucca, jades, banyan and palm grew all the way to a glass ceiling and you could see stars up there, as if they, too, belonged to Scotland. Anne loved looking into the tangle of plants at Lochranza Court. She felt it was alive with shadows and stories that couldn't be captured in words.

Someone to love, someone like you.

The corridor was quiet at night, but even if someone passed, Anne wouldn't notice because she was so absorbed in the plants. It was silent but she could almost hear the busy life of the undergrowth. She forgot why she was out. Her basket of washing would often be sitting there in the morning and the warden would find it and know it was Anne's.

HER OLD SELF

She left her washing the day she read out Harry's biography and her mind was a bit unsettled. Harry didn't come often enough. It was only a car journey and she'd promised an editor some prints. She'd been back in her flat for a while and the rabbit was looking at the microwave. She was going to use the speakerphone to tell the night warden there was a noise at her front door but then she realised she could answer the door herself, so she got up and took off the chain. 'Mrs Quirk,' the voice said when she opened the door. 'It's me, Russell. I was round today to test the smoke alarms. Can I come in and talk to you for a minute?'

Maureen heard them speaking through the wall. It didn't happen often because Anne didn't have many visitors, since her grandson was away on service and her daughter wasn't that welcome. It was nice to hear because Anne used to have such a lot to say, and now she went up and down because of her health and she could be silent for days. Maureen turned down her television and guessed it was a man's voice; maybe one of the neighbours had taken her in a cup of tea. That's nice. Maureen continued to watch television in silence. Nothing in the room was old, no pictures, no wood and no books, nothing with a memory. Esther had once asked her why she had no photographs of her grandchildren. And nothing of her own mum and dad, especially her dad. 'They just gather dust,' Maureen said, 'and the shops want a fortune for frames nowadays.'

She had gone that morning to see the warden in her office. She kept her own cup and saucer there, but, for some reason, that day, Maureen didn't bother with tea. 'We should have a drink,' Jackie said. 'It's your birthday. It's a nice glass of fizz we should be having.'

'Birthdays. I'm past caring about them.'

Jackie closed the door and they spoke about Anne.

'How long?' Maureen asked.

'I don't know, darling. Maybe a few months. It's a shame because we've tried to keep her here. Her mind's so alive. We've really tried. But it's getting to the stage where she can't cope in the flat. Even with you and me covering for her.'

'She can't do the cooker.'

'The kettle. She can't work the kettle.'

'And then there's the rabbit.' Maureen kept biting her bottom lip in an unconscious display of pity. 'She's not quite as bad with the rabbit,' she said. 'She still likes to know where he is, but she's not trying to feed him the way she was before the summer.'

'You always say "him",' Jackie said.

'Well, that's what Anne does.'

'The whole thing's horrendous, Maureen.'

'I know.'

'To see it happen to such an intelligent woman.'

'I know. Feeding the rabbit. It was me opening the tins. But she seems to have moved beyond that now. I don't understand it. Every day she's different and some days she's like her old self.'

'She can still talk. And she has a strong imagination. That's probably what keeps her going.'

'But it probably makes her seem better than she is.'

'Exactly,' Jackie said. 'It's mild dementia, but it's progressive. That's what the health workers are saying. The people at the Memory Club are monitoring the whole thing, to see how bad she is. We've been hiding it . . .'

'The whole community's been hiding it. We don't want them to take Anne into a home.'

'It's always the end,' Jackie said. 'But then, you can only cover up for so long. Then you're not doing the person any favours at all, really. You have to let them go.'

'Oh, don't say that,' Maureen said. 'Not yet, Jackie. She's still all right and we can —'

'I'm just saying,' said Jackie. 'It can't go on forever, and these health workers, they know what they're doing.'

'Yes.'

'We can't have residents setting fire to things.'

'No.' They sat in silence for a moment. 'Maybe my Esther would have an idea of how to make it easier,' said Maureen. 'She's very well qualified and she has a secretary.'

'Aye, well,' Jackie said. 'It's worth a try. But Anne will be moving out at some point, Maureen. That's just a fact, hen, and you need to start preparing for it.'

Maureen was staring at the desk. 'I saw some of the pictures she took when she was a young lassie,' she said. 'Unbelievable, Jackie. You really wouldn't believe them if you saw them. Just taking an ordinary thing like an old sink full of dishes and making it, well, you know, I don't know anything about these things.'

'Beautiful,' Jackie said.

'That's the right word: beautiful. As if life was just pictures. Like things you would see in an old magazine, you know? And when I asked her about her photography she said it was one of the things her late husband Harry did for her when they were young. He was a teacher and he taught her the new methods. She said it was Harry's technique that made the photographs special.'

'Is that right?'

'That's what she said. He knew about chemicals.'

'Oh, my,' Jackie said, 'it's great to have a man who knows things.'

Maureen replayed the conversation in her mind with the sound down and the mumbles coming through the wall. She didn't know what she'd do if Anne ever left Lochranza Court. Maureen recalled when she saw her with a whisky in a crystal tumbler and thought, Good God, here's Anne. A wee lady she is and she knows her own mind.

BEFORE THE WAR

The young man was nice and he made his own tea by pulling back the tape from the cooker and boiling a pan of water and finding a tea bag. Anne noticed his face was red but it calmed down. He looked like all the boys look nowadays with their cropped hair but he wasn't wearing a boiler suit like before and his shoes were polished. She sat down and said to herself that the fellows can certainly iron their shirts nowadays. He had things to say about the courage of the soldiers and he felt they were doing an amazing job and he said it took something special to sign up and go out there and fight.

'They have to go,' she said. 'It's the war.' The boy put down his cup and adopted a serious expression, which caused him to blush again and look worried.

'Mrs Quirk, I said something today and I shouldn't have said that in front of you. I'm sorry.'

'What's that, dear?'

'I said about the news. That a soldier from around here had died in Afghanistan. It was on the radio in the van. And I shouldn't have said that, Mrs Quirk. I listened to the report again. I'm sure it's nothing to do with you because they always contact the families first.'

'The men have to show courage,' she said. 'And go and fight for their country.'

'Mrs Quirk—'

'That's what Harry said. And he was right. You take it on the chin and that's true, son. You have to stand up and be counted. You're all the man you'll ever be. And when you get the call, that's you.'

'I'm daft sometimes. And it's been bugging me since yesterday . . .'

He looked a little bit like some of the photographers she used to know. They were always out on the streets, those guys. They wanted to get away from studios and portraiture, all that stuff, lights and props, airbrushing. They were always young and confident. 'You work for the Council?'

'That's right.' He was a nice-looking man. He looked like the photographer Roger Mayne. She remembered seeing him in Manchester with Harry one time, this thin-faced, serious man with a lock of dark hair falling over his brow and these pictures he'd taken of children in London.

'Those were fine pictures,' she said.

'They said the soldier who died was part of a big operation to do with a dam. I wrote it down.' He took a note from his pocket and read from it. 'The Kajaki dam. They said it was a big job to bring electricity to the Afghan people.'

'I thought I was an old hand,' she said. 'Then I met Harry and all the younger ones. I'd been away from it for a while, looking after them in Glasgow. Then I came to Blackpool and met Harry. He changed the way the pictures looked. He showed me how to bring out the light, the eyes, the background, you know, and he taught everybody.'

'Are you talking about your husband, Mrs Quirk?'

'Harry. You remember him?'

The boy took his cup to the sink and ran it under the tap while Anne talked about them, the Young Meteors, the group of photographers surrounding Harry at Manchester in the 1960s. It did occur to Anne that the boy might be too young but he seemed part of it, the men who worked for *Picture Post* and for Kodak and . . . maybe she was boring him.

'I'm really sorry, Mrs Quirk,' he said. 'I didn't mean to upset you and I should watch my mouth.'

'You're okay.'

He stared at her. It took him a moment. Then he stroked her hand and said he met a lot of elderly people because of his work for the council. His eyes were young. 'I hope that wasn't your

[107]

Luke,' he said. 'My brother said they would definitely come round and tell the family ages before it was on the radio.' He stood up and picked up his keys from the breakfast bar. Anne hoped he would stay because she wanted to talk about what to do with the stuff that was still down in the darkroom. It was nice to take pictures of children, she thought: they were only small for a short period of time and then it was over, wasn't it?

Maureen noticed it had gone quiet next door during the time she was on the phone to Alice. She didn't feel guilty but she hated to think it troubled Anne. It wasn't as if Maureen didn't have a family of her own: they were a full-time job, three grown kids and grandchildren into the bargain, and she only phoned Alice to make sure she understood everything that was happening. Since the rabbit, some people, some neighbours, had said that Anne's daughter was too absent. But Maureen understood families and she wasn't afraid to use the phone to try and help. It was late in the conversation that she turned to the day before.

'Have you heard from anybody?'

'Should I have?'

'Not especially, no.' Maureen pursed her lips and gathered herself. 'That nurse was in again this week,' she said. 'Yesterday. They like to get your mother talking about her childhood and all sorts.'

'All sorts is right,' Alice said.

'The illness makes her confused.'

'She's always been confused when it comes to the past. The fact is, Maureen, my mother's always had issues with her memory. That's what makes this so . . .'

'Heartbreaking.'

'Sad, yes. It's sad. Sad for us. Because it's now too late for my mother ever to face anything. If I was being unkind, I'd say that her illness has caught up with her character.' Maureen sometimes felt a twinge at the idea that the criticism coming from Alice was general, as if Anne's daughter was making comments about all mothers when she spoke about Anne and her problems. 'Now she's fantasising about a rabbit,' added Alice, 'but she was always fantasising about something. We're used to it.'

'The rabbit comes and goes.'

Alice responded with clarity. The people on TV, thought Maureen, are seldom so clear. 'We're used to my mother having relationships that keep us out. It's one of her things. At least, it's one of her things with me.'

'You're a mother yourself,' Maureen said.

Alice swallowed hard and let the implication fade. She had never been the mother she wanted to be – it wasn't allowed. And now she had to depend on the next-door neighbour to keep her informed about what was happening in her own family. It was pitiable, really. Anne had failed as a mother on nearly every front, but fantasy would carry her all the way. Everybody, including Alice's own son Luke, would pity the sad life of sacrifice she had framed so perfectly for their eyes. Alice knew better. But why did that knowledge feel like a curse?

'Mother seems to have told you a lot,' she said.

'That's what it's for, the Memory Club.'

'And she spoke about Harry?'

'Oh, yes. A lot about Harry.'

Alice felt that people kept her out of having information until she didn't want it anymore. 'Well, thank you for phoning, Maureen. I really appreciate you taking the trouble.'

'It's no bother,' Maureen said. They paused. The call hadn't gone well, but Alice didn't want to appear angry.

'I pray for them at morning Mass,' she said. It was clear that Alice needed to take strength at the mention of Harry.

'Were you his child, Alice?'

'Yes,' she said. 'He got her pregnant.'

Each wanted to hang up, but they kept hoping for something more, a clever development in the conversation that would turn it into something nice. Maureen said her father was the person she missed all the time. 'We used to run away to Glasgow together when I was wee,' she said. 'Just me and him and we had the whole day to ourselves. He used to take me to the perfume counter at Arnotts. We'd buy soap. And on the way back . . .' She paused and Alice felt kindly towards her. 'I always wished the train belonged to us and that we'd never have to get off.'

'I had none of that,' Alice said.

'He called me Mog.'

'I don't think my father even remembered our names.'

'Whose names?'

'Ours,' Alice said. She spoke reluctantly, feeling that she had gone far enough with Maureen. There was such yearning in Alice's voice, as if she wished more than anything for things to be certain, but she knew they couldn't be. 'I'm not sure,' she said.

ALWAYS

It was only a fraction of the stuff from Atholl Gardens, but the linen was washed and ironed, laid out and tied with blue ribbon, looking like old stories that had yet to be told. Over the TV set Anne draped an Edwardian tablecloth that had come from Canada after the death of her mother. She placed the ceramic rabbit on top of the tablecloth to hold it down and then she glanced at him while she moved between the bundles, unfolding the material and holding it up and tutting.

Jane, Jessie. Wait a minute. There was Grace. And Anna. Nobody came to the house in Glasgow once they were gone. It was just me up there. Before Luke was born I would build a fire because the pipes were frozen. My fingers used to get cold and they were stained with developer most of the time. I went to the camera club, that's right. I used to massage that stuff into my fingers to stop the irritation. Camphor ice.

She didn't notice her neighbour enter but didn't flinch when she saw her. 'Good heavens,' Maureen said, stepping over the bundles. 'Did you decide to have a wee spring clean?'

'Stuff from the aunt-hill,' Anne said.

'I thought I heard a man's voice earlier.'

Anne seemed distracted. 'We were talking about camera work. I had to come back from New York and I didn't want to come back, Maureen. I wanted to take pictures.'

'You were very good.'

'It's in there somewhere.' She pointed to the bathroom. 'A lot of negatives and things like that.' All of a sudden she seemed upset. She lifted a pillowcase and dabbed her eyes with it. 'But Jessie used to read to them all in their beds at night,' she said.

'Who did she read to?'

'The aunts.'

'And could you get away sometimes and see Harry?'

'I drove a car then.'

'Oh, I wish I could drive,' Maureen said. 'I never took the test, you know. We took the train. My dad loved trains and we were always on them. Away days, they called them. I was an only child. He used to squeeze my hand and say I was his favourite person. Just like that.'

'I had a nice father, too,' Anne said.

'We were lucky.'

Anne looked up as if she suddenly appreciated Maureen. 'I've always had good neighbours,' she said.

Maureen put her to bed and then went to bring a cup of tea from next door. She placed a sleeping pill on the saucer, to see if it didn't relax her, but it turned out Anne was fast asleep when she got back so she just took it herself. She felt Anne was on her own, really. She had all these people and all these stories but it didn't amount to much. You have to be ready to put the past behind you and learn to rely on yourself.

That's what I did, thought Maureen. I never needed a man to make me into somebody. No way. I could stand on my own two feet. But her mind changed as she handled the cold linen. She didn't want to admit it, but she understood how it sometimes took another person to turn you into your better self. And that's what happened with her and Anne. In the old lady's company she felt more like the person she ought to have been. Anne's interests touched Maureen, revealing a bit of her to herself. Maureen had just finished the audiobook of *Wuthering Heights* and she thought of it as she looked at Anne lying asleep. She couldn't imagine unquiet slumbers for a woman with that kind of nature and all this linen.

Maureen lifted a nice glass from the trolley and poured herself a whisky before coming back and sitting by the bed. It sometimes confused Anne to hear Luke's letters, but Maureen wanted nonetheless to read them to her in a good, clear voice, capturing the words he'd written down. With the glass balanced on her knee, she took out a folded letter from the pocket of her cardigan.

I told all the boys to write letters so I better write one myself, eh? This is the one and only Captain Campbell here of the 1st Royal Western Fusiliers writing to you from the roasting desert.

As she read aloud the clock was ticking and the whisky tasted of smoke. The letter was full of news.

So that's it, really. We're in Camp Bastion and getting ready to push off. I'm not allowed to tell you where we're going but it's a good one. I've got the usual team here, Flannigan, Dooley and young Lennox, who spend all day playing ping-pong and slagging each other off. The major is here too and is doing his best for us, so if anything happens to me you'll know it's just bad luck. Main thing is I'm thinking of you. Keep smiling, Luke.

Maureen finished the letter and put it away. It said a lot for a young man that he could write a letter like that. Just to let the people at home know he loved them, just to do the right thing when it's dangerous and he knows they must be worried with all the stuff they see on television. She poured another whisky and walked to the window. Half the things her own family said they probably didn't mean. They were all right, really. You have to forgive people if you want to get along, yet it wasn't the future she had expected with her children. She'd thought it would be holidays abroad and big dinners by the pool with all the women asking her opinion.

The darkness outside made a mirror of the window and the room looked back at itself as Maureen sat sleeping on the sofa with the tumbler in her hand and the linen stacked beside her. She opened her eyes with a start and found the siren was sounding. She got up slowly and went over to wash the tumbler and place it on the dish-rack before going into the bedroom. 'In the name of God,' said Anne.

'It's the fire alarm,' Maureen said. She unhooked Anne's dressing-gown from the back of the door and brought it to her. 'We'll have to go into the courtyard and be counted.'

'What is it?'

'The fire alarm. This is every other day. I bet you it's that Mr MacDonald again in flat 29.'

'McDonald's? Like the hamburgers?'

'No, it'll be toast. But a pest, Anne. Why he insists on making toast at midnight I'll never know.'

CHIAROSCURO

The road was black out there and the sea was black and the shore was blacker than the road. Anne could see the people gathered in the courtyard and the scene was entirely made of light as it passed through the glass doors of the reception area. Anne saw how the light picked out the eyes and the cheeks and the ears of the people standing against the blackness. She'd seen charcoals like that, where a person's eye was a dot of white and a nose was nothing but the smallest stripe.

Housecoat, slippers. And somebody said: 'Effing freezing out here, Jack.'

'What time is it, then?'

'Better ask the warden.'

Anne knew it wasn't a fire. It wasn't a house on fire. It was Mr MacDonald from flat 29.

You want fresh chemicals touching the film. You have to agitate the tank, keep it moving, swirl it, Anne, that's the secret if you want good contrast. Get the chemicals rolling but not too much, darling, or there will be blemishes. Right there. Oh my the safelight's out, love, would you believe it? Go down to Woolworth's, would you not, and see if they've got the bulbs, ruby-red. And get the other ones for later. It says here: 'A yellow-green or orange safelight is used for bromide papers and lantern slides, and a yellow or amber safelight for contact papers.' He was serious and then not. Keep your hands to yourself, Harry; oh stop it now, you're daft.

Anne was shivering in the cold and Maureen came up with a blanket to put round her shoulders. 'This is a bloody pantomime,' Maureen said with a look on her face. 'The third time this month. They should tape up his cooker. I don't see why your cooker's taped up, Anne, and his is still going and all he ever does is set fire to things.'

'Oh, stop it, Harry,' said Anne.

'This has been a long and complicated day for you,' Maureen said, and she stroked Anne's cheek.

'We could walk along the prom.'

'Not tonight, Anne. It's awful cold.' But then she took her neighbour by the arm and walked just a little way down the path leading to the bandstand. Anne looked and smiled to see the warm colour on Maureen's face, the street lamps drawing out her eyes and the black distance making a perfect background as they walked along the front. Two yellow blinks appeared out there in the part of the sea where the water was darkest. Anne stopped and Maureen stopped.

'What was that light?' Anne said.

'The Isle of Arran.'

To Anne it was all the walks. She couldn't name them perhaps but she could see them in her mind. The ones she took as a child by Lake Ontario with her mother and father. The boating pond at the Menier Camp where she strolled with a Leitz Leica, 1948. It was all of these and other places as the night enclosed the promenade and the lighthouse again blinked twice. 'I had a friend,' she said. 'We used to go rowing in the boating pond. A long time ago. They called us the Two Annes.'

THE ADDRESS BOOK

They didn't need the fire brigade. It was all done with a phone call and an opened window. Anne, back in the flat and sitting up, looking through the pages of her address book, found postcards of places she had liked when she was no longer young.

Campbeltown.

Girvan.

Blackwaterfoot.

Oban.

She knew of a morning in Oban with curls of butter at the guesthouse table, porridge and oatcakes, mackerel paste. The house was high on the hill above the port, under the pine trees, a place to be with Harry. Looking at the postcard, it wasn't the house that came back to her but the breakfast table and the night before, the sound of him asleep. She read a story in an old, water-damaged book she found in the bookcase. She couldn't have said the title of the book or the name of the guesthouse, but she could remember the story about the Lady Appin, who kept a painting of her lover in her private bedroom, a soldier who then died in the foreign wars. Anne couldn't have told you his name anymore, not a whisper now of his name, but Lady Appin locked her door and wept for a year and picked at the paint until the canvas was totally blank. 'Maybe I can live,' she said, 'because now he lives nowhere but in my mind.'

She placed the postcards at the front of the address book. It had been with her since her days in New York and later she got it bound in red leather. She opened it at the letter T and a photograph fell out, a black-and-white snap of a boy and girl. After staring at it for a long time, Anne went and got the scissors and slowly cut the photograph in half, placing one piece in the book and dropping the other to the floor.

By the sea, by the sea, by the beautiful sea.

You and me. You and me.

'Documentary work is the future. It's the truth, darling, the whole truth and nothing but the truth,' he said. One time he left a note pinned to the door of the flat in Blackpool saying he'd just driven over on the off-chance and would be back for the Illuminations because Jayne Mansfield was turning them on and a Canberra bomber was doing a fly-past.

'All my love. See you Saturday.'

When she was with him he only had one life. She fell asleep playing that song in her mind about the beautiful sea, his eyes in front of her, Harry's eyes. When the room was dark a single beam fell onto the bed from outside and lit the address book, where a cut picture of a young boy lay on the open page.

4

'It doesn't flood the valley because there's a good old dam holding it back.'

'What you talking about, Major?'

'I'm talking about the Helmand River.'

Scullion breathed out and nipped his cock. If you nip your cock in the wrong place you get piss on your boots. This was one of the helpful, sometimes philosophical facts that the major could retail at random. 'What in the name of fuck is that noise?' he said.

There was a guy peeing beside him. 'Don't worry,' said the guy. 'You're cool. Stick with the programme. That's not incoming fire, it's just the rations truck choking on its Corn Pops.'

'Its what?'

'Corn Pops, dude? Don't you eat breakfast in that dump you come from?'

'We eat porridge, like the best human beings.'

'Not us, Daddy. Not the Canadians. I'm talking Reese's Puffs. I'm talking *Froot Loops*.' The colonel laughed and it was one of those laughs that worked its way into a grunt.

'That shit you people feed your children should be banned,' Scullion said. 'It's toxic crap. No wonder those kids have two fucken heads and a massive need for semi-automatic weapons.'

'That's America, dude. Keep us out of it.'

'You're just America-on-ice.'

'Whatever.'

Scullion stared at the mountains and thought about the dam while the sun sparked off the convoy's mirrors. He peed into the bushes and spoke again. 'But there's drought and poverty down there, corruption like you've never seen and Terry bandits in their mud huts, begging to die for Allah. In time people will forget about the dam.'

He licked his lips and thought of R. White's lemonade. In his memory he could see a whole crate of it in the cellar of a pub in Dominick Street, Mullingar, in the old, grey days before the heat. The colonel put away his dick and turned round to face Scullion.

'But we can't forget it. We can't forget nothing because we're running a mission here.'

'The good thing is we'll be giving those kids electricity once the turbines are installed,' Scullion said. 'That's if we can pay enough bribes to the Taliban to let the power flow.' A giant Mitsubishi crane roared past behind them. 'That's the job. And if we can haul all this kit up the valley and get the machines turning, then the Kajaki operation – this whole fucken thing right here – will have been the biggest public relations coup of the entire war, my dear boy.'

'I ain't your boy.'

'You're all my fucken boys.'

'I'll have you remember I'm a colonel with the 1st Royal Canadian Regiment.' He smiled at Scullion: he knew his type. Everybody knew everybody's type and they mistook it for experience.

'Telling you straight. This operation's a PR megaphone,' Scullion said.

The colonel licked the salt from his middle finger. 'Well, fuck that,' he said and poked the air twice. 'Fuck all that. If it's all about giving the ragheads a bit of hydro, that's cool with me. But if you're telling me we're risking soldiers' lives just to climb up there for a photo op, so our armies can justify the Yankee dollar. Fuck that.'

'It's all in a day's work,' Scullion said. 'That's our mission, that's our task. So don't knock it, Sookie. You'll be back in Hog Town whacking pucks before you know it.'

As they rumbled along, Scullion tried to imagine Alexander the Great riding into the land of bones. Weren't the brown plains and jagged mountains a hostile shadowland, a place of dark minds filtering the light? He saw old armies coming with their cigars and their bagpipes to slay the enemies of civilisation. He saw men with mules and brass bands dying of cholera in the boiling wastes of the southern desert. In his mind he pictured Alexander's handsome face, young and fair with a cut lip, a hero driving his units through the snow-filled passes of the Hindu Kush, leading other men through clouds of mosquitoes and over the rapids of the Oxus, and greeting them with handshakes one by one as they arrived at the place of battle, their sarissas already crusted in blood.

Earlier that morning, Scullion had sat on the short wall of an abandoned compound to speak to Rashid. He considered the Afghan a good soldier: just the sort you want to be teaching to protect his country. Scullion imagined Rashid to be like the local helping hand in colonial life, a smiling khitmutgar from the golden period, a child-man, subject to sentimental affection from the clubbable men of England.

'But don't forget I'm Irish, Rashid,' said Scullion. 'I'm probably more like you, when all's said and done.'

'You are tired, sir,' said Rashid.

'The boys are fine. They have each other. A senior officer has to stand apart.'

'Yes, sir.'

'Though some officers don't know it.'

'Yes, sir.'

'You know who I mean?'

'You are speaking of Captain Campbell, sir? I see you do not like each other as you once did.'

'He's the judge and jury, my friend,' Scullion said. 'But you see he knows nothing about life. He thinks we are all just characters in his drama. He can't see anymore why we are fighting. Such men lose faith and then they blame their brothers. I've seen it before.'

'And you, sir. You still have faith?'

'I have a task, so I do. My task is to help push the operation to a successful conclusion.'

'But you are tired, sir.'

'That's true.'

'Very tired.'

'Luke has read some books. That's something. Shame that it makes him see sickness everywhere.'

'But you are sick, sir.' As he said this, Rashid raised his patch to itch the skin around his eye and Scullion saw a gnarled, ragged hole. And, right there in the open air the major felt sick: he looked into the dead socket and his mouth went dry. Scullion knew finally that his nerve had gone. The years of shredded bone and sudden cries and blood on the grass were behind him, and he was lost, not knowing what to say or how to be. Just this blank disgust holding him there and sapping his spirit.

He spat a plug of chewing gum onto the ground between them.

'Pick that up,' he said.

'Sorry, sir.'

'Pick it up.'

Rashid was silent. Scullion always liked the way he took his time to talk, searching through the concept before lighting on the word. 'I want to learn how to speak more like you,' he said. 'In pictures.'

'You will, Rashid.'

'For my own people.' Rashid picked up the piece of gum and put it in his mouth and he stared at the major with an unreadable expression. 'Dust,' he said. 'I like the taste of my own land.'

It was hotter than usual and Scullion gave orders and checked supplies among his group and at various times that day he shivered with a secret revulsion. He didn't know why.

A commander in Bosnia once told him he had no politics. It was the day after a young fellow Scullion was mentoring got shot in Vitez. 'You're a typical modern soldier,' the commander said, 'partly because you trust nothing. Everything's doable and everything's bullshit. You think like a flame-thrower, Scullion. You want to burn away the enemy and scorch their minds, without knowing what their minds are.'

'Is there another way?'

'We need to find one,' the commander said.

'Well,' Scullion said, 'you've slept peacefully in your bed for fifty years.'

'Peacefully? I don't know about that, Charlie. Any peace we've had is because we're not really thinking. If we actually understood what we were doing in the world we wouldn't ever sleep again.'

Around midday, Scullion poked his head out the top of the Vector and spat down on the road. 'Fucking A,' he said. As they moved up the track a flock of partridges scooted over the wall of an orchard. Scullion's eyes followed the birds as they flew into a field and then a larger bird dived down to a puff of feathers. You couldn't be sure of anything because of the heat and the way reality was bent by the temperature.

'Hawthorn sixty-eight. This is zero.'

The radio was loud in the Vector and he could hear the boys crapping on. 'Shut your gobs,' he shouted down. 'If it's hot weather you want you should try Kuwait in July.'

'What?' asked Lennox.

'Our fucken rifle grips were melting out there.'

He ducked back down and saw Captain Campbell sweating on the bench with his shirt off. It was a furnace and the heat's weight was dragging down their eyelids, but Luke stared at the major with a face full of accusation. He couldn't empty his mind of how Scullion had missed the ambush. It made him sick to think of it and he could still see the major climbing from the Vector after the firing stopped, that look, as if fatigue and horror had taken over at the end of a long march.

CULVERT

They came to a farmyard that was known to Luke. He hadn't seen it before but it existed in his head, grey stone walls, a run of trees by the road and a covered ditch hewn from the farm into the field. A man and a small boy were walking away from the building and the boy carried a helium balloon on a red string. 'That's weird,' Dooley said. The farm was bombed out and the boy didn't look over at the soldiers.

'The Yanks give them out to the kids,' Scullion said. 'Why the fuck are we stopped here?'

Luke watched the child going off, a large Disney princess in an aqua-blue dress floating above him. 'I want these rifles clean,' Scullion said. 'Get your wire brushes out.'

'It's forty-eight degrees, sir,' said Luke.

'I don't care if it's the fucking *Towering Inferno*. I'm sick watching this section sit on its arse.'

Luke turned to the boys. 'Open your kits. I'm taking a radio and we're going to check out this compound. Okay?' He looked back at Scullion. 'You and me, sir. We're going to check the safety of this shed.'

Scullion put on his helmet and raised his rifle and followed the younger officer into the farm. Rashid walked from the vehicle behind and Luke noticed his shirt was soaked in sweat. 'It is okay,' Rashid said. 'This farm is safe, you can go in.'

'And how do you know that, Rashid?' Luke turned and squared up to him by the broken stones in the yard. 'Would that be your fucken sixth sense or is it your priceless contacts with the enemy?'

'This building has been cleared.'

'By whom? Not by me.'

'We have the surveillance plan.'

'No, Rashid. Your head is a surveillance plan. I don't fucken trust you as far as I could throw you.' Rashid stepped back and put up his hands and shook his head like a professional.

'We are the same rank. I will not be disrespected.'

'No? Well, you can take your one beady eye and fuck right off over there, Captain. I am having a private meeting with Major Scullion of the British army. Fuck off, I said.'

The boys liked it. They liked his style. And they liked nothing more than sudden anger directed at a local. They thought Rashid was all right but a bit of a crawler, and the captain's way of sorting him out had them enthralled over in the Vector. Rashid just walked away and none of them turned their heads as he passed. When Scullion and Campbell went inside, the boys just fiddled with their rifles and then dropped onto the road. They started a game at the edge of the field with a few Royal Scots, playing football with some empty water bottles in a plastic bag.

There was chicken shit on the floor. Scullion flicked a gum wrapper and turned at the wall to look up at his young friend. 'He's one of us,' he said. 'You should be nicer to our allies.'

'He's irrelevant.'

'A little keen, maybe.'

'He's got nothing to do with our section.'

'He's with us,' Scullion said. 'Mainly, he's with us. And you can't blame them for having maybe a . . . heightened sense of desecration, what, with everything that's going on?'

'It's not the 1840s,' Luke said. 'And this is not your private army.'

Scullion made a show of listening carefully to him and then he walked to the far end of the room. Light came from the internal courtyard and he seemed to absorb the light and draw strength from it.

'Listen, Luke. Are you homesick?'

'Don't make this about me.'

'But are you?'

'I've been homesick all my life.'

'Good. That's a good answer. You're an intelligent man and you should pay attention to these facts.'

'I'm not your pupil anymore.'

'That's right. Your contempt has run ahead of your wisdom. And you no longer have a use for me.'

'This unit . . . this regiment has need of a senior officer in the field, sir, who does not absent himself during a major firefight. Can you explain yourself?'

'As a matter of fact . . . I can't.'

'They said you fell asleep.'

'I wasn't asleep, Luke. I was in the Vector. I was on the floor of the Vector, to be accurate.'

'And you decided it would be a good idea to leave a group of your own soldiers, average age eighteen, to survive and then recover from a heavily armed ambush by unknown enemy forces? You decided this was the best way to deploy your experience, did you? The best way to exhibit your leadership?'

'I didn't decide anything, Luke. I was frozen to the spot and that is simply what happened.'

'You're a fucken coward!'

'So it would appear.' Scullion didn't flinch. He didn't move. And as the seconds passed he seemed almost relieved.

'I find that hard to believe.'

'So do I. But it happened. Plain as that. I couldn't move.' He spat his gum onto the ground and looked at it. 'Do you know how many countries I've fought in, Captain?'

'I couldn't guess.'

'Just about all of them. Wherever we had a decent amount of hostility. And here's my hand on my Northern Irish heart to tell you I was never scared in any of them. In fact, I was overjoyed.'

'That's what they say.'

'You know the phrase "They have blood on their hands"? Well, I have blood on my hands, comrade, buckets of it, all in the cause of something good and something noble. Democracy.'

'So you decide to launch your new career as a white feather just at the very moment when my boys are in danger? You leave them to a firefight in the dark, do you? Exposed on a hill? What the fuck is happening to you, Charlie? Are you losing your mind?'

'I might be. It might be that.'

'Not on my fucken watch.'

He sniggered. 'Little Luke Campbell, who joined the army to find his daddy. Ends up confronting real-life danger and real-life fear. Shall I phone your mammy, Luke – get her to come up and turn your Xbox back on? Get you back to your nice wee world of video game combat, eh, my friend? Piling up the points. Topping the leader board. This nasty world of real people and unexpected turns doesn't really suit you, does it?'

'You're sick, Charlie. That stuff with your wife has made you mental or something.'

'Oh, we're all mental. You think all this fighting was making me wise? Making me braver? Here's the lesson, brother: it wears away at you; there's less of you every day.'

'There's less of what?'

'Less life. Less cause. Less morality. Less belief. Less judgement. Less energy. Less fucken hope. Just less. Know what I mean?'

'You know what, sir: I don't fucken think I do.'

'Well, you should. Captain Sharp-as-a-Needle. Mr Up-at-the-Crack-of-Dawn. Where's your fighting spirit now? It's not just about me, all this. When you joined this regiment you wanted to police the world. What a sight you were. You wanted to arrest every bad guy with a mobile phone. No territory was too hostile for Private Ego and his wish to shape the future. That's what made us friends. What happened to all that?'

The major's words burned into him as they had in the days when he felt ideas could make him a better soldier. 'Your private troubles,' he said, 'are threatening the lives of my men, and I won't stand for it.' Luke stepped forward and was up in the major's face. 'I'll destroy you first. Soon as this mission is over, I'm reporting you.'

'You've waited all your life for this, little Luke. I hope you're enjoying your moment.'

'The boys needed you . . .'

Scullion was shaking and blinking, and as he turned sideways he put his hands under his armpits. 'And I needed them. I did. But I wasn't available and it makes me sick to my stomach.' His face flushed when he said those words and he looked as if he might vomit on the farmhouse floor. He bent over, taking deep breaths with closed eyes, and when he looked up thirty years of humanitarian fatigue was on his face. He opened his mouth to say something but didn't say it and then tried again. 'I don't sleep,' he whispered, 'and I may never sleep again. Those pills you gave me – I need more of them. I need to stop my insides turning.'

'You need to leave, Charlie.' They could hear the revving of vehicles outside.

'I don't think I can. They'll have to kill me.'

'Don't be daft, Major,' Luke said, suddenly younger again. It made him sad to see how willingly Scullion accepted blame. 'The whole point of what I'm saying is you're not fit for the boys. They need you. All your experience and what you have to offer.'

Scullion slung on his rifle. 'All my experience,' he said, laughing in Luke's direction and twisting his mouth. 'All my terrific experience and all the army's experience, too.'

'There's life after this,' Luke said. Then he turned from Scullion

[131]

and walked out of the compound, leaving him. He didn't look round and just marched out through the door as if there would be a parade ground out there on the other side, a place of flags and proud families instead of a culvert spewing dirty water into a poppy field.

CONSTITUTION

When they weren't on duty Flannigan called him Luke and sometimes Jimmy-Jimmy, a joke on his Glasgow accent. The two had got to know each at the barracks in Salisbury and grown close at Camp Bastion. Luke tended to look towards Flannigan for basic back-up. During the second day of the Kajaki mission, while the boys bantered in the moving Vector, Flannigan looked over and remembered what Luke had said after the fighting had stopped on the ridge. He said his father had died because of an ambush in Northern Ireland. He said he'd hardly known him but had always lived with the idea of his bravery. Flannigan saw how mortified Luke was by Scullion and the way he'd hung back from the action.

'It doesn't matter, lad,' Flannigan said. 'He was stoned and he's probably not used to weed like that.'

Flannigan was ten years younger. He was clever in a way that had nothing to do with books. Like Luke, he was two guys, the guy in the van and the one in his head, but Flannigan had a stronger army constitution than the captain. He knew that great people often turned out to be rubbish and he thought it normal. That night up on the ridge, after the guns stopped, after the tracer went dead and the Apaches disappeared, the platoon stood around in a state of mellow disbelief. The smoke still hung over the camp and the stars, good God, the crazy stars were out for real.

THE SOUNDS

The convoy had stopped again. It was an improved part of the road, so the sappers and ordnance guys didn't trust it and were out checking for roadside bombs and tripwires. The boys in Luke's group didn't move when Scullion opened the passenger door and jumped down. Lennox had *Now* magazine down his shorts and was chuckling and saying something they'd heard before about a tattoo he wanted.

Luke was filling in a form. 'What's your Zap number, Lennox?'

'LA104,' he said, still laughing at his own antics. He pushed the magazine down further but made a serious face. 'My last wish is to be buried with the Mondeo. Please make a note. You can drive it into the sea off the Ballygally Holiday Apartments. That's where I was happiest.'

'The Real IRA will do that for free,' Flannigan said. 'Though I think we'd rather hand you over to the Fundie Jundies. They will eat you and your Ford fuck-up live on the interwebs for everybody to watch.'

Lennox burped and made a face.

'Stop crying, bitch,' Dooley said. 'You'll get a funeral. They'll say: "The ginger cunt was much missed by his comrades. Much saddened by his death but pleased as fuck to see the end of the plank's shite car. They were also delighted never to hear another word about his moose back home who was stinging him for cash-money every week. Duracell dobber got her up the duff and the

[133]

whole family of lazy tink bastards screwed the benefits system forevermore. The End.'"

'A beautiful story,' Flannigan said.

'Very moving,' Lennox said.

Luke folded the form and got to his feet. He pulled on a brown T-shirt and screwed up his face at Lennox. 'I thought you had a child?' he said. 'How can you be responsible for a fucken child when you're such a chozzie bitch?'

'Happens all the time,' said Lennox, removing the magazine from his pants and grinning. 'It's nature, innit?'

Captain Rashid of the ANA was sitting in the other corner with a small book in his hand. Half of the banter went over his head. 'Roll another fat one, Rashid,' Dooley said, looking over. 'Another giant bifta for the tea-break.'

Rashid just smiled at him. Luke thought there was something un-adult about the Afghan soldiers, disorganised, smiling at nothing, not really caring. The only thing they really knew was fear, the threat of reprimand, the anger of their commanders. And Luke found it hard to imagine what such men said to themselves. Rashid only had one eye but they imagined he'd put it out for the boys if they said it was routine. 'He's not your average arse-licker,' Flannigan said. 'There's something extra going on with him. He listens. I think he believes in the surge more than all our officers put together.'

'He's like a child,' Luke said. 'He does what he's told.'

'You don't like him, Captain, do you?'

'No, I don't. He plays at being loyal.'

'Ah, he's all right,' Flannigan said.

Later, Scullion was up-top on the vehicle behind. The sun really seemed to pulse that day and give out harm. They were over the mountains and an emerald-green lake had appeared on the other side. Ibex were drinking at the water's edge and several old men waited by the halted vehicles, men with few teeth but much knowledge, Scullion reckoned. What were they waiting for, the future, the past, ammo, or money? The major had no authority and his attention was parched by the heat and the dust. When they waved at the convoy and held out their hands, Scullion couldn't rightly see if they were holding pomegranates or grenades.

He climbed into the Vector and grabbed a book from the dashboard. He had been avoiding Luke but now he smiled over at the captain, one of his old smiles. 'I think we should cheer things up around here,' he said. 'You know where we are? Near one of the ancient sites.'

'Does it have a strip joint?' Lennox said.

'Wind it in, bumboy,' the major said. 'I'm talking about ancient ruins. Get your ginger nut into thinking mode, soldier.' Scullion threw the book to Luke and moved to expel the whole day's tension. 'This'll be a good one, Captain. You'll get a buzz. Ever since Trinity I've wanted to see these places out here. Footprints. There are certain things war and wives can't put down. And one of them is curiosity.'

'Tappeh-ye Mondi Gak,' Luke read. It was too humid to think and Luke was feeling miserable about the argument. He knew the major wasn't fit but Luke was shopping for a quick resolution, something to tide them over until the mission was done and he could think straight. Scullion was off his head but at least he seemed proactive, wanting to do something, and Luke reasoned it might be better not to fight him. There was no point stewing in the sun and mulling over what they'd said.

'Come on,' Scullion added after a moment. 'We can't sit here. I'm going down to see what's what with the ordnance crew. If the work's going to take hours we're off on our holidays. Pack your bags, girls.'

The major trooped off and Luke tried to swallow his doubts. Flannigan looked at him for assurance and he just shrugged. 'It's madness to leave the convoy,' Luke said, 'but what the hell, Flange.'

'He's the boss,' said Flannigan.

'Well,' Dooley said. 'Let the madness commence. The major's right. We're fifty miles from the dam and a fuckload of bullets. Things are in dog order round here, sir, and I for one can't sit boiling my spuds off waiting for a pack of greasers to sort out the vehicles up front. If we're here for hours, let's follow Emperor Mong into the land of Ali Baba. You never know. We might find a Coca-Cola out there.'

Scullion's insistence was a feature of the weather that day and not open to change. He came back with the news that a big IED scan was under way and that the Royal Engineers were fixing the axle on the truck carrying the crane. They wouldn't be moving for three hours. Scullion called in Bawn and Kilbride, two privates from the next vehicle, and ordered them to man the Vector. 'Leave your shit here,' he told Flannigan and company, but Luke insisted they take their rifles and two radios.

'I don't want guns,' Scullion said. 'This is a cultural outing.'

'Nice distinction, Major,' Luke said. 'But either we take our assault weapons or we're not moving an inch away from this convoy.'

'I'll remind you, I'm in charge,' Scullion said.

'You'll be wanting to protect your section, then,' Luke said.

The two men stared at each other for a moment and then Scullion smiled.

'All right, girls,' he said. 'We're taking a trip. Look lively and bring your bang-sticks like the good soldier says.'

Scullion commandeered a jeep and steered it off the line. He drove onto a patch of desert and Rashid came with extra water. When Luke said there might be flak about them absconding from the convoy, Flannigan pointed to other servicemen wandering free. A team of Canadians and Dutch were already setting up a makeshift volleyball net. 'The line is two kilometres long, Captain,' Flannigan said. 'Jesus, it's fine. Remember in Basra we used to go sightseeing all the time. The boys get sick waiting.' A second jeep carried two of the Royal Caledonian boys and a couple of the Canadians and Scullion waved the vehicle alongside. He hadn't been so keyed up at any time since the platoon left Camp Bastion.

'What's with the wheels?' asked Lennox.

'They're the bomb,' Luke said.

'Seriously the bomb,' Flannigan said.

'White motherfucken Land Cruisers,' said Lennox. He rolled his tongue and spat on the ground. 'Brand-new.'

'Bought for the ANA by the Americans,' Luke said.

'No way.'

'Yes way.'

'Holy mother of Jesus,' Flannigan said.

The major had his hand on a map. Rashid was rolling another joint and kept indicating places of interest. At one point, Rashid wetted his hand with saliva and dampened the area under his eyepatch. Scullion saw it and it made his stomach heave. It was a new thing: Rashid now did that to him, made him anxious, revolted.

But as usual with the regiment, events moved faster than thoughts, and the quartet of 1st Royal Western Fusiliers, Flannigan, Dooley, Lennox and Campbell, climbed into the back and all felt rewarded when the air-conditioning kicked in and went turbo and seemed to blow the heat and the dust from their brains.

Dooley put his rifle on the floor and pulled out a CD. 'Stick this mother on,' he said, handing it over. Scullion looked round when the music filled the car and he grinned the grin of a middle-aged man finding freedom again in the sound of a metal band at full pelt.

'What the fuck is this?' Luke shouted.

'For your musical delectification,' Dooley said, holding up the case.

'Delectation,' said Luke.

'Whatever,' Dooley said. 'Brain Drill. Featuring the fastest drummer in the world, Marco Pitruzzella.'

'Turn that off, our kid,' Flannigan said. 'It's fucken unbearable.' The car bumped over the road and white dust billowed at the second Land Cruiser coming at the rear.

'Jack up the volume,' said Lennox.

Luke dropped his shoulders. Everything was cool and the boys were happy. It was irregular to go off-site but stuff happens and it wasn't his job to commandeer everything. Scullion knew they were close to the kind of holy ground where lapis lazuli lies under the dirt. They passed a man on the road who was holding up a fistful of windscreen wipers.

Rashid said a few words to Scullion and then he closed the map and stared into a group of trees. Looking back on that day, they'd understand that Rashid had been in charge, he'd planned everything, directed it, without ever seeming to be other than his usual subservient self. He had the gift of patient belief and the habit of silence. They were three miles from Tappeh-ye Mondi Gak and Rashid felt the coming simoom, a red mist of hot sand. The Land Cruiser was like a bubble of air in the local bloodstream, and he hoped the mist wouldn't mess with the car's radiator or upset the plan to get to the ancient site and from there to Bad Kichan. The music was loud and Rashid looked towards the mountains beyond the bank of trees, the mountains plain and beautiful and dark blue in the crags. In the foothills of De Mundagak Ghar a boy in brown scarves stared down at the road. Rashid saw him and rolled down his window, and, putting his arm out, tapped the door twice. Rashid glanced round at Scullion and saw he was miles away and beating the steering wheel in time to the drums and the boys were singing in the back of the vehicle. When Rashid lifted his eyes again to the hill the boy had gone. Luke later understood that this had been the ANA captain's gift to his people, to let them know, as promised, here and there along the way, that the British soldiers were making progress towards the village.

THE PROPHECY OF THE PETROL

'What is that?'

'An old water wheel,' Rashid said. They walked past it and away from the vehicles to see the ruined fort. It stood alone in the desert, a doorway, a piece of wall, an arch maybe, a rampart like a broken tooth. Scullion felt he saw sand blowing off the white ruins and it excited him. The poet Shelley came into his mind and he wanted to talk about that with his young friend, but, when he turned, he saw Luke was remote. Some fellows get eaten up by the army and forget what it's all about.

He climbed up to the fort and stroked a wall and looked through the remains of an old window. 'The lone and level sands stretch far away,' he recited, and when he stood back he felt his stoutness, a sudden feeling of increase, next to all this thinning beauty. When he looked again through the hole he saw a lone camel walking in a daze.

The Scottish boys from the second jeep came up the dirt track to the fort looking stoned. 'Hey, Dooley,' Flannigan said. 'Here come the Jocks and one of them's got a shite Gucci leg-holster the same as yours.' The soldier he was talking about carried a six-pack of bottled water and had a T-shirt wrapped round his head. Luke recognised him as the lance corporal who had sat in front of him during the briefing in Maiwand, the boy who spoke about Scullion's reputation.

'Any you diddies want a beer?' the boy said, smiling up. He had a Browning pistol in his leg-holster and an SA80 rifle over his shoulder. Luke turned round when he heard the accent and caught a bottle of water. Rashid passed a new joint to Lennox and walked down to the vehicles.

'Where you from?' Luke asked.

'Ayrshire,' the boy said. 'I'm Mark.'

'Whereabouts in Ayrshire?'

'Dalgarnock.'

'My gran lives in Saltcoats.'

'Just up the road,' Mark said. 'I went to St Andrew's. They pulled it down to make way for the new school.'

'And my mother lives in Troon,' Luke said.

'That's mad. I used to go to the Pavilion in Ayr, the raves up there. Do you ever go to the Metro?'

'The club in Saltcoats?' asked Luke.

'Aye. I got a knock-back from there, man. I'm like, "You can fight for your country but you cannae get into a club . . ."'

Lennox passed them the joint and Luke and the boy smoked it while Dooley set up some of the water bottles. 'Target practice,' Dooley said.

'You shouldn't waste water, dude,' said the Canadian. He had driven with the Scots boys in the second vehicle.

Scullion came down from the fort and he seemed high. 'I reckon everybody drinks too much water, anyway,' he said. 'In Ireland when I was a kid nobody drank water. I can honestly say my mother never once set a glass of water down in front of me.' He sweated as he said it and the sweat ran into his eyes. He dragged his hand wearily down his face and wondered if the fort had anything buried around it. He would kill for a little Hellenistic carving or a bracelet to take home.

Luke's eyes locked on to the bottles. The light was coming through them and caused a rainbow stripe to appear on the white wall of the fort. The boy Mark tipped the rifle off his shoulder and took aim, the joint dangling from his lips as he crinkled an eye. 'Die, motherfuckers,' he said and looked pleased as the water exploded. Scullion enjoyed the boys' laughter and felt nauseous again at the metallic smell and the echo in the valley. He hoped he'd remembered to put a 355 radio in the car in case he got lost or the convoy moved or something.

'It's fucken boiling out here,' Lennox said, wiping sunblock on his neck and shoulders.

'Twos up on that,' Mark said. Lennox squirted the stuff in his direction and they all laughed.

'Cumshot,' said Flannigan.

'I'm totally wasted,' Dooley said.

The blue sky above the fort, the blue sky, thought Scullion, throwing a stone down into the gully. 'Alexander the Great dug wells near the Oxus to get fresh water,' he said, 'and the water was bad. You know why? There was thick black liquid seeping into the water.'

'Black liquid?' said Flannigan.

'Oil. The general's advisers said it was a bad omen. The advisers. They said it warned of troubled times.'

'Did they get rich?' Lennox asked.

Scullion ignored him. It was a sign of leadership: knowing exactly when to ignore people and for how long. 'It's the first mention of oil in literature,' he said, and Luke, the younger officer, his former pupil, turned briefly out of interest but let his interest die. Luke lay on his back with a hand over his face, palm open to the sun, and felt sure that whatever happened after the tour he might never again see a day like this. An entire version of himself was moving into the shade and he experienced the mild distaste that comes before a change, the fear of nostalgia.

'They don't build them like this anymore,' said Flannigan. He looked at the ruin and spat in the dust.

'We don't build anything,' Scullion said. 'That's part of the problem out here. Even the Soviets built apartment blocks. All we do is help bring in metal containers. Drop them from the sky, promise to helicopter them out at the end. Life's complicated, boys. Look over there: the ancients had windows, ventilation. You won't see that in a shipping container. We're all just part of a transit area nowadays.'

The elder had a fistful of gambling chits and he squatted down with his brothers to flick quails. They all looked up when the soldiers came into the village in their loud jeeps. Scullion drove to the end of the only road and stopped on a humpback bridge, next to a school where children could be heard chanting in a study circle. The CD stopped when Scullion turned off the engine. He rolled down the window. They could hear the water running. A woman spread a light blue burqa on the grass.

The village was fresh, Luke said later, green like an oasis, and after the hilltop the air seemed soft. Maybe it was the children's voices and the noise of the quails, a life not to do with heat. Everything in the desert emerges from heat and goes back to heat, but in Bad Kichan there was water and activity and tins with labels on them. 'Keep your eyes open,' Scullion said. One of the local men came to the vehicles with his hands up. He spoke rapidly and Dooley released the catch. The major turned to find Rashid. 'Is he speaking Dari? Tell him to fuck off.'

'A wedding today,' Rashid said. 'The man offers you blessings.'

'That's some crazy-ass mumbling,' Lennox said.

Scullion looked nervous. 'Tell the old fox to back off. I can speak a little Pashtun if he wants to bless.'

'He is younger than you,' said Rashid.

'I don't care if he's sweet sixteen, Rashid. I want him to get the fuck back from this squad. That's an order.'

'An order, sir?'

Rashid's good eye was clear. He was the only one of the group not feeling nervous and his sense of command, his entire presence, had altered when he spoke, and it altered further as he stepped through and touched the shoulder of the local man. Whatever he said made the man tap his chest and walk down the track to where the villagers had gathered. Rashid turned to the boys and put out his hands and smiled. 'Welcome,' he said. 'This is a feasting day and custom says you must join to celebrate.'

Children followed them and Scullion handed out packs of coloured pencils from his thigh pockets. He laughed as they grabbed them and he gave them sweets when the pencils ran out. He was feeling good because you only get worried when there are no children, when the place is quiet and the people are inside. Luke had the same thought. As they walked up, Scullion could see past rickety doors into the low mud dwellings. One house revealed a huddle of eyes, men sitting on a red carpet, and he stopped at the door to examine them. They were around a television set, watching an old tennis match between Borg and McEnroe.

The street was busy and there was music outside the *hujra*, the guesthouse, where three chickens' heads lay in a puddle of blood. Rashid handed a case of water to Scullion to give to the elder and as he placed the water at the man's feet Scullion said, '*As-salaam alikum.*'

'*W-alikum-as-salaam,*' the man said.

'*Khair Yosay,*' Scullion said. The ANA captain turned to Scullion and a smile creased the contours of Rashid's short, dark beard as he said, 'Your accent is very strange.' Luke peered into the pomegranate grove at the side of the guesthouse and saw a group of boys there, all dressed in brown. Some of them touched their breasts as he looked and he did the same. There was a wall around the grove and Luke could see a cart loaded with fruit. Silently, he heard co-ordinates and radio crackle in his head and he imagined an aerial shot of the village. Calm the fuck down, he

[144]

told himself. Stay on it. He counted heads. He couldn't be sure but he thought one of the boys in the grove, the one in the long waistcoat, was holding a mobile phone. Luke tried to work out what was going on and he wanted to be friendly but he hated the phone and how they all stood still.

'Let's not hang about here,' Flannigan said.

'You're fine,' Scullion said. 'Listen, guys. It's cool. This is how we bring peace to these people.'

'What, by barging into a private wedding?' said Luke.

'Showing face,' Scullion said. 'Taking an interest. A wee bit of civilised banter. A glass of tea.'

Luke saw a heap of cartons against the wall labelled Nestlé Fruita Vitals. 'We need to get out of here.'

Rashid stood still. Scullion looked again at the leader of the village shura and bowed to him and wished he had a cigar he could offer him. Whatever Scullion said, the sweat was pouring off him and his mouth was dry, yet he believed, deep at the centre of all this rising alarm, that something existed in faith or memory that would serve them well. Whatever it was, he believed in the code. He was from County Westmeath and he knew about gangs and he knew about boys who wanted to be the big man. He'd known them for thirty years and they didn't piss on their own doorstep. He looked over at the soldiers in his party and felt they were each a version of himself. 'Let's not insult this gentleman's hospitality,' he said.

Mark looked at a low wall where a row of skewered kebabs were cooking on a grill. Beside it, on the dusty ground, were several basins of stew and rice. A bowl of almonds caught his eye as he stood up straight and looked at the sky and thought of a Chinese restaurant back home. He and Lisa Nolan used to go there for curry and chips and he thought of good times and a trip they made with their friend Father David. He never expected to see a sky this blue or almonds in a copper bowl.

The young bride came down the road wearing a white head-scarf and a dress of many colours. Dooley thought of his sister's wedding in Skibbereen. Lennox moved out of the way and followed the sound of clapping into the house where the people danced. For a moment, standing there, Private Flannigan felt that everything tilted in the direction of these people, because of their happiness and the young groom's way of looking at his wife. The soldiers went in and out of the house with their rifles up and Luke noticed the boys in the orchard had stepped closer to the road. Scullion was clapping his hands to the music, beaming and nodding, and when he turned he saw Luke moving towards him and swiping the air, saying, 'We have to get the fuck out of here right now.'

The boys in the orchard started throwing rocks. One of them struck Scullion in the chest and he turned open-mouthed to see a smear of men shouting and flailing in the first seconds of panic. He grabbed Rashid's arm to stop the gun but Rashid held it straight out and it was pointing at Mark, the Scottish soldier, who was standing in the middle of the road facing them, shouting '*Come ahead ya dirty bastard!*' Rashid shot him point-blank in the face, blood gushing from the man's mouth. Rashid shouted a name and instantly the kid with the mobile phone rushed forward screaming and Luke turned his rifle and shot him dead. At the same time, Dooley lunged out with a bayonet and stabbed Rashid in the neck. Lennox saw the Scot fall in the road with his face covered in blood and he saw Rashid collapse on top of him, then he turned and opened fire into the orchard. In a second or two they were all shooting into the orchard, and Luke joined them, his heart going mad as he shouted over the noise.

An old man wearing pink came out of the *hujra* with his hands clasped together in supplication, crying. Was that crying, thought Dooley, or was he laughing? The bowl of almonds seemed to explode next to him as Dooley opened fire again and the old man spun and fell backwards through the door where the screaming seemed to swallow him. Scullion dragged the body of Rashid along the road and fired into him. Then he took out his service revolver and shot him in the eye, standing over the body and staring down. By now the Canadian colonel was bent over Mark, the young lance corporal, blowing into his mouth and after a minute or so the colonel looked up with blood on his face and shook his head because it was no use.

At the edge of the orchard, among shattered pomegranates and grey rocks and blood, the boys of the village lay in a heap. One wasn't yet dead and he opened and closed his mouth. Luke would remember the whiteness of the boy's teeth as he opened his mouth to breathe and dropped his small hand to the ground. The women wailed. They wailed everywhere. Scullion was now bent over the mangled body of Rashid, speaking to him, asking him why. Flannigan dragged Scullion off the body, shouting, 'Got to go, sir. Luke, take charge. We've got to get away from here.'

'Jesus fucking Christ,' Lennox said, looking at the mess on the ground.

'Luke!' shouted Flannigan. 'We've got to get Charlie out of here. We've got to go!'

'Bosh!' Dooley said. 'Fucken killed the bastards. Dirty Taliban scum. See ye! Fucken see ye!'

'Holy Christ,' said Lennox.

Scullion was looking at the dead ANA captain and Flannigan tugged him by the arm. 'Just leave it, sir. A no-use traitor bastard.'

There were rose petals on the road. Luke saw them and the blood running into the dust at the edge of the orchard and his eyes were stinging with sweat. Suddenly he came up and pushed Scullion nearly off his feet. He grabbed his shirt and pulled him in and locked eyes with him. 'You caused this. You fucken caused all of this.'

'Leave it, sir,' Dooley said, pushing the captain back and separating the men. 'Let's go.'

Scullion was wild in the eyes. 'This is *yours*,' Luke said, walking away from him. 'Good fucken work.' He waited a moment. 'Okay,' he said. 'Moving out!' There was screaming coming from the *hujra* and the women appeared in the road beating their chests, raising their hands. Dressed for the wedding, they cried for their sons.

The Canadian and Private Dooley walked ahead to secure the retreat and Luke ordered a couple of the others to carry Mark's body. The dead soldier's hair was matted with blood and white dust and his pal from the regiment was holding his hand and weeping. Dooley opened the passenger door for Scullion and he got in without a word. He wasn't there, Dooley said later. 'The lights were on but nobody was at home.' Luke and Flannigan walked back up the road from the *hujra*, their rifles pointing at the village. And when they reached the bridge Luke cast his eyes at the school and saw a line of children's faces at the open window.

'Charlie base. This is call sign 722. Over.'

AIRLIFT

Beside the whop-whop of rotary blades, Luke stood with the commander at the edge of the convoy. 'There will be a full investigation,' Emory said. 'Questions. Big fucking questions.' But Luke wasn't listening. The camouflaged underside of the Lynx lifted away, creating a wind that blew the dust into a dense cloud. 'You chose to leave his body,' said the commander. 'He was Afghan National Army.'

'He was not one of us.'

'We are all one of us, Captain.'

'Yes, sir.'

'We are forging on. Nobody's going back. We are fifty-nine miles from the delivery point and that is where the action is. Major Scullion will stick with the platoon and we can discuss his jolly outing into bandit country back at the base.'

'As you wish, sir.'

'It's not as I wish. What I wish is that the British army did not harbour such fucking idiots.'

'Yes, sir.'

BANN RIVER

The operation had to be completed that night and they were in the Vector moving towards Kajaki. They said little, feeling everything, eyeing one another and hanging their heads as they breathed in the hot aftermath. They would remember Scullion sluicing himself with sterile water, but was it fury, confusion or regret that dimmed his eyes and made him grunt and rub his sodden hair until it tufted into spikes?

The old life was over and Scullion knew it. As the vehicle bumped along and then rejoined Highway 611, he recalled that he'd once imagined the world could be put right and made whole. He had been a man who liked the era he lived in and was well suited to it. He loved the metaphysics of the new wars, where one spoke of freedom, of delivering security, but as he put down his head and meshed his trembling fingers he pictured slain Bosnians by a shopping precinct in Srebrenica. He saw corpses in burnt-out cars on the Basra Road and rebel soldiers lying dead by a runway north of Freetown, their eyes open to democracy. He saw those boys in the orchard. And it was all a mystery to him now, all at an end, the resolutions, agreements, interventions, because the people who police the world are never ready for the world's ingratitude. Eight construction workers in Teebane, blown to pieces by the IRA. His first acquaintance with gore. A culvert bomb on the Drum Road. His platoon got to the crossroads in minutes from the barracks in Omagh. That's what the journalists don't see. That's what the politicians and the mothers never see.

Luke was staring the other way.

'You all right, Charlie?' Flannigan said.

When he turned his eyes they were clouded with failure. 'People let you down, son. They do bad things.'

Luke had come to the end of his own dark corridor in the mountains and Charlie Scullion was merely a name he would give to the mistakes that led him there. He had suspected in Maiwand that the major, despite his stories, his reputation, was not up to the job, and he had looked away as the enemy made an opportunity of their weaknesses. Luke and Scullion were not so different as either hoped: they ran their battle from the centre of some persistent idea of themselves as good men, and, in this way, they resembled the politicians who paid for their boots and gave them their language. Luke wasn't sure how a life works, how your story accumulates and regresses, how it speaks, how it hides, but he'd know it eventually. As the vehicle rumbled on and the daylight dwindled, he knew he had played his part in the disaster at Bad Kichan.

'It sounds bad,' Lennox said, 'because I feel sorry for the Scottish lad, but I'm just glad it wasn't one of the platoon.'

'It was bad luck, that's all,' Dooley said. 'The soldier stepped forward at the wrong time.'

'It was more than that,' said Flannigan. 'It was bad everything. It was just bad.'

Scullion stared at the ground. It was Operation Grapple. The Croats were trying to cleanse the Bosnians from the Lašva Valley. Three hundred people were murdered in a cinema in Vitez and the boy next to me, Second Battalion . . .

'How old was the kid today?'

'He was twenty-one.'

The convoy joined the decoy units for the final push. They went past canals and villages and climbed to the high fields around Kajaki Sofla. Crossing the Helmand, they took turns to look out and see the beautiful green of the river and the many sunflowers growing on the banks. They got their full battle kit on and Scullion looked up and told them to affix their radios and bring out the light machine-gun.

'The Mini-Me?' Dooley said.

'There's two here,' Scullion said. 'Let's get this over with. Docherty brought in two after the last stop.'

Kajaki was one big choke-point, a lot of vehicles waiting to go in and a lot of Terry down there. This was the fight they had come for and it had to be over quickly. Night fell and Luke could hear the Chinooks moving ahead of them, softening up the gun positions around the hills. The men fixed their bayonets and checked their ammo outside under a hanging herb that smelled of peppermint. Scullion came with information about Taliban gun-mountings in the town but he didn't offer any speeches. He just looked into the desert.

Scullion put his hand on Luke's shoulder. He didn't respond, but when he looked up he hated the expression in the major's eyes. It was dark now and a burst of red and orange appeared over the tops of the trees. Scullion clapped Luke again and the younger officer widened his eyes. 'Please fuck off, Major. It's my only request.'

'We have a battle to fight,' Scullion said.

'Then fight it.'

Luke climbed up and examined the scene from the top of the Vector and thought of the little town of Bethlehem they knew at school, the white buildings on the hillside and the stars. Except this was godless territory and the night ahead would be brutal. 'We better get a few rewards after this,' Dooley said. 'A few shakes of the choccy-tree. The lads have been through the mill today and a few beers might be in order.'

Scullion led his own platoon over the hill. They could see the floodlit dam and he wanted to press home. 'If you haven't got a wife or a child, follow me,' he said. The boys turned to Luke and he shrugged and stared into the poplar trees and the centre of Kajaki Sofla. It was either a slow or a fast descent but you had to get there. A commander came up and a mortar brigade and they took up positions and started shelling. The directive was to repel incoming fire, then to shell into enemy positions and move forward, taking the fight down to the insurgents who controlled access to the dam. Within seconds of the rounds going over, the return fire was brutal. There was smoke on all sides and bullets tearing past or thudding into the ground. Out there, somewhere in front of them, a machine-gun was being fired so furiously by one of the Canadians it glowed orange in the dark. Scullion feared it might give away their position, but the enemy was too chaotic. He snapped down the night-vision goggles on his helmet and assessed the activity on the road and around the buildings. He spotted a gap and began firing tracer rounds towards it, which gave the platoon a bead on where to direct their fire.

'Go on, my son,' shouted Lennox to the Canadian. 'Go on. Give the fucktards a pounding.'

'I've got disco-leg over here,' Dooley said. 'Fucking dizzy I'm tellin' you. Let's go!'

'Don't move forward yet, Doosh. Wait for the signal.'

'What we waiting for?'

'An order, Dooley.'

Red tracer fire streaked across the hills and fell prettily into the town. The arcs of red and green appeared more sluggish than they were, like an illusion of movement, a strobe, out across the hills and into the static night. But down there in Kajaki Sofla the bullets arrived as a hail of ripping metal. Car windscreens exploded and copper bowls ricocheted down the alleyways. The enemy manned its own batteries from the rooftops and their rockets scudded over the inclines, shearing the trees, falling short for the most part and lying phosphorescent in the fields. He looked up, they all looked up, and suddenly the pattern in the air was not a light show but a constellation of death. Luke wasn't a gamer as he watched the fire but a man seeing action in real time, a miasma of efforts and consequences. He met the realisation calmly on the hillside as the guns blazed and the boys shouted into the dark. He looked up and experienced a short invasion of mortality and a surge of adrenalin. He was just a man and he faced what was coming with a singleness of heart. He knew standing there that the string of lights began and ended in fear.

He took his soldiers down the irrigation ditch and found cover behind the rocks. Enemy mortars were exploding just in front of them and they held fast, while troops from other regiments ran ahead and took up position. Luke knew where he was. A sense of documentary reality came over him as he pressed his face into the rock and waited his turn to take the boys forward. His breath was short and he saw jackals scattering higher up. He heard the shouts of the other soldiers as they stormed into the gully, moving in formation according to their training, and as he heard them he thought of the geography around each man.

They were near the street. Every soldier had his rifle raised and was picking off targets below. With goggles down, Luke could see the enemy scurrying from one building to another. Fire appeared at the windows of the engine house above the dam. In the final push off the hill, the enemy had a clear shot into the ground in front of the allied soldiers, the last 200 metres leading down to the road and the end of all hope for that day's insurgents. The allies were all over that part of the hill, shelling the hell out of the engine house and rocketing the vehicles on the ground. At the final clearing, Luke was making ready to go forward, listening to instructions from the commander on the radio, when suddenly, without warning, on his left-hand side, Major Scullion came dashing out from behind a clump of rocks. He was firing his assault weapon and roaring in a blur. 'Charlie!' shouted Luke. 'We can't cover you from there, get back.'

'Major!' screamed Flannigan.

'What's he doing?' Dooley said on the radio.

'Hold back.'

'Jesus fucken Christ,' Flannigan said.

The radio was going mad. 'What's the fucken matter?' a voice said. A mortar landed a short distance in front of where Scullion ran and Luke saw the shrapnel tear up a tree and Scullion was down. The shouting increased and suddenly the ANA troops led by Docherty and the 1st Royal Western team surged down onto the road. They pushed forward and the explosions were massive and the sniper fire cracked out, then the Apaches came in and suddenly the engine house was gone. The whole platoon tumbled over the rocks like a body of water, except for Luke and Flannigan, who held back and took advantage of the air cover and the Terry batteries going silent to rush into the clearing. They found Scullion sitting as a child might sit in a sandpit, planted on his bottom with his legs out, except that his right leg was severed and lying apart from him. The other leg was a mess. He sat with his eyes wide open to the scene before him, smoke rising from the rags of his trousers and his hands down flat.

'Jesus, mother of God,' Flannigan said.

'You're all right,' Luke said. He rubbed the blood out of Scullion's eyes and reached for his meds. Fingers were missing on Scullion's right hand but he continued to stare out and pick at the rags of his trousers. He was shaking as he saw the leg a few feet away and touched the sheared, bloody bone of his knee. The bullets had stopped coming and it was weirdly quiet up there, the dark about them and Scullion murmuring, which seemed a good sign, while the men tried to keep him from passing out. 'Look,' said Flannigan, 'Jimmy-Jimmy's here. We're all here.'

'What's the score with these trees?' Scullion said.

Luke stabbed the morphine needle into the major's stomach. He returned from some place in his head and was again the boy in training. He took charge and had the old logistical zeal, the clarity of thought. He pulled out the field dressing and ripped it open with his teeth. Scullion looked up at him and smiled. 'You're a bad soldier.'

'Come on, sir. You're going to be all right. Hold my hand ya auld fucken wanker that you are.'

'Come on, Charlie. Keep your eyes open,' Flannigan said. 'We're not having a kip out here. Come on.'

Scullion had stopped feeling around his knee and his smile continued as Luke radioed for a stretcher. They were down from the convoy in minutes and the medic from the parachute regiment said one of the boys was religious and good at prayers. 'Don't be fucken daft,' Luke said. 'He's going to be fine.' One of the guys lifted Scullion's torn-off leg by the boot and wrapped it up in a piece of plastic.

'You're great, now. Okay, fella. Just keep the head,' Flannigan said. 'Keep it together, sir. Jimmy-Jimmy's here and the boys are coming up for a fucken smoke in a minute. Dooley wants to tell you about that moose of his, the bird he's going to marry because she's a staff nurse.'

Scullion was lying on the stretcher and his face was grey. Luke wiped his brow and tried to say everything was cool, they'd soon be out of the zone. The major's smile went cold after a moment and he started whispering. *'Or had I but riches and money in store.'*

'Come on, sir.'

'Cop on!' Flannigan said. 'Give us one of your songs. Give us a few verses, ya mean bastard.'

'*It's there on the banks of the lovely Bann River,*' spoke Scullion.

'Keep going, Charlie.'

'Oh, fuck,' he said.

A bit of a tune came into it, nothing much, but Flannigan picked it up and Scullion got the words out. '*In all kinds of splendour I'd live with my dear.*'

'Go on, lad. It's a beauty.'

'*My name is Delaney, a name that won't shame me.*'

They had to make it to the top of the hill because there was nowhere for the chopper to land. Luke and Flannigan stayed at the side of the stretcher on the way up. '*And if I'd had money, I'd ne'er had to roam,*' Flannigan sang. His eyes had filled up and he wiped the tears as they jogged. Over his shoulder Luke could see that the convoy had broken through and was at the gates of the dam and the trucks were rolling down.

'*But drinking and sporting,*' whispered Scullion, '*night rambling and courting . . .*'

'Go on, sir,' said Flannigan.

'Keep it together, Charlie,' said Luke.

'*Are the cause of my ruin and absence from home.*'

5

LOVE ME DO

In the waiting room, Alice looked at the frosted glass and wondered why receptionists are always so impatient and puffed up.
Always, she thought. Did they want to be doctors themselves,
and that's why they hate giving out forms and taking calls about
appointments? It made sense. You don't want to spend your life
feeling secondary to the person upstairs. It pleased Alice to allow
a thought like that to flourish silently in a boring room, as if she
had now become, at this point in her life, a lesson to herself, the
kind of person on whom no small thing is wasted.

'I'm not sure,' Dr Sabin said. 'It's complicated.' He had taken
to wearing tweed jackets and knitted ties. He offered Alice a
mint from a little vintage tin showing a smiling kid and a Union
Jack. 'The truth is, we're all getting older and your mother is
eighty-two.'

'It's the hallucinations, as I call them,' Alice said. 'It comes and
goes all the time. Some days she's quite normal. But yesterday she
was talking as if it was the 1960s. Just talking about the bands and
the short skirts, you know. Not recalling it but blethering to me,
and to Maureen, her neighbour, as if it was all happening now. I
mean, that's quite hard to take when the person was always so –
well, intelligent, I'd call it. My mother has always behaved as if
the truth was the biggest thing. The photographs she took when
she was young were all about that.'

'Was that her skill, taking photographs?'

Alice looked at the window and sighed. People's offices always said so much about them, the old, soothing prints, the sweets, the boxes of wine glasses sitting on the filing cabinet. 'Oh yes,' she said. 'It's a sad story, really. Sad, I'd call it. She was a name. A bit of a name. Anne Quirk. Her photographs still turn up in a few collections.'

'Really?'

She looked at him. She waited. 'Anyway, she gave it up. Then she started going to Blackpool just before I was born and she met the man who must be my father.'

'You didn't know him?'

'I saw him a few times. His name was Harry. She met him at a night school or something. A young woman who'd lost her goal. And suddenly there was this Harry and he was a photography lecturer in Manchester. He was in with that group of young photographers who were out on the streets and in the factories, you know, recording it all, and it gave her another chance. She was the only woman – I mean, among the photographers.'

'They didn't get married?'

Dr Sabin found it interesting to talk to somebody who didn't have angina or a common complaint. People tend to forget you're human when you're a doctor and what he liked most was conversation. So the appointment with Alice ran on, the doctor wishing to expand his knowledge of this strange family who had travelled the world, who had talent, stories. The old mother was even quite famous, she was saying.

'No, they were never married. She got pregnant. She's got some information about Harry written down. I think he wrote it.' Alice shook her head and the silence that came said enough.

'We can move on if you like.'

'It's hard to talk about. It's hard to know what's true. Harry was a war hero. Harry flew the spy planes. But I've never seen any of the medals she talks about.'

'They're a bit overrated, those things,' he said. She chose to ignore the doctor's easy familiarity with all the world's predicaments and situations. He was a bit like that. She came quite regularly to see him and always left feeling better, but it annoyed her the way he found every problem so familiar. It was clearly a part of his effort at cheerfulness and she found herself hoping he was a secret drinker.

'Other people's great deeds,' Dr Sabin said. 'They're sometimes a bit hard to take. I know I find that.'

'I was never able to ask.'

'Why's that?'

'Because, you know, the truth is so obvious to some people that they don't feel the need to share it. In fact, they resent being asked about it. They just want everyone to behave as if their story is the only story. And the people who ask questions in that situation are treated like traitors. It's a form of control and a kind of bullying.'

'You describe it very well.'

'I've had it all my life.'

He told her to take her time. Sometimes Alice would just shudder at the memory of things. 'Okay?' he asked.

'She always left me with other people. I was really brought up by the neighbours.'

'Is that right?'

'Yes. It's a thing in Glasgow. Somebody should write a book about the role of the next-door neighbour. She's got the same thing again with some woman who lives next door to her now. Maureen, she's called. We don't really know anything about her, though she's learning a lot about us, I'm sure. Same old story: the neighbour's in charge.'

'And you can't speak to your mother about the past?'

'Too late, doctor. Too late. For years I tried to please her and be more like her. She thinks I'm boring, I'm conventional, and I am those things, to people like her. Married to the wrong person. Too interested in the wrong things. You know. But the fact is, my existence threatens her story. I used to think she might love me more by realising I was all she had left of Harry. But that's not true, Dr Sabin. My father has never gone because the great story of him only grows and grows.'

'You feel you've been overshadowed?'

'You can say that again.'

'Really?'

'Oh, yes. I've been sacrificed.'

'You might be wrong.'

'Maybe. I used to think it would be possible, one day, to get back to a kind of reality – you know, about her own achievements, her photographs, everything she did. But it wasn't possible. She just transferred her worship of Harry onto my son, Luke. She always wanted a son. He's always been close to her and now he's coming back.'

'He's been in Afghanistan?'

'He discharged himself. Or something like that. And now she's so far gone it's like all her fantasies coming home to roost. None of the lies were shot down or set to rights, and I didn't get to talk. I didn't get to ask about my father or get a grip on the past.'

'Their past.'

'It's my past, too,' she said.

'I see.'

'I will never be able to ask her.'

'And that's important to you?'

'It was. But it's too late.'

'Her life's not over,' Dr Sabin said. 'And yours is very far from being over, Alice. We'll keep talking.' He stood up and walked to the window and stood looking out at the sea. 'We have a lot of it now, with the ageing population,' he said. 'And dementia presents insidiously, so that patients, carers, family – doctors, too – we all find ourselves only slowly understanding it. But it's true that dementia can dramatise some of the issues the patient might have had with memory and so on.'

Alice stood up. 'Dramatise. Yes. With memory. It's as if my mother turned to something else when she gave up her photographs.'

'Something else?'

'Make-believe,' Alice said. 'Fantasy. Like all her hopes went sour and she just couldn't take reality anymore.'

'Perhaps,' he said.

'I've always been made to feel I lack faith.'

'I agree there's drama in it while it's happening,' Dr Sabin said, 'but I can tell you from experience, Alice, that life reveals itself, in any case. I see it every day in this room. Time shows everything.'

She lifted her coat off the back of the chair. 'I didn't ever think it would be so hard. So hard to face it.' She could feel her eyes well up and her breath staggered from one sentence to the next. 'I would love to spend half an hour with the woman who made those pictures.'

'She hasn't gone,' he whispered. 'Quite the opposite. She's coming back. And maybe you could prepare to meet her half-way. Between the person she is now and the person she used to be. Enter into the spirit of where her mind is going and allow her . . .'

'She's never needed my permission for anything.'

'Well, maybe she does now.' They sat in a state of hesitation for a few seconds and the seconds seemed long. 'There's been too much denial in this family,' Alice said.

'Maybe so. Maybe in all families. But your own counselling might mean you can help her by helping yourself. Your mother isn't your enemy. She isn't your only resource. She's losing parts of herself and gaining others. And if it's possible, Alice, you might take it less personally.'

'I worry that her lies shaped my life. I worry that I only took up with Sean, my husband Sean, because of her war-hero thing. I was always trying to keep up. My husband was a soldier and I lost him and I used to worry I would lose my son the same way. You don't see the connections in your life until it's too late to disentangle them.'

'So, Luke's on his way home?'

'Yes, he is. I think it's been hard for him. He's been through a lot out there and I want him to know, when he comes back, that he doesn't have to talk about it if he doesn't want to.'

The doctor turned. 'We all have something to hold back,' he said. 'And maybe some of us depend on other people's mistakes to make us feel better about our own.'

'So, it's my fault?' She produced a ball of tissue from her sleeve and held it against her nose.

'Not everything reduces itself to the question of fault, Alice. Most things don't, in fact.'

'Right.'

'You've coped well.'

'I don't think so. Sean and I thought we would live for a hundred years. And when he died it was going to be me and Luke against the world. But Luke chose my mother, just as she chose Harry.'

'You feel the men got the better deal?'

'God, yes,' she said. 'What were the men really like? God knows. Because they always got top billing. The boys are the heroes in this family.'

'She didn't like women?'

'She loves women. Her friends. The woman next door. The girls she knew when she was young. She just doesn't particularly like the woman she gave birth to.'

'Just remember, she's not well.'

'I think her mind's gone. I told you about the rabbit?'

'Yes, you said.'

'Caring about a fake rabbit. What's that about?'

Some smiles aren't smiles. What he did with his mouth was more like an acknowledgement, a firm admission that some mysteries must be endured and never solved. He sat down and laid a hand on the mousepad and put a finger to his lips. 'Nobody takes me seriously,' he said. 'But the thing I wish I could prescribe isn't available in the pharmacy.'

'What's that?'

'They don't keep it in bottles.'

'What?'

'Time,' he said.

She got outside and breathed the sea air, taking her time, moving on very precisely to another self. You have to dust yourself off and get on with it and that's that, she said. Alice could drop in and out of her own feelings and now she wanted a latte. She walked down the street to the Marina Cafe thinking of something entirely new, and, once inside, she waited. No one was there and the sweet jars lined the wall, the jukebox playing 'Love Me Do' to the mirrors and the clean tables.

BLUE

Maureen said she wanted one of those sky-coloured radios and a light blue rug for the living-room. Not exactly the same blue everywhere but very similar and kind of summery. 'I've never been one for dark colours,' she said. 'People with black sofas and brown curtains, heaven help us, they want their heads examined. There are such nice things in the shops and our Ian's handy with a screwdriver, so if you go to IKEA you can just get him round and he'll hammer it together, because you don't want those men coming, you know, the ones with the van. They make you smile. They charge you a fortune and leave a right mess in your hall.'

Maureen always said she had too much time to think.

'I love them to death, but . . .'

Maybe her children had betrayed her by seeking happiness elsewhere. She'd think it mad if anyone said it, but her children saw how affronted she could be by their ambitions and their progress. 'Nobody is prouder of their children's success than I am,' she'd whisper. And she did enjoy their achievements in a boast-to-the-neighbours kind of way. But she didn't like what comes with success in one's children: the independence, the sudden confidence, the distance, the self-sufficiency. That was all bad news from her point of view. More than bad news: it was selfish. They should be holding themselves responsible for the way she felt, as if only their guilt could assuage her. And, because of this, it was impossible for her ever to let them see that she was happy. Maureen was a woman who kept her good times a secret from her children for fear they might stop pitying her.

The great secret was she liked her life. The routines at Lochranza Court suited her down to the ground and she loved her friends. But that didn't stop her from leaving messages on the voicemails of her children, messages that ended with a few tears. She would sniff into the phone and slowly her bad feelings would become an aria of blame about them not doing enough. In all their adult lives – and Ian hadn't been a teenager for twenty-five years – Maureen had never sat her children down together at a table for a meal. And it wasn't because she couldn't cook or couldn't buy a chicken. It was something else: making a meal would have suggested a level of well-being that some part of her, some sad part of her, couldn't bear them to witness at the same time. She resented their spouses as if they had cast a spell on her children and made them forget who they were.

She had put out a lovely spread for Alice. Cut sandwiches sat on plates, pieces of Victoria sponge, amid the mugs and spoons at the kitchen table. Good God, thought Alice: sugar in the tea and all this cake and it isn't even lunch-time. 'She measures out her life in sugar spoons,' her mother cracked one time, when she was well. And it was true Alice always worried about her weight.

'Oh, what the hell. Who cares?' Maureen said. 'It's just us two. If we're not good to ourselves, who's going to be?'

Coming along the corridor that day, Alice had enjoyed an unexpected feeling of belonging. Some days she experienced a random turn for the better and it usually didn't last. She suddenly admired the housing complex and saw it as a wonderful cooperative. She said to herself she hoped that when her time came, they would bring her to live in a place like this. With the Yamaha organ and the board games, the large-print books, the knitting patterns, it seemed made for tired wanderers, except that most of the people in there had lived all their lives in the town. She thought she probably deserved a place at Lochranza Court after all her upsets, before realising that was the sort of thing Maureen would say.

Each flat had a ledge by the front door, like a low concrete table, which the resident would crowd with ornaments. Flat 21 had a collection of porcelain dogs with sad eyes, jowly faces and hanging ears. Maureen's daughter once said it was a black hole of empathy. Flat 20 had a host of fairies hopping about in eternity on gossamer wings. 'Life is much more interesting if it scarcely exists,' said their surprised little faces, their slender hands. Alice was heading to Maureen's place, but passing her mother's she saw again the photograph on her ledge of a shipyard and a red poppy stuck in the corner of the frame.

'That photograph,' Alice said, putting down her teacup, 'the one outside my mother's door. It's one of hers, isn't it? One of the ones she took years ago?'

'Yes,' Maureen said. She was washing the butter knife in the sink. 'It was one of the pictures from those suitcases she keeps in her bathroom. But she says there's a lot more of her stuff somewhere.'

'And why get them out now?'

'Well, your mum being the way she is, it's good to get things out and try to remember, you know? The nurse in the Memory Club, she encourages that kind of thing. Get stuff out, she says. Get the old albums out and stir up the memories. So in the evenings your mum and I have been pulling things out and I've been making piles of them. We thought we'd put that one outside the door for people to see.'

The late-night tasks. The letters to Luke. Alice couldn't be sure she wasn't envious of Maureen. It's the sort of thing a daughter should be doing with her mother. And yet she was grateful to the neighbour because she knew that Anne would never have enjoyed doing those things with her. Anne trusted strangers, and so, quite clearly, did Maureen: they liked a new person's willingness not to jump on the things you said, questioning everything and doubting you. Families did that but strangers didn't. And so Alice swallowed another insult when she was told about the picture. The photographs were coming out of the suitcases and it was a good thing. And when she thought about it, well, it probably was a good thing if the past could emerge, at last, without her mother's editing.

'They're fantastic pictures,' Maureen said. 'And I suppose they show you what Anne was like in her prime, you know, long before this started happening to her.'

'I couldn't tell you,' Alice said. 'Some people hide away in their prime. You can't know them.'

'And you only get to them later?'

'That's right. When they need you.'

'You know I help her with her letters?' Maureen said.

'I do, yes,' said Alice. 'It's been very kind. I appreciate it. Especially you helping her keep in touch with my son. We're an odd family.'

'I could show you odd. You should see mine. One minute you're the best mammy in the world and the next minute you could be missing and they wouldn't notice.'

'I don't think this tour's been easy for Luke,' Alice said. 'The Ayrshire boy who died. You know about that? Well, Luke was there. He saw it.'

'Aye. You and I spoke on the phone, remember? For a terrible moment we all thought . . .'

'Yes.'

They sat in silence for a moment. Maureen felt Alice was a bit strange that day, a bit stressed or something, but frankly, it was hard enough trying to keep up with Anne without worrying about her daughter as well. 'Anyway,' Maureen said, 'it's not only the letters from Luke. Anne's been getting other letters, too, and there's one that seems quite important. It's from Canada.' Maureen brought it from the cutlery drawer and handed it to Alice. The envelope was marked with crayon and with various stamps and crossings out. The name of the place it came from was across the top of the letter. 'The Art Gallery of Ontario,' read Alice. And when her eye dropped to the foot of the page she read out the whole address: '317 Dundas Street West, Toronto, Ontario, Canada M5T 1G4.'

'That's the address. It's a woman, I think,' Maureen said, twisting her head to get a better view of the letter she'd already looked at many times. Alice went on in silence and pressed her own lips with a finger when she noticed they were moving. The curator who wrote the letter said she was writing about 'Mrs Quirk's photographs', and she used the words 'honoured' and 'intrigued', 'visionary' and 'important'. It said the gallery was planning an exhibition of lost women photographers and that Anne Quirk was an artist with a connection to Ontario. The word 'marginalised' appeared in the third paragraph, and, further down, where Alice noticed a teacup stain, it spoke of 'permission'. Alice felt a sudden weight of responsibility reading the letter. She wasn't at all sure what to think so she folded it away immediately and put the envelope in her bag.

'Isn't that something?' Maureen said.

Alice found it hard to say anything. She simply stood looking at the images on the television, staring at them before realising there was no sound on, then she turned with damp eyes to the centre of the room and tried to regain her composure. In some rooms you don't notice the contents so much as how carefully they've been polished.

CENTRAL STATION

They say oil and water don't mix. But those people never walked out of Cowcaddens and turned at the corner to face the card shops and their helium balloons, the windows displaying teddies and jokes in all weathers. They never walked down Sauchiehall Street in the pouring rain and felt the oil in the rain that waxes your skin and makes you belong to Glasgow. She turned into Renfield Street and immediately thought of the exhaust fumes from the old buses and the neon signs above Central Station that used to glow in the dark with ads for sugar and whisky.

It was 1981 again. The days of Sean and her with bags of chips after nights at the Apollo. If you meet a man who can make you laugh, then stay with him forever. And that was her Sean: he could make a dark night and a poke of chips something you'd want to remember. She could see the two of them walking down Renfield Street with the neon above and Glasgow standing cold in the exact present, their fingers all salt and vinegar. She could still feel the warm brown chip-paper inside the *Evening Times* with the print coming off on her hands. They could ignore the news then because it wasn't about them and she saw Sean balling up the paper and chucking it into a bin, pulling her in for a kiss.

She always got nervous walking in the city centre with Sean, the green, white and orange buses and the whole Rangers and Celtic thing and him a soldier beginning his service in Belfast. It was a sectarian time and you could get into trouble, but those nights out with Sean seemed to glow pleasantly in her mind.

Bell's Scotch Whisky. 'Afore ye go.'

'Afore ye go where?' Sean said. 'I mean, they're saying: "Drink whisky, afore ye go."'

'Before ye go out.'

'But if you drink Bell's whisky before you go out for the evening you'll be drunk by the time you get there.'

'True.'

'So what does it mean, "Afore ye go"? Drink Bell's whisky, before you die?'

She remembered laughing. Creasing up. The laughter in your youth that comes before everything.

'Before ye go to bed? What does it mean, Alice? Before ye go into a meeting? Before you go on holiday? I'm asking you: what does it mean, the advertisement for Bell's Scotch whisky? Afore ye go? But what is *go*? And what is *afore*?'

'And what is *ye*?' she said.

'Exactly!' Sean said. 'What is the ye that must have Bell's Scotch whisky before he – or, okay, she – goes?'

She remembered it all. She remembered his teeth and his laughter and the scent of Brut. The fact that his eyes seemed glassy when the buses passed. It was the teeth and his smell she liked the best: nobody could touch Sean for teeth, and they stopped again to kiss outside McDavit's kilt shop. 'Shall we have one?' he said, looking up. 'It's your nation. It's your community. All of you having one before ye go.'

'Why don't we?' she said. 'Ye need all the help you can get in this life, afore ye go.' The grin that comes before everything. And then he took her arm and led her over the road to the Horse Shoe Bar for a whisky and a comic sermon on Irish songs. The pub darkened now in her mind as she made her way but there would always be something about that place, always a light on. It seemed so long ago and Glasgow seemed so changed as she fought through the rain to meet their son.

ELECTRIC BRAE

She didn't see him right away. She passed the bar in the Rogano and walked to the back of the restaurant, and there he was in the last booth, over by the kitchen. Back of the bus, back of beyond: that was always Luke when he was wee. And there he was now with one of those tall beers in front of him. White shirt, nice sweater. Her own son deep in the pages of a book. She stood on the carpet and just watched him for a moment. He was typically thin but he looked tired for a young man.

'Mum,' he said.

She hadn't expected to feel his resolve when he hugged her but it was the strength she noticed. She saw his exhaustion but his arms still had certainty and pride in them: it was always that way with soldiers, the bravado, the private fight, the clean shirt, the shoes much brighter than bombs. She closed her eyes and patted him wordlessly in the middle of his back. She didn't ponder for long his state of mind because she noticed as she patted him the gauze of rain still clinging to his jumper. 'Good God, son. You're damp. Did you come out without a coat?'

'I'm only five minutes away.'

'But it's cashmere,' she said.

'Mum . . .'

'Right you are.'

She wouldn't be the mother. You can't, really. After the battles and the helicopters you can't come storming in with advice about raincoats. There was something different about Luke as he sat across from her. Not determined, but achieved. Some people would have counted it a loss in him because it seemed that the softness had gone. Looking at him, listening to his low murmur as he spoke about the flat and the joy of sleeping in his own bed, she felt she was looking at Sean.

'You look good,' she said. But she wasn't sure. His life was telling on him. He didn't know he was young and he probably never would: any day now he'd be thirty, then thirty-five, then you're in your forties with that tremendous sense of no turning back and nothing really proved. It would take a nice woman to renew his spirit and get him on the right track. That's what she thought, conjuring with the next set of problems before the present ones had settled.

'This and that,' he said, answering her question. 'I've been walking a lot. I went up north. Climbed a bit. And I went down south to see about things.' She ordered the Pinot Grigio. She thought it overpriced but it was the nicest they had by the glass. She saw he was more anxious now and shorter of breath and she tried to shelve the feeling that he was more available now, as victims are. He wasn't a victim, he was somebody who needed time, she thought, the thing they couldn't prescribe at the chemist. The waiter came with two small cups of Cullen skink.

'Gordon will tell you all about it when he comes,' she said. 'He's making gallons of it now for his company. You know about his company, don't you – Homeland Fisheries?'

'He's selling fish soup?'

'Well, you know. Prepared fish products. Ready to cook. Instructions in the pack. Fish cakes. Mussels. He won an award for best home delivery company.'

'Good old Gordon,' Luke said.

'He's all right,' Alice said. She paid her dues to Luke's mocking tone. 'He works hard.'

'It's a busy life,' said Luke. 'Smoked haddock.'

She giggled, took a sip. He noted a certain fierceness about her, the pursed lips, the eyes. He could tell she wanted to get close to him by having an argument. Families do that. But he'd been away awhile and wasn't sure he could face it.

'Aren't you proud?' she asked.

'Of what?'

'Scotland.'

'I know we're supposed to feel proud. But maybe we ought to earn that feeling.'

'You *have* earned it.'

'No, I haven't.'

'Everybody feels proud, Luke.' She drank nervously from her glass and put her elbows on the table.

'Before we get totally leathered on national pride,' he said, 'maybe we should first work out how to be proud of being in the human race. I would like that. I would like that first.'

'You were fighting for your country.'

'I was fighting for Flannigan and Dooley. For Lennox and Scullion. Is that a nation?'

'Your friends? It kind of is, Luke.'

'There's no nation, Mum. There's only people surfing the Net. People like your husband sending cod in parsley sauce to people in France. And the money pouring into your life via PayPal. And every person imagining the world as he wants to see it, just like the guy in the turban behind the wall with an explosive vest who thinks he's going to Allah. He thinks he loves his country, too. And he thinks his country is being exploited. And he thinks his pals are a nation.'

'You don't believe that, Luke. You were brought up in a country with traditions and you loved them.'

'It's a game, Mum. A great game. We only believed in it for as long as it lasted. I love my country for its hills and its inventions, not for its sense of injury, not for its sentimental dream that there's nobody like us. I've been out in the world and I can tell you they're all bloody like us: desperate and tired and fighting for a way into the modern world. I don't know what convinced you that building walls would make you better inside.'

'You're on the wrong page. It's changed. This country has a flag!'

'Dump the flags and the drums and the pipes. They're for the museum. Like all the junk of all the nations.'

'Those countries you've fought in want to kill us. Those people hate civilisation.'

'Oh, Mum. Stop reading the *Daily Mail*. The band of people who want to kill us are just psychopaths and criminals. They won't last. And they've never even heard of Scotland. Jesus, those people couldn't point to their own country on a map.'

'But you can.' She went on to tell him he was rootless and cynical. It was a nice conversation, hopeless, going nowhere, but full of the possibilities they each denied. They came alive arguing with each other and so did the country.

'I might be rootless,' he said, 'but I'm not cynical. I love improvement, but I can tell you it doesn't often arrive in a tank.'

'Well, remember where you come from,' she said, 'if you care for improvement. That's what we do up here. That's what we've been doing for years now.'

'Don't rest on your laurels.'

'You come from here, Luke.'

'Do I? I come from here? A person might come from lots of places at the same time and a young person's sense of humanity won't confine itself to Dundee.'

'Oh, Luke!'

'Don't Oh-Luke me. Those people in Afghanistan are poorer than you could ever imagine, and they can't read the books containing the words that they're willing to die for. But the biggest armies in the world can't stop them imagining. That's the truth. They want their tribes and they want their enemies. And so do we.'

'Oh my,' she said. 'Some nations are decent, Luke, and if they want to spread that to backward places then it's worth it.'

'Decency?' Luke said. 'Do you know why I've been drummed out of the army, Mother? Do you want to know exactly? Because my group went into a village where there was a wedding. A small village. People preparing food and playing games and looking after goats. And we were led into a trap but we massacred the whole fucken lot of them. We sprayed them with bullets. We

[179]

weren't even supposed to be there. It wasn't part of the mission. But we killed them all. Some of those boys were no more than thirteen or fourteen.'

'I'm sure you—'

'Don't be sure, Mum. Don't be. I was out of my fucken head.'

'Don't swear, son.'

'It was a slaughter in broad daylight. We were smoking spliffs. We were listening to heavy metal. Scots boys. Irish boys and others. All from proud nations. All from freedom-loving nations with statues to philosophers. And then we went into this village . . .'

'Son.'

'No. It was chaos. You want decadence? You want rootlessness? Come to Bad Kichan. I could've fired bullets into every building. Into the lady in the wedding dress and the old men and the animals, too. All of them. Just blood. Just the enemy. I didn't know if I was firing for decency or just gaming. It wasn't real to me and it's not real to anybody. So. That's what I've been doing on my holidays, Alice.'

'Good Lord.'

'Don't talk to me about proud nations. That was me. Spreading decency to the world because we have so much to spare.'

'Oh my.'

'I'll never put a uniform on again.'

'No.'

'I shamed it and it shamed me.'

Alice was remembering how Sean was the same. He started off believing in all sorts of things for Ireland and by the end he thought the players were part of the same rabble. Maybe it was just hard for soldiers to keep faith. But if Gordon was here he would put Luke straight on a few things. Nationalism was the way to live in a small country. England had been in charge for long enough and look at the mess they'd made.

'One of our own boys got killed,' Luke said. 'A boy from Dalgarnock. Aged twenty-one.'

'I know. We saw it on the news.'

Alice slowly shook her head and eventually the mussels came and she ordered more wine. She dipped a piece of bread in the bowl, tasting garlic and herb butter. Being in the Rogano made Alice feel part of something elegant. Gordon might bring her here for St Andrew's Night and he knew the chef from the markets and was trying to tie them into an online shop. Luke went outside and when he came back she saw something weary in his handsome face. For the first time, she saw how he might look when he was old. It was a shock, really, because she had never seen his father old. Sean was twenty-six. 'You still at the smoking?' she said.

'I'll shake it,' he said. 'I always start again during a tour. Just being with the boys. They all smoke.'

Alice didn't know why she needed courage to pat his hand. 'They said on the news it was drugs. They said the soldiers were smoking drugs.'

'It catches on. I mean, the boredom. And the Afghans smoke it all day and all night. The boys are like nineteen.'

'But the major, he wasn't nineteen, was he? And the newspapers say he was worse than any of them.' Luke knew there had been stuff in the papers but a public hearing was unlikely.

'Mum. Just leave it.'

But leaving it just wasn't Alice. Luke could hear the vague, distant pleasure in her voice as she said the things he didn't want to hear. 'But you'd think a man that age – I mean, practically my age – would know better than to smoke that stuff and then go into a place . . .'

'Mum.'

'. . . taking boys who can't see what they're doing in that state and it was children at a wedding.'

He couldn't help it but his teeth were gritted when he said it and he felt the heat in his face. 'Fucking. Stop. Talking,' he said and he stared hard at her. There was always something weird about Alice's make-up, as if she didn't really believe in make-up and was trying it on.

'No,' she said. 'You're right.'

'I just can't talk about it anymore.'

Under the table her hands were shaking. It was just like Sean all over again, Sean talking to her, trying to explain something that men don't want to explain. And even Luke's voice was the same as his father's talking about the army. She had the old feeling of not knowing what to say. She didn't want to provoke him, but what about the practical things? Was he out for good? Would anyone be prosecuted for what happened? Would he just live in Glasgow now and settle down and maybe keep away from all this stuff that preyed on his mind?

'Can I just say something, Luke?'

'Knock yourself out.'

'No, not like that. Nothing big.' She took a gulp of wine and looked away. 'I was never able to ask her anything about myself.'

'You mean Gran?'

'That's right. I can't ask. I can't say, "What happened in my childhood?" or "What was my father really like?"'

'Why not?'

'She made it impossible.'

'But why?'

'I don't know. And I've always asked myself, "Why can't she speak to me?" Everybody has questions.'

'Yes.' He could see far down into Alice just then, the quiet, lonely life of his mother who was never free of them all.

'I always felt my presence wasn't called for.'

'Mum . . .'

'It's fine. You learn how to live with these things.' She took another drink. 'It was always clear I got in the way of some story she had built about her and my father and what they did, who they were. If I had any doubts or any questions I had to put them away. That's my life.'

'Maybe that will change,' Luke said. She looked at him and knew she was looking at him with all the love she had.

God bless him, she thought, for thinking life was something you solved. 'I was so envious,' she said, 'when you were a boy and the two of you were reading those Dickens novels. You were like a gang. You and my mother and her favourite authors.'

'They were just books.'

'No, they weren't. They were passports. You and she went to unknown places together and I was left behind.'

'Anyone can read them.'

'Don't pretend to be shallow, Luke. You know what I mean. She taught you how to look for more out of life.'

'I suppose she did.' He could see the pain in her face.

'She never told me who I was,' she said. 'Just who I wasn't.'

'Don't get upset, Mum.'

'Some people make life bigger for other people. And I've always been on the wrong side of that bargain.'

He just felt awkward. He wasn't going to say things just to soothe her because she was too shrewd for that. He didn't quite see it but his instinct was still to hold out against his mother, to stall her sentiment and deny her all the small benefits of possession. And she changed the subject after sniffing to clear the air. 'All that stuff you're saying, about not belonging anywhere, that's just the war talking,' she said. 'It's just because of what you went through in Afghanistan. It's all the stress and what have you. But I think you know where you belong.'

He felt his phone buzz in his pocket and reckoned it would be one of the many texts from the boys in the platoon. He wished he could dive into the carpet and swim to a time when allegiances were clear. The thing he loved about Glasgow was that you never felt truly alone there: a sense of community upbraided you at every corner, but as his eye wandered vacantly over the floor he felt pinched by the local style. 'Well, Mum,' he said at last. 'I wanted life to be more than us. Much more than us. Maybe that's why I went away in the first place.'

Alice was looking at the old wallpaper. 'The way my mother spoke to you when you were a boy,' she said. 'She hardly spoke to me at all when I was a girl, and there were these long absences, when she was away somewhere, Blackpool probably or on holidays with him, and I stayed with the neighbours. My father I only saw a few times and I can't picture him ever once lifting me up. He was awkward. He once gave me a doll but I felt it had belonged to somebody else.'

'Mum.'

'No, it's all right. It was different with you and my mother. I remember you saying to her "What's colour, Granny?" and she pinched your cheek.'

'I remember that.'

'And she said, "Colour is light on fire."'

LANGOUSTINES

When Gordon turned up he was pleased to know the menu better than anybody else and he wanted to argue about fisheries and good governance but Luke asked if they could change the subject. Alice blushed and looked at her husband. They knew Luke was wrong. Gordon stroked his moustache with his bottom lip as a way of not speaking up, though to him it was a pity about his stepson, who obviously went away too young and no longer understood the priorities of his country. He knew nothing about policy and taxes or what makes a people, and now, God help him, he was like those kids who think their country is Google.

'You're just not going deep enough,' Luke said. 'Money has imploded. Religion has gone mad. Privacy is disappearing. The ice-cap is melting and children are starving to death. And you want to sing an old song about national togetherness.'

'He does a couple of tours in Afghanistan and suddenly he's Bill Gates,' Gordon said.

'I did four tours in Iraq.'

'Of course.'

'You're not *thinking*.'

'No,' Gordon said. 'We're thinking, in our own country, about how it's important to ensure that elderly people can still get their medicine.'

'Luke,' Alice said. 'You've always had your head in the clouds. Always the idealist.'

'Out of touch with reality,' said Gordon.

'The games are finished. All bets are off,' Luke said. 'We're living in the big world now.'

'This is a big enough world for me,' Gordon said.

'So why make it smaller?'

'I thought you wanted to change the subject, Luke,' his mother said and she smiled without comfort.

Gordon was wearing a yellow sweater. He knew how to make money but didn't really know how to spend it. It showed on his face, Alice thought, wondering if she was just too caught up in the mystery of her own family's approval. That was it. When his langoustines came and Gordon sniffed them on the plate she realised his lack of style told against him in a way she tried to ignore. She loved him for his kindness and his politics but not really for himself.

'You'll come round,' she said to Luke. 'The whole country's slowly coming round and you will, too.'

After a while they talked about the business of Anne's photography and the letter that came from Canada. Alice said the photographs were just another part of Anne's secretive life. She had kept it all back for her private self and her times in Blackpool. 'If the offer had come even ten years ago', she said, 'we'd all have jumped on a plane to Toronto and been proud to see her having her moment.'

Luke didn't believe it. He didn't believe there was ever a time like that, when Alice would happily have flown to Toronto to celebrate her mother's achievement. 'I don't think it's for us to say what happens,' he said. 'I don't know anything about photography but it's important for her.'

'She's just not fit enough,' Alice said.

'We'll see.'

'You don't seem to understand something, Luke. I know my mother. I know everything about her.'

But he could see it happening. He was certain the exhibition would take place and that his grandmother would be part of it. He had no idea what it would take, but he knew he would go there, that his mother would come too, and they would see for the first time what Anne had done. He pondered the possibility that his grandmother had once had a fresh vision of life and he wanted to place himself within it. Alice, too: he wanted to put her there, even as she said no. He wasn't angry at his mother for trying to bury the whole thing.

'Maybe someday,' she said.

'But let's try.'

She shook her head. It was too late for exhibitions and speeches and trips to Canada. It was enough that they take care of Anne and manage her illness. Alice said her mother didn't know the difference anymore between the past and the present, and Luke suddenly thought of an American poet he'd loved when he was a student, Wallace Stevens. After the lunch he would go to the bookshop and buy the poems.

'They're probably worth a bomb, her pictures,' Gordon said, checking his phone. Luke said he would stand by whatever decision Alice made about the exhibition. Anne's work, Anne's life, would take its own course regardless. And Luke would try to help his mother, just help her to overcome all the pain and the mess of her first life.

He felt the strange, loose spreading of the afternoon that comes after a few beers. He could say something. 'It's true. I wasn't always sure myself what was real and what wasn't.'

'When?'

'Out there. On the last tour of duty.'

'Why was that?' Alice asked.

'Too much gaming,' he said. 'Too much Dad.'

'I buried your father in his Royal Western Fusiliers dress uniform. Red hackle and everything.'

'It's over,' Luke said.

Alice just sat when he left the restaurant. Gordon was off talking to the maître d' and she could hear him laughing, his present-day-ness, all that, making him free.

BOBBY'S BAR

Maureen thought it was funny to see him after all the letters and everything. Just normal, wearing jeans. 'Don't ask me how I get to know these things,' she said to Alice on the phone, 'but apparently he was in and out the pubs down the town, the wee Saltcoats pubs, you know, that one by the railway station. This was after he saw you in Glasgow. These pubs: dog rough, if you ask me, but there you go. The men like these pubs on a Friday night. The girl who used to work in the wedding shop in Kilwinning was behind the bar. She says he had an alteration with some of them.'

'An altercation,' Alice said.

'That's right.'

'Dear God,' Alice said. 'I got a text back from him. He said he was fine and heading home.'

'You don't grudge a young man a drink, not after what he's been through. You would sooner he didn't get into arguments but there's no controlling men once they're together, sure there's not?

Anyway, he came in here in the afternoon after he'd seen you and before he went to the pub. It was funny to see him wearing jeans after the lovely uniform and everything. I'd only seen your Luke in photographs, you see.'

'He's looking thin,' Alice said.

'He's a handsome fellow,' Maureen replied. 'Anyway, he knows what he's about. I said if his gran wasn't in her flat she'd be down there drying her towels. He went off to see Anne and it was about an hour before I saw her in the corridor, dawdling back with her laundry basket. Quite happy. In a wee world of her own.'

Luke ended up in Bobby's Bar and at one point was standing beside a girl with platinum hair. She had lilac eyes and false eyelashes and was part of a hen night. She said the colour wasn't real, it was special contact lenses. He was talking to her and lifting shots off the bar and throwing them back, red shots, one after the other. His vision was blurred. He crooked an arm around the girl and she didn't care one way or the other. 'She's spoken for, by the way,' her friend said.

'That's cool,' he said. 'I'm off duty. Everybody's off duty forever and that's it.'

The friend just shook her head. She couldn't decide if she liked his face or not. He was nice and tall but he seemed like trouble. 'You're a bit of a thinker,' she said. She thought he must've been a student before or something like that, the way he had a bottle of Evian in the pocket of his bomber jacket.

'A thinker,' she repeated.

'Oh aye. That's me. Rudyard Kipling.'

Most of the men at the bar were older than him and they couldn't be bothered with hen parties. They might put a coin in the pot but they were busy talking to each other and looking up at the television to see the scores. Luke passed out the Red Cola shots to the girls two at a time. 'Who's the one daft enough to be getting married?'

'A real man, at last,' the lippy one said. Some of the men at the bar looked round and shook their heads. Luke had been shy as a student but he could remember one day walking to the Andersonian Library with the army leaflets and thinking he might be an officer and women would like it. He had been doing an essay on Thomas Hardy and one night he dreamt he was walking in uniform towards a pile of rags. He couldn't remember the girl in the book he was reading, or the soldier, but he remembered the feeling of power he had, the sense that a woman had taken off her clothes for him and was nearby.

The girls took pictures.

Shrieked.

Downed shots.

Kelly with the lilac eyes grabbed a handful of money from the pot held by the bride-to-be. 'Our turn,' she said, smiling a lipstick smile and squeezing into the bar. Luke wondered what her friend's wedding would be like and imagined men outside the function suite smoking on the steps. The noise of the fruit machine seemed to infect his sense of things, a robust, well-lighted anxiety in the corner. Maybe he had never been enough of a lad to really connect with the whole platoon. He remembered their fear that something big might never happen.

'What's your name?' the girl said.

'Captain Campbell.'

'You're in the army?'

'I was, aye.'

'We could tell.'

'How come?'

'There's lots of squaddies in this town. And you can just tell them by the way they stand.'

'Right.'

'Not many drink in here, though.'

He looked at the bottles and the masses of postcards and Celtic memorabilia. 'My name's Luke.'

'Check how you stand up straight. And check out your haircut and all that, the tanned face.'

'Maybe I went to the Sun Splash.'

'You kiddin'?' her friend said, eyes bright. 'There's nothing you can tell her about fake tan. And that is not a fake tan you are wearing. Take it from the experts.'

Kelly smiled and handed him a shot of something very sweet and green. 'Apple Sourz,' she said, and the barmaid put the bottle down on the counter. The barmaid seemed to know the girls at the hen party and the bride especially.

'Oh, that's pure disgusting,' one of them said.

Luke ordered a lager top. The girls left in a flurry of plans and proper nouns, places to go next, battle cries and whispered invitations. The lilac-eyed Kelly stood looking for a second. 'You're a honey,' she said, reaching up to kiss him on the lips. Then her fingernails cascaded goodbye in the air.

'I think you're in,' the guy next to him said, nodding in a pair of paint-spattered overalls. The girl behind the bar was looking over at Luke like she knew him. He drank his pint and tried to ignore the buzz of the fruit machine and the telly. Maybe my grandmother never really knew the people in her life, he thought. Maybe none of us do. We didn't put in the hours. A man in a Celtic top was holding up the European Cup in several of the photographs pinned up behind the bar.

'A whisky please; a Talisker.'

There was a barman behind there, too. He reached up and served Luke a decent one. Hand-poured. And Luke felt his mouth was instantly on fire, the whisky burning off the sugar and the nonsense of the previous drinks. His tongue shrank. His family was known for bravery but maybe it had never actually produced a brave man in all these years. He was drunk. The alcohol was now clearing a path to the loneliest part of him and when an Irish song began he stepped outside to smoke.

He had a text from Flannigan in Liverpool, out on the lash with his brother and his schoolmates.

Squad of horror-pigs down here lad total cocknoshes man I h8 them.

Dooley was struggling down in Cork, already champing at the bit to get back for another tour:

Hey Jimmy-Jimmy. Not seen the ladz or heard much fm the bitches but bored man still thinking about Ops. Weird shit sir and douche bags in the papers don't know nothing. Totally misinformative. Im in car park waiting for Rosie to get off fuckn work have you seen the ladz?

He smoked and used the thumb of his other hand to text back his mother.

Thanks. I'm down seeing Gran but going back up to Glasgow tonight.

He wondered if other people had to think before leaving kisses. The Kilmarnock bus via Pennyburn passed and he took in the emptiness on the upper deck. Nothing is emptier than an empty bus. Seagulls drifted over the railway station and music came pounding from one of the lounge bars at the end of Countess Street. Lennox sent him a smiley face, the third that day, a solitary smiley face. To Luke it said all the things the ginger nut was trying to say. He could see Lennox talking like a hero in some Belfast pub with the boys around him lapping it up. Then Lennox would go to the jacks and piss his wages into the metal trough remembering faraway mortars and shouts down there in the valley. Leaning on the tiles and texting smiley faces to the captain.

He wrote back:

Hey Andy. Keep smiling mate.

There's no such thing as a quiet drink. Not for Luke, anyway, and not in Bobby's Bar on a Friday. Luke went in and out of the general cheer and at one point was chuckling to himself on a bar-stool as the noise level rose. A man in an anorak came up when Luke was past caring about military decorum or the last train. 'I'm not being cheeky, pal,' the guy said, 'but can I ask you, were you in the Royal Caledonians?' Luke turned. He swayed and the man with his hands in his pockets was still speaking. It was a question. 'Is that your regiment?'

'Who's asking?' The man was on a reluctant mission but he had something invested in carrying it off. Honour, Luke supposed, and honour was the thing that ruined a man's happiness. He wiped his mouth and gripped the bar. Next minute he was over in the corner talking to a very fat man. Even in drink, Luke could see the man was wider than the copper table, covered in empty tumblers and packs of Regal King Size.

'I think you knew my son.'

'What's his name?'

'Mark McNulty.'

Luke knew right away. He had known the boy was local. He'd known there was a chance when he came into the town. And even through the fog of drink he knew it was the boy's father, the soldier called Mark who was killed at Bad Kichan. He suddenly saw the boy in the terrible heat of Helmand, smiling kid, eager as anything, one of the detachment squirting him with sunscreen by the ruined fort. Looking into his father's face and putting his hand into his, Luke saw again the boy's fury as he shouted in the road and he saw Rashid lifting his gun and shooting him at close quarters. He saw again the boy being hit and the copper bowls erupting and the blood that came from the boy's mouth.

'I recognised you from the papers,' Mr McNulty was saying. Luke was still standing next to the tables. He wanted the boy's father to come outside to speak in private, just for a moment, because he hadn't expected to meet him like this and he was trying to become the captain again despite being drunk. The gesture the man made with his hands made it clear he was stuck and didn't want to move outside.

'We won't be long,' he said.

'I wasn't with the Caledonians,' Luke said, sitting down. 'I was a captain with the Royal Western Fusiliers.'

Mr McNulty stared.

'We have a long tradition of combat. Fighting in war zones all over the world.'

'What is this, a careers talk?'

Luke wasn't sure what to say. He wanted to open up with something official and grand, providing a dignified context to the condolences he intended to offer. It was hard to do this after all the drink. 'It's a long tradition, Mr McNulty and . . . many men have given their lives.'

'Oh, aye. Very good. And do you have a long tradition of taking twenty-one-year-old boys off the beaten track and having them murdered by people on your own side?' The man was red with anger, his hand shaking over his glass and then quickly wiping his mouth.

'Mr McNulty, we were ambushed. There was nothing we could do. He was a brave soldier.'

'Oh fuck off.'

'We . . .'

'Just fuck off. Brave soldier. He was a silly wee boy who thought he could see the world. Fucking running into bullets since he was about eight years old. And then he really ran into one, didn't he? They say he wanted a square-go with the Taliban and next thing he's back here in a box. Broke his mother's heart. He's over in the graveyard, Captain. My wee boy's over in the graveyard and you can tell me whenever you're ready what it was for, because they sent some medals, but maybe you can explain them to me, each one: the silver one, what was that for?'

'I'm sorry, Mr McNulty. This isn't the place.'

'It's as good as any place.' He looked up at the two behind the bar and shouted out, 'Hey, Brian. I didnae realise you were inviting the British army into the bar these days!'

Luke was staring at the man and he tried not to think about his own father and how he had died for Ireland. 'I'm not going to argue with you, Mr McNulty. I'm just very sorry. Your son was a brave man and it shouldn't have happened.'

'Oh, he was a fucking pest. Joining the army. I don't know where you're from but we're not army people. And he goes and gets himself fucking killed into the bargain.'

'He did his best.'

'No, he didn't. He died, son. He died for nothing. And people like you can say what you like. You sent my boy back in a box and now you're drinking in my pub.'

Luke stood up.

'He didn't die for nothing, Mr McNulty.'

'He was a fucking idiot.'

IF U B WEIRD WITH ME I'LL B ANGRY

How easy to go from being one with responsibilities to being nothing at all in a nightclub queue. A man who was boss of a platoon section out there in history, an officer, yes, making decisions in the hot fuckery of life, now swaying in the line for the Metro with a nearly dead iPhone in your hand and surrounded by people ten years younger.

If u b weird with me I'll b angry.

That's what the text from Lennox said.

And to the clubbers you're just a pissed guy with no friends. You're a dude in the wrong clothes. So you start a conversation with them and they're a bit embarrassed at first but they pass you the joint. And after a while in the queue you buy some coke off the boy in the white high-tops and you stick it in your boxers and get past the bouncers by straightening up. You expect nothing of the kids but they surprise you by proving you right. Inside the club they veer off into a red pumping chasm of secret belonging and you wander to the bar where some boys gather and you find it hard to believe they're the same age as Dooley.

You drink sambuca. Jägerbombs. And then the girl Kelly comes out of the smoke all sweaty from the dance floor. You kiss her and she says 'You're really nice' but she can't put her number into your phone because your phone is dead, and anyway the laughter. She pulls you onto the dance floor and she whoops and you say 'I don't dance' and yet the lights bring you out and you find some version of yourself you didn't know. You try to talk him down and then you give in to the lights and the girl is lost and you're still there.

Oh, Luke. You never put in the hours. And then a minute comes that brings you out of yourself. You see the girl again and she's laughing big-eyed and you like how it feels and you tell her to follow you up to the bogs. You snort two more lines each and then you fuck in the cubicle, the girl talking ten to the dozen with the music deep below. Her legs are balanced on your forearms and you're fucking her standing up and kissing her neck and she says something good. You're back downstairs, you see the lights again, the kids with their hands in the air. You hear the old dark emptiness behind you and you turn and smile, feeling for one mad moment you're at home in the beat. The music is beautiful and you take a mouthful of water, so cold you could drink the sea, and suddenly you're outside the club. You float over the pavement and crouch by the door of Cancer Care, puking your guts up, and then you suck from the bottle in your jacket pocket, rub some coke on your teeth and think of Scullion.

A box was sitting in the doorway of the charity shop. It contained books and shirts and a small fire extinguisher covered in stickiness and dust. He took it. When he walked down Windmill Street he felt exposed again, as if the mirrors of the cars were conscious. He looked round to see a closed chippy and a washing-machine repair shop, and there, in darkness, facing the sea, was the Army Careers Office. He didn't look in or think about anything much, he just raised the fire extinguisher above his head and threw it at the window. He expected an alarm but the glass didn't break and he staggered away.

A boat was roped to an orange buoy. The water came in around it and a bird stood on the prow, the boat rocking, the bird looking into the night and cawing as Luke sat on the wall. It was perfectly dark out there. The bird would attempt the crossing if she could be sure to make it. Luke just stared at the creature and willed her to go, as if, with a surge of courage, she might conquer the reality of sky and whatever else.

Lochranza Court was behind him. He looked back, seeing a dim light. The corridor was never dark and it amazed him suddenly to think what stories the building must contain. His gran was there and the lady next door, Maureen, the one who wrote the letters, she must be asleep, also. He wondered if the women slept well, or did their experience keep them awake? He could still see his mother in the restaurant the day before, the worry on her face as she spoke about never knowing who she was. For the first time in his life he felt sorry for his mother and wanted to know more about what had estranged her from the woman who lived across the road. Once the war is over, what is there but life? He pulled the jacket around his ears and looked at the building, just thinking of them.

When he visited earlier that day, he'd found his gran beside the window in the laundry room, and he'd been sure she was speaking to something in her handbag, perhaps the rabbit. She looked up and called him Harry and then she remembered his own name. She took his hand and said yes, of course, he was Luke and he had been away. Just sitting in the room, he realised there was so much to find out about her, so much to do for her. And perhaps for all of them. He said he was home now and she brightened. 'That's really nice,' she said. 'I want to go on a journey with you.'

'Where?'

'To Blackpool.' She rubbed his hands by the window and touched the object in her bag and said very clearly to both of them that life was only what you made it. 'They were our best years. Lovely times. I think there are photographs down there in Blackpool.'

'You've wanted to go for ages, haven't you?'

'Yes. Since the snow.'

Sitting on the wall, he smoked a cigarette, watched the water. It was a loss of spirit that had occurred in him, a loss of make-believe, that's how he thought of it, and he knew it meant he would have to start again. The waves arrived on the sand and they bubbled there and he liked it, seeing the white froth and how it disappeared in front of him. He later wished he could capture the peace he had known over those hours on the seawall as he looked into the black distance, the lighthouse on the Holy Isle beating out a message just for him. The mountains of Arran he felt he had seen in another time, a recent one, but there was no gunfire or flares, no broken sleep, no enemy below, just the mountains themselves, the steady return of the fishing boats and the light that came with the morning.

6

SELLY OAK

'You're in England now,' the nurse said. 'You're not in Afghanistan anymore, do you hear me?' That was the first time he saw the room, though Scullion knew it wasn't seeing in the normal sense because everything was blurred with a milky radiance. And then, one at a time, he counted the colours back into his life. She was moving tubes about his face. For minutes or days he saw her green tunic. She was chatty, the nurse, and her head came in and out of focus, lifting, prodding, reminding him of school. One day a pair of blue surgical gloves fluttered over him like a hawk. A yellow drink came with a straw but he couldn't.

Three weeks in Critical Care. 'You're doing great,' she said. 'You're in *Birmingham*.' Scullion wanted to say this was a contradiction in terms but he couldn't speak and didn't know if his mouth was moving. *Try to be nice.* Sunlight broke through the blinds one day; then he heard Madeleine, her voice by the bed and her hand smoothing his hair. He couldn't afford to be miles away now that Madeleine was here, the spouse of doom, passing small pink sponges into his mouth.

'Drink, darling,' she said.

He smelt her perfume. Anaïs Anaïs.

It came in small bottles. He fell asleep. And when he woke up again he imagined he saw a goat's bones on the sand and staring down from the mountain a boy with brown eyes. What

[203]

if evil came and held your hand and said you were in England?

She sat in Kehoe's pub in one of the snugs. He saw her. It was twenty-five years ago and you couldn't smoke a cigarette without Madeleine taking half of it and kissing it down to the filter. She had a perfect smile and he loved the way she knew more than she said about everything. She just laughed instead of boasting. He called her Kitty because she loved Parnell. Back in college they had sex every day and he remembered her spraying scent into her bathwater afterwards. Sitting in the bath with her knees up to her chest asking for a puff, she looked as if trouble had been banished from her life. Disaffection was never going to touch this sweet woman, the Kitty who gleamed and the Kitty who smoked.

He lay thinking of her. Heart monitors beeped in the distance and every day more detail arrived. Madeleine was always there in the morning and he began to wonder if she'd forgotten that she hated him. 'Don't you remember, Maddie,' he said to himself, 'the day you woke up without children? And your husband was off in the sand again looking for snakes and vermin. On tour again. He wasn't the Charlie you'd known, was he? Him hiking round the world killing people because the government wished voters to see they were taking a strong line.'

Wasn't *Charlie*, he thought.

'We wanted different things didn't we, Mad? I was fighting out in some shithole and you were booking rooms in expensive hotels. That's right. We wanted different lives and we grew apart and these things happen to the very best of people, don't they, Madeleine? And you just wanted someone to be kind and to look at you that way again.' So she changed the locks and gave his books to Amnesty.

'It's hard,' she said to her friends in wine bars, 'but some men, you know, they're nice in bed, they're good to you, but they're just an absence when it comes to it. Poor Charlie. He just wants to be with the tented people.' And now she stroked his head and called him darling. This woman who would float forever through his mind in summer dresses.

'We tried to save the left leg. The other one was off when you arrived. But we had to amputate, old boy. It's too bad. It's just too bad, but you'll recover.'

Scullion lifted a hand, bending one of three remaining fingers. 'Yes,' said Colonel Pettifer, the chief surgeon. 'Both legs, old boy. You've lost an eye and your mouth is damaged, but we'll fix that. And the fingers, obviously. But I wouldn't worry too much about that.'

The heavy sedation wiped Scullion's questions. For weeks he roamed in a field of floating reds before he saw white carnations. A week later it was lines from 'The Charge of the Light Brigade'.

'Forward, the Light Brigade!'
Was there a man dismay'd?
Not tho' the soldiers knew
Some one had blunder'd:
Theirs not to make reply,
Theirs not to reason why,
Theirs but to do and die:
Into the valley of Death
Rode the six hundred.

He spoke the words to his own face in County Westmeath, the clear eyes of his boyhood, and he knew the boy's wonder would only awaken to grief. He'd never given himself good advice and it was too late. Was that Madeleine holding the blunderer's hand, counting the days, saying all would be well now between them?

'Patience,' the surgeon said.

'The wounds are healing and it's all about . . .'

'. . . commitment to getting . . . that's . . .'

'And then you won't know yourself.'

The tubes came out. One day: the theatre. A journey under lights and the operation on the mouth. The nurse said mud and dirt had been embedded in his gums, causing infection. Pettifer picked out the material with a silver tool and then he bent over to show him the grains on a swab. 'Grass from an Afghan field.' All the while Madeleine spoke about the good eye. He was in England now and many patients walk again.

A day came when his mouth had healed enough for him to try getting out a few words. He took his time. It was slow. And the first words he spoke were not curses or woes, not instant requests or questions about the legs. He simply said enough to make it clear that Madeleine should leave. He was sitting up and he could see the outline of her blonde hair, her white blouse, and he imagined her looking at the stumps of his legs and seeing that the whole man she disliked was gone.

Two weeks later he could say much more to the nurse. 'No sentimentality. You can write it on the end of the bed.'

'Like "Nil by mouth"?' she said.

'That's right. Nil by sentiment.'

'You're back with us. Goodo. Sentiment? I think you'll find that sort of thing's in short supply round here, Major. Shame about the lady, though. She was here for weeks.'

'She comes from money,' Scullion said. 'Or they pretend they have money. What they really have is debt. Those people live with so many lies they forget the money thing is false, too. And one day you just have to get away from them.'

'Too much information,' the nurse said.

The day he dismissed her, Madeleine went back to the family quarters and phoned her sister in County Clare. She was crying. 'The thing Charlie will never understand', she said, 'is that he'll always be all right because he'll always have himself. He'll never see it, but there's a sort of complete selfishness in him.'

'You did your best,' her sister said.

'He doesn't have it in him to be pitied.'

THE TOLLYGUNGE CLUB

One day he smelt food. It was coming from the corridor and it marked the return of routine. 'This is how it works,' Pettifer said. 'You'll be going off to the High-Dependency Burns Unit. You'll need skin grafts and a cataract operation to improve your good eye. After that, the real work begins – the legs. We're going to seal them and then you'll be off to Headley Court in Surrey. You're not old, Major, but you're not in the first flush. The training is hard work, let me tell you. It's six months before you're off the stubbies and walking on prosthetics.'

'Prosthetics, really?'

'Yes.'

'We had better get a move on, Colonel,' said Scullion. 'It would be lovely to be able to walk to my own disciplinary hearing, don't you think?'

Pettifer just smiled the way people smile when they don't want to get involved. 'Keep fighting,' he said. Scullion wasn't sure if blushing was actually an option anymore, but the words embarrassed him and he wished he could go to sleep.

He spent the long afternoons thinking about a new life in India. He thought he could just about bear it in Calcutta, the slow, fading intensity, playing billiards at the Tollygunge Club with the gardeners, eating mangoes, reading Saki and drinking gin and tonic. He could see it so clearly he almost believed in it, a life of displaced authority in warm weather, a life of impotence. He was only two days in the Burns Unit when he asked for paper and started trying to write out the logistics. There was money from his parents' old pub in Mullingar: he could pay for nurses. He could talk to strangers or start a charity or write a book. With his childish legs in front of him under the blanket, Scullion knew that his great companion had always been his imagination. He asked the welfare officer if she could bring him *The Jungle Book*. He could see himself sitting under the twisted boughs of a banyan tree, hidden from the sun, recalling the Great Game, a blanket like this over his poor legs and a drink in his hand, the mind alive, his eyes scanning the horizon for elephants.

'Hello, Charlie,' he said. It was Luke standing in the doorway with a bottle of Talisker and a bag of cakes. He had walked all the way from Birmingham New Street thinking of what to say.

'Is it yourself, Captain Campbell?'

'It is.'

'Well, fuck me with a flute band,' Scullion said. Luke smiled and walked over to the bed. He thought better of shaking the major's hand so he clapped his shoulder.

'I'll pass that request on to the regiment. I'm sure we could arrange for the old Western band to march up your hole while playing "Amazing Grace", if that's what you really want. I mean, it's quite a strange order but look at the fucken state of you. You can have anything you want.'

That was well done. Well managed, thought Scullion. He laughed and pulled himself up on the pillows. Luke was pleased to see he could still laugh and he realised, watching him struggle, how much he had always been intimidated by the major. Scullion began speaking hospital small talk while Luke considered him, realising, while he listened, that he was now in a position of power. Nobody else but Luke had fully witnessed the major's meltdown. Nobody else knew how reckless he had been in making them go to that village or how his judgement had collapsed before the mortar attack. Scullion had abandoned the boys to danger more than once, they both knew it, and the facts of the matter told against them both. The facts ridiculed them as soldiers and mocked the legend of Scullion's war. At that stage it hadn't gone beyond blame into a collective sadness; indeed, it lay heavy on Scullion's own head, on his features, his scarred mouth, twisted now as he stared from the bed and tried to talk.

'Sit your arse down.'

'How they treating you?'

'They dance around. The nurses. Doctors. You're lucky if you see the same one twice.'

They discussed the hours after he was hit. He didn't remember the song or the tourniquet, the morphine, the airlift. He didn't care so much about the weed-smoking or the gamer mentality in the field. It was all nothing in the end, the sound of a different drum. 'We ran into some bad luck. Or I did. And the wee boy did' was all he wanted to say.

'It was a fuck-up,' Luke said.

'We brought light to those people . . .'

His bad eye was leaking. Luke handed him a swab from the top of the bedside cabinet. Another silence. 'You nearly died.'

'One thing I've learned. When death smiles at you, Captain – you've just got to smile right back at it.'

Luke didn't mind the fakery. The man was in pain. Or was he actually proud of all the sacrifices?

'We achieved a lot,' he said.

'Fucking zero,' Luke said.

'We deployed with confidence.'

'The mission to make the country stable has made it less so and only the Taliban rose in confidence.'

'Ah, fuck it,' Scullion said. They were silent for a minute and Scullion wished he could resurrect the banter that had drawn the boys together. But when he spoke he found he was grasping for something larger. 'Some of us are just two-sided men, Luke. The moment we look at anything we see its exact opposite. It's a way of life.'

'I understand, sir. Let's talk about something else.'

'You think I failed.'

'I think you've suffered.'

Scullion's smile had something wrong in it. It took the world at its worst and gave it his blessing. 'Holy fuck,' he said. 'I sent my bitch of a wife away. I lost my legs. One of my eyes is fucked for good. And you *think* I've suffered?'

'It was a terrible tour.'

'That happens.'

'Not to me,' Luke said.

'You know, Luke: some things are simpler than others. Maybe you just chose the wrong career.'

'I know I did.'

'You'll be appearing at the tribunal? And you'll be talking to the journalists downstairs?'

'I thought you liked the truth, Charlie? Wasn't that your thing? Alexander the Great and all that? Truth and enlightenment? Pulling the savage peoples out of the dark ages? But now that a few papers want to ask what happened, it's loyalty, is it? It's sticking together for—'

'The regiment!' he shouted.

'Oh, Charlie,' Luke said. 'Is that the best you can do?'

He walked to the cabinet to lift the cakes, setting them out slowly on a plate and placing it on the edge of the bed. 'This has nothing to do with the regiment,' he said. 'It's to do with a bunch of kids from different regiments being mistreated by their superior officers.'

'Is that what the boys say?'

'The boys don't know what to say. They've gone back home to see their families and pine for another chance to be heroes.' Luke took one of the cakes and picked at it.

'You always had judging eyes,' Scullion said.

'Calm the fuck down, Charlie. I came on the train to see you and there's no point talking shit.'

Scullion was one of those actors. He had any number of selves to call on and he didn't favour one in particular. That's why he could do things other people couldn't do, because, to him, at some level, it was always another person doing it. He was always above it. 'I don't know what any of you want,' he said. 'You're all the same.'

'Is there anything you need, Charlie?'

'I need a year. If I can make it to a year I'll go to India and none of you will see me again.'

'India?'

'I've never been happy, Luke. That's a lie. I was happy for a term at Trinity College Dublin. I think I told you. Me and Madeleine up the stairs listening to jazz records and that was it.'

'What?'

'That was it.'

'You were happy?'

'Yes.'

He spoke for a while about the early days, when he thought he would live in London and write a book. For a summer he haunted Senate House and the reading room of the British Library.

'Then you joined up.'

'I did.'

'Why didn't you just stay in that world?'

'It isn't a world, Luke. People who read books aren't reading them properly if they stop with the books. You've got to go out eventually and test it all against reality.'

'You're from another age.'

'That's what she said. What they all said. And I made the mistake once of thinking you were the same.'

'I just missed my da', Charlie. And I thought I could show the difference between right and wrong.'

'We all did.'

'That's right. We all did.'

'There was a generation of men wrecked by Ireland,' Scullion said. 'A fair few of us. I saw those dead construction workers in Teebane, the ones that were blown up by the IRA. I was young and I hoped at the time that I'd never see such carnage again. But time passes and I've seen more dead men than I ever imagined. Hundreds more. It makes you hard. I've been shot at from buildings in places you don't even know.'

He sat up straight and wiped his good eye. Luke imagined it was now trained only on the dark places.

'You should go to India,' Luke said. 'Go if you can and look after yourself, Charlie.'

Scullion put his head back on the pillows. 'We never had children. We were too busy trying to work ourselves out and we missed the boat. We missed our chance. And maybe they would have been my cause. Maybe that's what people do to . . .'

'What?'

'Gain a foothold. Make their own news.'

'Maybe.'

'She never forgave me. My army career was a nightmare to her and it killed our marriage.'

'Maybe.'

It was obvious to Luke that something final was taking place. He tried with words and gestures to reassure his old boss, but his heart wasn't in it, and his attitude clearly irked Scullion, who saw only disloyalty. Scullion suddenly winced: it was obvious the whole thing felt to him like pain, the dull unravelling of his command. Being unable to shout orders, he could only stammer, his bad temper entering in gasps.

'You don't know what I'm talking about, Campbell. What . . . what have you had?' he asked. 'Girlfriends? Silly girlfriends? You've never risked anything, never mind your happiness, never mind your legs.'

'People get over things, Charlie.'

'Good luck with that.'

A nurse and two men came in. 'Time for your scan,' the nurse said. 'The porters will wheel you along.' She started fussing with wires and tubes and Luke stepped back. When he came forward again he placed a hand on the major's arm.

'You taught me things,' he said.

'Like what?' Scullion said. 'How to put trust in the wrong people? How to become a two-sided man?'

'Maybe you'll write something.'

'Like what?'

'I don't know. You're the one with the stories.'

'History's always told by the deputies,' Scullion said. 'Men like you. You're just the right age for revenge.' Luke stared at his old mentor. Decency or pity demanded that he allow the major the final insult.

'Goodbye, sir.'

'This is real life.'

'Aye.'

Unspoken words softened the air. 'Why don't you wait here,' Scullion said. 'I won't be long at this thing and you can just sit and wait for me.' But Luke kept his eye on him as the bed turned and was sure the major understood they would never meet again. 'My hand's warm,' Scullion said. 'You don't get this in your video games, sure you don't, son.' Luke felt the years slide away as the major withdrew his hand. A look of complete spite came into Scullion's face and he blinked his crusted eye, then rested his head on the pillow as the bed moved off, steered by his new lieutenants. Luke could hear his old friend complain about the bumps as he vanished down the corridor, setting out on his long journey to India.

Maureen was setting the table in the breakfast room and getting all het up about an episode of *EastEnders*. Bloody napkins, she thought. The stress was too much, doing a lunch. It wasn't even the whole family, but she didn't do lunches. It was all because Esther was coming down from Edinburgh for one of her visits and she'd given her mother a stiff lecture on the phone about how normal it was, having your family round. Maureen felt it might be Esther's idea of a Sunday but it wasn't hers. It was a sheltered housing complex she lived in, not the Ritz.

Esther was like her father that way. She would just decide on a whim that everybody had to live according to new rules. Stanley used to come back from his jaunts, Maureen remembered, full of ideas about how they should eat more salad or start playing tennis. It would cause rifts between them that couldn't be healed. The children could still remember the time their parents decided to buy a gas fire. They had arguments in every showroom in Ayrshire and collected dozens of leaflets. Every Saturday and Sunday for months was spent looking for a fire, but still they couldn't agree and it somehow destroyed any good feeling between them. She wanted something plain like you might see in a modern office, and he wanted one with a flame, a novelty fire that could cheer you up. Their differences were silly but they became strangulating to the kids. Maureen then watched for bullying tactics in everything Stanley did: if he made a pot of soup, she would follow him around the kitchen with a damp cloth, cleaning the surfaces before he'd even had time to mess them up, pointing out how soup was his mother's thing, waving away his cigarette smoke, his pleasures. Maureen was young then but she behaved as if her life was a trial. And as Esther and her brothers grew up they realised their mother had never stopped being angry at their father. He was still a force of resistance for Maureen, a niggle, a source of objection that she couldn't stand, and now, in her later years, his invisible fire still sent a chill over her living room.

Maureen was not at her best that Sunday. Her mind raced back and forth between bitterness and scorn, and lavishly, early that morning, she began to exert herself making sure the lunch would be difficult. Them with their Edinburgh dinner parties and what have you. Out of the blue they decide they want catering in the middle of the day, Maureen thought. 'It's not the kind of thing we do in Ayrshire,' she whispered, 'and I'll be seventy on my next birthday. Them with their fancy cars and their pasta.' Esther was always dropping little hints about how her father loved having them over to stay and how the new wife was into cookery books and growing her own tomatoes. Maureen liked to say the new wife would have her eyes opened one day.

She hadn't seen Stanley for twenty-five years. Hadn't clapped eyes on him. Yet she'd added to her dislike of him every day, now saying he hadn't played a real part in the children's lives, hadn't got involved in all the struggles of bringing them up or setting them straight. She said Alexander's drink problem was completely Stanley's fault. She said Ian had never really worked himself out because he had no father to guide him. And Esther – don't get me started, thought Maureen. Esther thinks it's healthier to forgive the bad people than praise the ones who've been good to you. That's Esther. Maureen held up one of the new spoons, polished it and then set it back down on the table. They pay her well as a therapist, she thought, to hurt her mother and pretend it's all about honesty.

Esther arrived first and brought one of those sweet Italian loaves full of sultanas that Maureen secretly liked but always said was too rich. Scott and Jack, Esther's two, gave their grandmother big, self-conscious hugs, and she wanted to tell them to take off their massive shoes. It was all problems of size when it came to the family, big hugs, massive shoes, the small thanks she got, the exorbitant need for Wi-Fi. 'Can you not do without it for five minutes?' she said to Scott when he asked what the password was. 'We don't have anything like that in here.' She shook her head. 'We've enough to do just trying to keep the place clean and tidy.'

With his gelled hair and his love-bite there was suddenly something quite lewd about Scott. She was sure he was playing with a Harry Potter doll the last time she saw him. You can't keep up with them nowadays, she thought. One minute they're using your handbag as a magic cave for their Lego figures and the next minute they're advertising how they just had sex. No sooner did her family arrive in the living room than Maureen went into an anxious depression, their need for things belittling her somehow, taunting her, making her yearn for her normal afternoons when she was by herself. Esther's youngest was silent except for the bleeps and melodies that came from a small red device in his lap.

'You better turn that off,' Maureen said. She gathered up the coats and started for the bedroom. 'The fire alarm in this place is always going off and it's because these gadgets interfere with the system and break it.' Jack looked at his brother and the two of them just bit the laces around their necks and smiled into their sweatshirts.

Going off with the coats, Maureen was thinking of Stanley, realising how much better he seemed to her now that she never saw him. He had once been as handsome as Tony Curtis. He was a fine boy when he was young and Maureen felt proud then to have him. He drove lorries all over Europe and would bring back bottles of perfume for Maureen that nobody else owned, and what a laugh he was. 'My father had no time for him,' she always said and her story never varied. 'He saw him for what he was, but my mother, of course, she thought he was fabulous. Stanley would come in and ply all the old women with drink. He had trouble handing in his wages or staying at home for a week, mind you, but to everyone else he was the great Stan. He always had contraband, as he called it. This was before you could just drive to France to buy drink. He brought all these things from the Continent and my mother and the rest of them thought he was just the best in the world. He always had stories. They thought I was the queer one.'

Standing in her bedroom, with the coats in her arms and the window clear and polished in front of her, Maureen wanted to scream. In the next room they were bustling about, talking and upsetting her cushions and opening the fridge, and it all felt to her like an invasion. She hugged the warm coats and wished they were her nearest-and-dearest: she could just lay them down for the afternoon and then brush them off and send them home. But the actual people? Maybe it's me, she said to herself, maybe it's my problem, but I just wasn't cut out for that way of life. Families and what have you. They would put years on you. She felt guilty when she thought about it later, but there was no getting away from it: her family made her feel like she couldn't really breathe. Her mother had always made her feel the exact same way, as if she had so many things to prove. And she didn't have the means to prove them so she might as well not try. 'Stanley lights up a room,' her mother said to her one Hogmanay. 'But you've always got so much on your plate, Maureen.' She used to dream he went to Spain with her mother and her mother's friends. Her father was never in the photographs that appeared in the dream, but years after her divorce, long after the kids had families of their own, she would see Stanley drinking sangria from a leather bottle in a bright yellow place in her mind.

The bedroom felt like an old, reliable friend. Maureen looked at the pillows and the mirror and almost whispered to them, speaking out her frustration. 'I mean it when I say I'm lonely,' she said to herself, 'it's true in the night, but when they come I don't like it.' The sentence mortified her but she added more. 'When they take off their coats I feel mugged by everything they expect.' She knew it wasn't fair, that in her mind she lived like a servant when in reality she ruled like a queen. But she couldn't change, she would never change, and it was her habit now to say they were 'hurting' her if they complained. 'And why would anybody hurt a person who lived on her own?' She could tell Esther thought this was some kind of strategy to get her own way.

'See the family: I could run a mile.' This is what she used to say to Anne next door. 'I could see them far enough.'

'What's wrong?' Anne said. 'Don't you enjoy your family? They all seem so nice.'

'They're a handful, Anne. I'm not kidding you. It's not easy. You don't know the half of it.'

For years her children had witnessed it on their mother's face, how put-upon she felt by them, how aggressed by their basic wishes. They tried to understand it. Family life, to her, was a complication best left to television. She liked greeting cards because she could buy them on her own and send them on her own, and she despatched all responsibility when she posted those cards.

The soaps were her haunting counsel. She watched them and got ideas about how the members of her own family were less than they should be. She said it broke her heart, but, in a sense, she liked it when people let her down. It made her feel justified. Alexander was an alcoholic and a genuine worry to everyone, and there was nothing she could do. He was angry and messed up, his life was out of shape, so he just blamed his mother. She could see that. The other two, Ian and Esther, confused her much more. They had spent years trying to supply her with a new perspective, to little effect. They kept trying and they kept hoping their lives would please her but Maureen had formed a heady resistance to their idea of family bliss. Esther reminded Ian it was a condition she suffered as well as a decision she made. And if she ever took the trouble to compare herself to her own mother, she would see that the same pattern had been repeated. Old Sadie had liked who she was with her friends but not who she was with her family. She hardly ever invited them round, and she, too, hated finding her cushions on the floor. Maureen sometimes felt like a person being punished for no reason.

Stanley said people didn't really know her. Maureen remembered Esther repeating what he'd said as if it was news from God. 'Your mother used to be light-hearted and full of fun,' he also said. Maureen didn't want to hear it from Esther, but it was true. The children think they know everything but they don't know the half of it. 'I used to make cakes and there'd be flour everywhere,' Maureen said to herself in the bedroom, 'and halfway to Carlisle he'd open his piece-box and find these perfect wee cakes.' Maureen knew that Esther had brought it up – what Stanley said – in the hope that the information would boost her mother's self-esteem.

It's one of Esther's favourite expressions, said Maureen, and some of us don't need boosts and don't want self-esteem, we just want peace and quiet at the weekend and for the past to stay in the past.

She counted to ten in front of the window. Ian was coming down the path with his daughter and his face was serious, but when they came in she heard the usual cheers. Esther always had to kiss everyone and now she would be greeting her older brother. She'd be lifting the little one and squeezing the poor wee thing to death. It would soon be over, Maureen thought, laying down the coats. The audiobooks were by the bed and Maureen looked forward to that. You get to a certain age and it's just too late to start changing. 'Hello, son,' she said when Ian entered the bedroom with more coats.

'Cold out there,' he said.

'Well, that's November for you.' She looked down to see her newest grandchild padding in behind her father. 'And look at this wee lady with her chubby face. Ah, Bonnie. Come here till I see you, darlin'; take your shoes off now, there's a good girl.' Bonnie came waddling forward in her winter wraps with her fingers out like twigs, and, when she lifted her, a real smile broke over Maureen's face. She patted down the fluffy hair and smelled the winter on her granddaughter's cheeks. 'Have you been a good girl? Have you? Have you been a good girl? Well, Bonnie, my wee pet, I've got a treat for you, so I have. Yes I have.'

'Don't give her sweets, Mum,' Ian said.

'Don't be daft.'

'No. We don't give her sweets.'

'Oh, don't be silly. Just a wee sweetie, eh. She deserves a wee sweetie just like any other kid.'

Ian wondered why she didn't just say 'fuck you'. It would've been easier in a way if she had. Fuck you and your plans and your decisions that are different from mine. Fuck them. And fuck you for coming in here thinking I should respect them, because I don't, I think they're nonsense. As well as that I think you lot are all out of touch with normality. All children want a sweetie and what kind of grandmother would I be if I denied my wee grand-daughter a sweetie? It's you and Esther. You're that stressed you can't let your kids be at peace.

Why didn't she just say it and be done with it?

She pulled open the drawer and picked out a bar of Highland Toffee and a Kinder Surprise. She didn't hand them to Bonnie but placed them on top of the chest of drawers next to a framed picture of Stanley and the children at Butlin's in 1973. She turned to Ian to see what he was going to do about it and he flushed before he spoke.

'Mum,' he said. 'There's a reason we don't want the kids to have these things. It's because we had four or five fillings each before we left primary school. And because our dad had his first heart attack at the age of fifty-two. So it's not really a matter of whether Bonnie *deserves* a wee sweetie, because what she deserves much more, my daughter, is to not grow up with a mouthful of scabby teeth and then have heart disease at an age when healthy people are thinking about running a marathon. That's my choice as a parent. Okay? Is that all right with you?'

'Oh shut up, Ian. I'm not in the mood today.'

Bonnie emerged from the bedroom with the chocolate egg and Esther could see that Ian and their mother had already had an argument. She noticed the slow progress of Maureen's befuddle-ment and a slight limp as she made her way to the kitchen coun-ter and handed the plates to Jack. She wished she could just go and hug her mother and tell her this was a happy occasion but it was years too late. That's what happens. She looked at Maureen as if she suddenly had a clear idea of her and took the plates herself from Jack. 'I'll help you, Jigger,' she said.

'This Parmesan's smelly,' Scott said.

'Don't say "smelly," Scooter.' That was Esther. She didn't like the boys to use words like 'smelly' or 'toilet'. Something could smell strange or you might visit the loo, but 'smelly' was definitely out of bounds, and so was 'belly' when you could say 'tummy'.

'It was all they had in Tesco's,' Maureen said.

'You're better buying it fresh,' Scott said. He always got more sophisticated when his father wasn't there. Esther considered it a sign of maturity or something, probably meaning he would cope better at university. They sat down. Maureen wasn't eating what was on her plate. At times she thought she should have tried much harder to keep Stanley. Tried much harder to please him and make him happy. When it came to it, she let him go as if her disappointment in him – her sudden hatred – was simple confirmation that men weren't worth a button. She liked to tell herself that everything would have been different with the children if she'd had a man in the house. Perhaps Stanley would've protected her against their need to be special all the time.

She lifted a fork. 'I don't know why you wanted Italian,' she said. 'Every time you have your lunch nowadays you've got to decide which country you're going to.'

Esther looked at her mother and chewed her food a few times more than was necessary. 'There's certainly a lot more choice nowadays,' she said.

'You call it choice. I call it harassment,' Maureen said. 'It's

[223]

like the bloody Olympic Games in that Tesco's. Italian. Chinese. They've got a whole bloody aisle of Polish stuff.'

'Well, there's a lot of them living here,' Ian said.

'Too many,' replied Maureen.

'I don't know where we'd be without them. Half the building sites would be lying empty for a start. And taxi drivers. You couldn't get a British guy to get out of his bed on a Saturday morning if the town was on fire. These Eastern Europeans will work all night.'

'Taking jobs,' Maureen said. 'And bringing their giant jars of vegetables over here. And biscuits. It's not even biscuits they eat. Those things are like bars of soap. You'd get bubbles in your mouth if you sat down to eat one with a cup of tea.'

Over the years, Ian had come to accept her complaints as a kind of sickness, a complete resistance to the idea of forward movement, and he only blew up when it seemed directly to affect his own child. Esther, on the other hand, had an obvious pact with Scott and Jack, to be themselves no matter what Maureen said or did, but Esther could get nervous. She knew, for instance, that her mother would find it difficult when she began a story about the cocktails they had every weekend at tea-time.

'Cocktails,' Maureen said. 'You all think you're film stars and this is Scotland, not bloody New York.'

'Dad made me a mojito,' Jack said.

'A mosquito?' said Maureen.

'There was hardly anything in it,' Esther said.

'Well, if you want to get them started on drink that early, it's up to you. I'm just telling you it's the slippery slope.'

'It was just a bit of fun, Mum.'

'That's how it started with your brother.'

'Let's not go there,' Ian said.

'Take it from me,' Maureen said. 'Giving drink to young men is not a wise move. Alexander was at it far too young. And your father, the great man, was giving him pints of lager when the boy was about fifteen years old. Somebody saw him down the street the other day with a bottle of vodka in a plastic bag. The middle of the afternoon, when all the men are at their work. Vodka! I was mortified.'

Esther looked at Ian. She knew it was going to be like this. She knew she would be sharing looks with her brother, rolling her eyes at the dawning of impossibility over the lunch table. She sipped her fizzy water and saw that her mother would never change and that the healthiest prospect was just to love her as she was. And that's how she played it. She mustn't be brutalised by her mother's frustrations and she counselled herself always to seek new ways to think well of her. Love is hard work and you don't get anywhere just by feeding your resentments. She thought she could steal a little goodness back just by stopping to remember how lovely her mother had been to the woman next door. She once read a paper that said if you love someone then you're always ready to let them start again.

Maybe they'd like the ice-cream, thought Maureen. People always cheer up when it comes to the sweet. 'I'm sorry I'm not very good at these things,' she said suddenly to them all at the table. Ian and Esther smiled and said everything was great and both of them seemed relieved to see her relax enough to say what she'd said. Sometimes you just have to accept that the people you care about are different from you, thought Maureen, but walking to the kitchen she realised she had a tear in her eye. The visit wouldn't last for ever and neither would her nice memories of Stanley, but there it was. As she opened the fridge she knew she'd never have chosen anyone else, even as the chill of the icebox softly caressed her hand.

ARIEL

Luke walked from the car and skipped over a puddle and smiled for no reason at the windows of the building. He looked along the seafront to where the prom disappeared into the thick of Ardrossan and took out a cigarette. The car ferry was halfway out and the seagulls wafted it on, before banking away like bombers and heading up to Largs. In the morning the coast always looked as if it was drying out, as if each town was in recovery from the bad weather and the night's racket. Feeling for his lighter he found his wallet and took out the picture of 5 Platoon up against a wall at the barracks in Salisbury. The major's eyes seemed fixed on something miles away.

It was the second time Luke had discovered Anne in the laundry room, and this time she sat facing the machine with the suds splashing up on the glass. He stood at the door watching her and noticed a smile, the smile she had developed long ago, an expression that he couldn't read. After a moment, she sighed. 'I like to wash and iron a man's shirt,' she said.

'That's not very feminist,' he joked.

She looked up. 'I had a job in New York.'

Luke went over and put his hand on her shoulder. She held a box of Ariel washing capsules in her lap and something in her attitude suggested she understood how to cope around a washing machine. She took a tissue from her sleeve and rubbed her nose with it, then she turned it over and used the clean side to wipe her eyes. Luke watched her and thought only an old person would do that. He would know he was getting old when he used both sides of a tissue. 'You used to come here before the war,' she said.

He paused.

'I did. It's your grandson, Luke.'

'I know who you are. You're the one with the flat in Glasgow and the uniform.'

'You're doing your washing.'

She inclined her head to look at him. 'You're the one with the imagination,' she said. 'A boy and a half. And why shouldn't we take pictures of a pile of old dishes if that's what we want to do?'

'No reason,' he said.

'Exactly. There's beauty in it . . .'

'Yes.'

'Art.'

'I agree. There's an art to telling the truth.'

'That's what the boys used to say – Harry and the boys. That was the style, I don't mind telling you. Get out of the studio!'

'Test your theories outside.'

'I've met you before,' she said. 'And you're quite right. No doubt about it. Go outside and see the people who have their hands in the sink.'

'You're talking about photography?'

'Everyday things,' she said.

'Yes.'

'I'll tell you something,' she said, tapping the box in her lap and sniffing. 'When I lived up in Glasgow there was heaps of washing to be done. Heaps. I think there were a hundred rooms in that house and a hundred chests of drawers in every room. It was a very big house. And I was quite young to be carrying all that washing up the stairs.'

'You came from America.'

'I came from Canada. Then America. Then Glasgow.'

'Glasgow must have been some place in those days,' he said. 'Remember those Annan pictures we saw of the tenements?'

She paused to catch her thoughts. She smiled. 'They were ghosts,' she said, 'those Annan kids.'

'But you understood the pictures – the light.'

She turned and waved a playful finger. 'So did you, Sonny Jim. That's the darkroom for you. That's why you're number one.'

Luke had gathered from his mother and from the warden that they were going to move Anne out. They said she couldn't manage anymore and even the Memory Club wasn't helping, though she still had bursts of clarity. It was time to place her in better care, they said, and Anne wasn't really absorbing this information, so they would be better just getting on with the task. There were a lot of things to box up. It was hard, too sad. The books and the photographic stuff would need a van to themselves. Luke was talking to the people in Canada about her photographs and various papers and they put him on to a person at McMaster University, a nice woman with an Irish name, who was going to be in charge of whatever they did.

'I'm happy, Luke,' Anne said. She just said it. He lowered his head and thought of Scullion and the boy in Bad Kichan, and he found himself exhaling slowly as he took Anne's hand. When she said she was happy it gave him the final push he needed to announce the excursion and defend her against whatever doubts. 'Here's what we're going to do,' he said. 'You and me. I've got a new car. We're going to pack some things and go to Blackpool.

You always used to talk to me about it, remember, the lights and the trams and all that?'

'Blackpool,' she said.

'We're going to go and see the Illuminations.'

'Nice, that. Will we take the train?'

Glasgow Central to Preston. And Harry would be waiting for me, if he could get away. Or it didn't matter if you had to manage by yourself. Work is work. You wouldn't believe the concentration. Masking is a technique whereby you hold back some of the light from one or two areas by placing a mask on the printing paper itself. It will affect the image you see and the reality you observe.

She asked again: 'The train?'

'I have a car,' Luke said. 'Now, listen. I'm going to work it all out and we're going together. You and me.'

'We'll pack some things.'

'We will so, Gran.'

'We'll pack some things and there's always lots to do in Blackpool.'

Luke had phoned his mother. 'There's a flat,' she said. 'Part of a flat or a room, anyway, and you'll find the number in her address book. She never wanted me to know about it. It's hers, the flat. And it doesn't matter anymore. Just go. It's a lovely idea.'

'It's tomorrow they're coming, right?' Luke asked.

'Tomorrow, yes. Monday,' said Alice.

'We'll go tomorrow, then.'

'You want me to come along?'

'Thanks,' he said, 'but just drive over here and help the cleaners once we've gone. I'll spirit her away.'

'All right,' Alice said. 'God bless.'

Luke was sitting out by the exotic plants that everybody called the jungle. His gran was having a nap and he wanted to arrange things. He hadn't spoken to Flannigan in a while and was out of touch with the boys and hadn't said anything about his visit to Scullion in Birmingham. 'So what about it, Flange?' he said on the phone. 'Do you think your fucken heap-of-shit car will make it out of Liverpool?'

'What you doing?'

'I'll be in Blackpool.'

'Don't sweat it, lad. I'll be zooming past all the horror-pigs on the road to get to the land of Kiss Me Quick. Just hit me up with the time and the place.'

They hadn't talked about the tour or the tribunal or any of the stuff that was in the papers. It just wasn't part of their training to pore over things. 'Shit happens' was the other motto, but, at the end of the call, the young private altered his tone and there was a pause.

'What is it?' Luke asked.

'I dunno, man. Flashbacks. She said I woke up shouting in the night and like fucken crying and shit.'

'And did you?'

'I did, yeah. It was like I was losing my nut. My head just full of Scullion, man, the boss lying there ripped to fuck. Remember his eyes?'

'Go on.'

'Blood, sir. His eyes were full of blood. Fucken leg blown off and blood pouring down the fucker's cheeks.'

'Aye,' Luke said. 'It was messy.'

'That's the difference,' Flannigan said. 'You're out. I'm nineteen. What the fuck am I going to do if I don't have the army?'

Luke didn't know what to say. He didn't yet know how to talk about the visit to Selly Oak or how to share the details of his own flashbacks. When he came into Lochranza Court that afternoon he had been spooked right away by a Remembrance Day appeal box sitting in reception. And when he was telling Anne about the night he went out on the town, the night he drank too much, her voice rallied and she said what he'd heard older people say to boys with hangovers, 'Hell mend you.'

'What, Gran?' He shivered. He'd thought she had said '*Helmand* you.'

'I better go, Flange.'

'You stayed so long, sir. Why did you stay so long in the army if you hated it that much?'

He wondered, as he often did, whether he should tell the truth or reach for something he half-believed. He had never really lived in a world where things could be said, but he said it now, in a lowered voice, as if posting an old letter he'd never got round to sending. 'I kept thinking I'd meet my dad and we'd change the world.' Luke wondered if Flannigan was just far too young to believe it, but it didn't matter, he'd said what he'd said and the kid went on to something else.

'It didn't feel real, being in Afghan,' he said. 'It was so fucken hot all the time.'

'I know it's a loser thing to say,' Luke said, 'but I stopped believing in it, Flange. I was never like that in Iraq.'

'Other people believe in it, sir. We just do our job.'

Luke paused to take that in. 'I hope I haven't embarrassed you, mate.'

[231]

'Don't be daft, sir.'

'Okay. I'll buzz you from Blackpool.'

'Roger that,' Flannigan said.

Luke was sitting on the wall, looking at the plants, when the two boys came up. 'Is that the new iPhone?' Scott asked. Luke's phone was sitting beside him.

'Yep. Top of the range.'

'Aw, man. I want that, like, *so* badly.' Luke knew they must be the grandsons of Anne's nice friend Maureen. It was weird for him to think that they weren't much younger than most of the guys in his section. The two boys spoke very easily: one of them said he wanted to be a DJ and the other said he'd study medicine if he could get in.

'I'd never join the army,' Jack said. 'No offence.'

They spoke about phones and laptops and sounded very keen on cool things. 'Wait here,' Luke said, after a second's hesitation. 'Just wait here a minute. I'll be right back.' He went out to the car park, opened the boot and lifted out a black bag of stuff and brought it back to the boys. They opened it and gasped: two Xboxes, all the wires, handsets, mouthpieces, manuals, and a jumble of Nintendos and games.

'Aw, man. Awesome!' Jack said. The boys looked at each other with big smiles and Luke felt sure it was right to return it all to the realm of fun. They put their long arms into the bag and pulled things out and from the bottom Scott produced a paperback book, Kipling's *Kim*.

'This stuff is so cool.'

'Don't stay up all night,' Luke said.

Anne woke and didn't know where she was. All the houses had become one house and one time. She could have been downstairs as a child in Canada, or was she inside the doll's house, lighted with the bulb Daddy put there at Christmas? She felt for a moment she might be in the parlour in Hamilton waiting for the doctor, her mother bad with the shakes, and red leaves spinning in the yard. She blinked and heard a rumble under the boards. *Jane Street.* She thought of the rugs she'd left in storage near Battery Park. A voice that came from the stairs made her think she must be in Glasgow, the big house, snow outside, Anne watching from the top window as the little girls in round hats made their way to school. She turned her head on the pillow and smiled to think of it. She pictured Blackpool, the darkroom at the top of the stairs. And she knew he would come. Harry would come and they'd put on a lamp and have a drink.

She sat on the edge of the bed. It was nice to have a place and a young man to help you take down a box. That's right, she said: the boy Alice had and he's now a leader of something. Luke. He wears the uniform and has to go out on night flights and what have you. He comes here and it takes an hour or two if the roads aren't bad. And when she thought of bad roads and night-time, all the stories drained away.

There was fog and snow over Germany.

You can forget you're by the seaside. And good God: you have to keep your wits about you in these places, Saltcoats, Manhattan. You had to keep your chin up. She thought she heard the phone ringing and then Luke appeared in the doorway with a cup of tea. 'Are we going to Blackpool?' she asked as he put the cup down.

'Yes, we are,' he said. 'First thing.' Sometimes her old artistic sense would jump out at him, as if it had waited.

'I hope you had a camera in that country you were in,' she said. 'Because that's a place for documentary.'

'It was all too real,' he said, 'though we struggled to know it.'

'You know fine well what's real. Did you and me not argue all day and half the night about it?'

'About what?'

'You know fine well. If you want a good photograph, stop messing about with models and start marching to a different tune.'

'Lovely.'

'That's what we believe.'

'Who's "we"?'

'Me and you and the rest of them.'

Later, in the other room, Luke lifted Anne's address book and sat in an armchair by the window. It felt good in his hands. He was amazed by the thickness of the book, all the names and numbers, scribbled or crossed out with different pens. Postcards were stuffed between the pages, images of young women he'd never met, a snap of him as a cadet, and, filed under T, an old black-and-white photo of a small boy. There were people in the address book from other countries, many in England: he realised as he flipped through the book that these were his grandmother's mystery people. Whole pages were crossed out and the word 'DEAD' was written in bold. His mother had told him to find the name Harry Blake and look for a Blackpool number. There were a lot of numbers for Harry, most of them with Manchester telephone codes, and though Harry was dead, none of his numbers was scored out.

'Who is it?' the voice said. He was speaking to a woman with a very thick Lancashire accent.

'My name is Luke Campbell. You don't know me. But I'm phoning on behalf of Mrs Anne Quirk.'

'Say again, love.'

'Anne Quirk. The photographer. She used to come a lot to the house, I believe. Not recently. From Glasgow. She looked after her aunts and would come for a break.'

'Mrs Blake!'

Luke hesitated. He looked at the address book and saw Harry's name again and took a breath. 'Yes.'

'Oh, Lord Jesus. *Mrs Blake!*'

'I'm her grandson. I'm afraid she hasn't been well. I was thinking of bringing her to Blackpool, to get her away for a week.'

'I knew something was going to happen today.'

The lady was cheerful and Luke thought from her voice that she was probably middle-aged. 'It's been ever such a long time since Mrs Blake were down.'

'Are you the landlady?'

'I'm Sheila, chuck. It was my mother that ran the house when Mrs Blake was down a lot. Oh, darling. I'm talking the 1970s and the 1980s now. Happen it's five years at least since we saw her. How is she?'

'She's not bad,' he said. 'She's forgetful. But things are changing with her flat up here. I'm phoning from Scotland.'

'From Glasgow?'

'No, from Saltcoats. Down at the coast. She's been living in a sheltered flat down here for years now.'

'Oh, aye. She flitted. I'm remembering now.'

'Did she come a lot?'

'Oh, when I was a girl, love. Mrs Blake would be down here

doing her work. Times have changed and we're not getting any younger. But her room's still here any time she wants it.'

'Her room?'

'Oh, aye, love. Mrs Blake's room. She's always had a room up the top of the house. Some of her things are still locked in the cupboards. It was always her room. Since before my time – during my mother's time. It's a little studio flat, actually. It belongs to her and just sits there.'

'There's nobody in it?'

'No, love. Mrs Blake was always happy for us to put guests in there during the season, you know, but we'd always keep it clean for her. We're not busy nowadays.' Sheila chuckled. 'We used to call it the darkroom. Was full of old photographs and trays and that. Aye, it was the darkroom. My mother would say, "Away up with the key and dust the darkroom, I think Mrs Blake's coming." Aw, I'm set up. You're coming down? I always loved Mrs Blake. You've made me feel all funny.'

Luke got all the details and answered the lady's questions about sheets and towels. 'Don't you worry, chuck. It will all be shipshape for Mrs Blake. God love her. The Illuminations are coming on later than usual this year, you probably know. Hurry down. It'll be lovely to see you both when you arrive. Only the other day my sister was asking about Mrs Blake and I told her, I said, I didn't even have a number. Aw, it's made me go all funny. My mother always said, "Now, Mrs Blake has paid for the flat, it's where she works, she's paid for it, Sheila, so don't forget to keep it good." Aw, what did you say your name was?'

He sat up through the night reading her letters, discovering his grandmother's younger self, a brilliant artist, someone ready to change the world. He examined the stamps, shuffled the blue pages, a privileged onlooker, wanting to make the connections and miss nothing that might bring her story to him as something he could keep. He saw her slow-burning heartache, her avowals of independence, her return to him, Harry Blake, whose divided nature dominated her life. His grandmother confronted him with an eerie, special power, this person he had loved all his life. He witnessed her spirit survive a series of trials he had never known about, and it made him love her more, while doubting the strength and consistency of men, including himself. He read the whole night long and in the morning he felt ready for the journey.

BEST BEFORE

She didn't know the word for it. Every time they left she felt the same way but she didn't know the word. It wasn't relief and it wasn't regret, but it contained both, the feeling she had when they gathered their stuff and took their coats and drove their cars up the Shore Road. Maureen would often stand at the window and wish she could call them back, start again, only better this time and happier. But the feeling only lasted until she dampened a cloth and she was now back in her own world, where no one could expect her to care about olives or fancy drinks.

Next morning she went to Anne's door and was surprised when the young man opened it. 'I just thought I'd pop in to see if Anne was all right,' she said, slipping the skeleton key into her pocket. 'And I brought in a wee plate of food in case she was hungry. It's nice stuff: Italian ham and these are called sun-dried tomatoes.' Luke brought her into the room and she immediately sensed a change.

'How are you feeling, son, now that you're back?'

'Everything's good, Mrs Ward.'

'Call me Maureen. You'll make me feel old.' She blushed because the young man had travelled the world and he probably hadn't time for neighbours. But her eye scanned the room and took in the bags and the ashtray. She didn't know how she would cope when Mrs Quirk went into a home. 'I'll miss her terrible,' she said to herself, and it showed on her face.

'I saw your family yesterday,' Luke said. 'Those big lads'll cause you a bit of trouble, eh?'

'Oh, they're lovely boys,' she said. 'So well-spoken. I mean, compared to how we were at that age. Very polite. They love to cook. Very busy lives they all have. They live in Edinburgh. My family's always busy with their jobs and everything.'

'Nice to see them, though.'

'Oh, aye. It's a breath of fresh air.'

Luke sat Maureen down and explained. He said Anne couldn't look after herself anymore. He knew they had tried, Maureen and the warden, to keep her here, but unfortunately the time had come to move her into a nursing home. He was going to take her down south, and while they were away the flat would be cleared. As he spoke, the tears welled up in Maureen's eyes and she pinched her lips. 'I'm not really sure,' he said, 'that Blackpool's the right place to take her. But she wants to go.'

'Don't mind me, son.'

'It's all right, Mrs Ward. You've been so good to my gran. And to my mum and me, as well. I want to thank you for the letters you wrote for her when I was out on service. It meant a lot.'

She cried very quietly, as people do who are used to crying and don't think it's a big deal. She just dabbed her eyes and pursed her lips after everything she said. 'Oh, it wasn't a bother to me,' she said. 'She's the best wee neighbour I ever had. A lovely lady was Mrs Quirk. And it's true, she wasn't herself and it's only been getting worse, hasn't it?'

Luke's phone rang and he put up a finger and went into the hall to deal with whatever it was. Anne was lying awake when Maureen put her head into the bedroom. 'Hello, Anne,' she said.

'Hello.'

Maureen lifted the blinds and talked about Scott and Jack and the family's lovely visit. She tucked Anne in and lifted an empty mug and when she came back from the kitchen Anne had her eyes closed again. Maureen continued to tidy, finding plenty to say to her sleeping friend. She heard when Luke was off the phone. Before leaving the room she folded some clothes over the chair and tidied the top of the bedside cabinet, bending down to pick up something from the floor, a severed picture of a little girl.

She had good days and bad days. The rabbit was the start of it all getting worse. Luke said he'd heard about it from his mother and saw it on the chair. 'I used to worry about the rabbit,' Maureen said, 'but really she wasn't so bad at first. She was still *at herself*. Still trying to put two and two together. But she's tired now, isn't she?'

'She's still with us, Maureen.'

'I know,' she said, wiping her eyes. 'The laughs we used to have in here. She'd have us all in knots. I'm not kidding you. The whole place. She could tell a story, God love her.'

'I'm gathering her things.'

'Right y'are. I'm going to help you get her ready for Blackpool, if that's all right.'

They spent the morning together. Luke squatted down by the fridge inspecting the stuff inside, the two shelves stacked with tins of soup and old jars of marmalade and whatever. 'Don't bother with that. I'll do all this with your mum during the week,' Maureen said. 'We'll organise everything. Just take what you need for the journey.'

'We're going to gather her work,' Luke said, 'the best of her photographs for an exhibition.'

'That's the people in Canada. The curator. I saw that letter. Has your mother come round to it?'

'We'll see.'

'It's so nice to have family, isn't it? Like Anne has you. I don't know where I'd be without my three. My daughter's a therapist. She stuck in at the school and now she's got a lovely house in Edinburgh. Ian, my eldest, he's a wonderful father. Very high up in IBM. He's all for computers. And the other one, Alexander, he's a nice guy, too. A bit of a rogue. You don't get two the same, do you?'

'I'm sure you don't, Mrs Ward.'

'They all drive. My God, it's like a car showroom out there when they all come to visit. But I often look at my three and say, Well, you didn't do too badly. It was a struggle but they turned out nice.'

They worked in silence for a while; then Luke said not to take down too many things before they went, so's not to alarm Anne just as they were setting out. 'You might want this,' Maureen said, handing him the photo of George Formby that had been pinned above the kettle. It had been there during all the time she had known Anne, looking down on them at night as they heated the soup and unfolded their lives.

Anne was squinting at the light and talking about holidays she had once taken with Harry. She would make comments and then go silent for whole stretches of the road. Luke found the moments of clarity really exciting. It was hard to admit that she was probably quite content generally and not just when she was talking sense and making him feel better. She seemed to admire the passing vehicles and she pointed without words at the mist over the houses on the road to Lesmahagow.

What is an adult? He'd always wondered. Was it a person who can speak when silent and who invents life, as opposed to just living it? At the wheel, Luke told himself she was the most adult person he had ever known. Some people would argue the opposite: that she had never grown up, that she had never faced things. But he was a happy student again, learning, over the miles, how to read a person by finding what character was available. She was brazen with words and actions no matter how baffled she seemed. No matter how far away she seemed, no matter how lost, she was with him, and he was determined to go with her as she slipped through the past into some brand-new element of the present.

'There's a reason I like you,' she said. She added nothing for a moment and then said it again. 'There's a good reason.'

'And what would that be?' he asked.

'You can read into things.'

'How so?'

'Stop fishing for compliments.'

'I'm not!'

'Well, then.'

'Well, what?'

'Then. Some people see a painting. They don't know what it is. Like that one of the place where the bombs fell.'

'What painting is that?'

'By the man who made his girlfriends have two faces.'

'Picasso.'

'That's the one. He painted a town.'

'Guernica.'

'Is that what it's called?'

'Yes, Franco bombed it.'

'I don't know what I was saying.'

'About how some people look at the painting of the bombed town.'

'They don't see the truth. They just see the paint.'

He took a deep breath. He knew as she reached for the words that she was uncovering the old ground of their sympathy. She'd used the example to him way back in the past – of how some people looked at *Guernica* and admired its form but couldn't understand why it couldn't just be an aerial photograph. But form told its own story, she used to say. And now she was struggling to say it again as the road vanished behind them.

'I don't know what it was about,' she said. 'Something about the man in Spain who never went on holiday because he hated photographs.'

'I know what you mean.'

'It's nice to have that, a person in your family who knows what you're talking about when you say about your work.'

'That's nicely put.'

'It's important,' she said.

'I agree.'

'Deep down,' she said.

'Drumlanrig Castle' flashed onto the windscreen with a load

of rain and grit. The wet cows in the fields got him thinking of those animals Scullion had liked to talk about, the endangered ones, the Asiatic cheetah, the goitered gazelle. When they passed another service station he thought of the melon stalls by the road in Helmand but the windscreen was now streaked with salt and he turned to her as she woke again.

'Vodka,' she said.

'Vodka? Well, not in here, Gran. I would've brought a hip-flask if I knew you were going to go all karaoke.'

'And tonic,' she said. 'Do we have that?'

After twenty minutes or so he turned off the motorway and stopped in Moffat. 'Turn around when possible,' the GPS said. Anne looked down at the voice and he turned it off.

'Who's that?'

'Just the map,' he said. 'We're on a detour.' He drove into the town and parked across from a cashmere shop. He noticed how curious Anne's eyes were and how young they seemed for a woman in her eighties. 'Let me put your gloves on.'

'Cold hands,' she said.

The hotel wasn't busy that afternoon and they got a nice table by the window. Luke came back with two vodkas and tonic and she smiled. 'I don't like that,' she said, poking at the lemon with a finger. He took it out and put it in his own glass and clinked hers.

'I'm glad you've got your gloves on,' Luke said. 'I don't want you leaving any fingerprints. I don't want people knowing I took my granny away and got her drunk.'

'People sing,' she said.

'Have you been here before?'

'This isn't Blackpool, is it?'

'No, Gran. You'll know it when you see it.'

7

THE DARKROOM

They crossed the border and Luke spoke of the letters Harry had sent to Anne in their early years. He wanted to help her picture things and put her story together, for him and for her, in readiness for Blackpool. He wanted to establish her good times. She didn't ask him how he had come to read them, as if their contents must have been known to him all along. 'So,' he said. 'You came to Glasgow from America about 1955. You gave up your apartment. You came back to look after the aunts in Atholl Gardens.'

'Is that my house?'

'Theirs. Up the West End.'

'Gardens.'

'That's right.'

'A lot of bedrooms.'

'You were looking after them. And after a few years you joined a photography club. Do you remember?'

'My Auntie Anna died.'

'You joined the Glasgow Camera Club.'

'Was it in a long street?'

'Sauchiehall Street.'

'I used to go there.'

'And in 1958 the club went to Blackpool. It was a trip. You all went down on a bus.'

'That's where Harry lived.'

'No. Harry lived in Manchester. You saw him give a talk at the Masonic Hall.'

'In Blackpool?'

'Adelaide Street. You went with your friends to hear him talk about photography.'

'Harry spoke.'

'Yes. He sent you a cutting about it that was in the paper. The talk was called "The Ethics of Documentary Photography". I think that's what it was. He wrote to you about it once you were back in Glasgow.'

'Is that right?'

'Yes.'

'My voice is different. I have an accent.'

'He spoke about Bert Hardy and the man who took the pictures of the children on the streets in London.'

'I know Bert Hardy.'

Bert phoned and said there's an editor from America who wants the youth of today.

Luke mentioned more dates and details he'd gleaned from the letters. He went carefully. Some made her nod, while others silenced her. Harry's letters spoke of these men, the Young Meteors he called them, who had a new approach to capturing life in Britain. 'And you kept going back to Blackpool. Did you have other friends there?'

'Harry lived near there, in Manchester.'

'Right.'

'We'd meet at Woolworth's. Under the clock tower.'

It was obvious from the letters that Anne had started taking pictures again when she met Harry. She was looking after the aunts, but she went to the Camera Club to escape, then Blackpool to escape, and the photographs she began taking were different from her previous ones. Luke couldn't understand what would make someone who had taken pictures of random objects suddenly want to photograph poor people standing at factory gates. He'd seen examples of both. He remembered seeing prints when he was a child and drawing on the back of them and never knowing where they came from.

She fell in love and it changed her style. That much he'd gleaned before they set out, reading the letters, thinking her thoughts. But he didn't know why she gave it all up again in 1963. He felt there must be an answer lurking quietly in her current confusions, but it lay deep down. When he was growing up he had questioned her about the photographs and she said it had become important to capture real lives. The conversations between them had made them close. It was like a kind of teaching. Yes, he thought: she gave him lessons in how to aim above himself. She made him unusual, and she helped him to believe that a readiness for art was equal to a capacity for life. 'Art is a moral adventure,' he said to her in his university days, and she'd winked at him. He'd got it. He was hers. She had no suspicion that this kind of hope would lead him into the world in a different way, but she supported him when he joined up, feeling it was all part of some secret quest that both of them understood.

'Harry liked the shipyards,' she said as they drove along. 'And they were lovely people.'

'The workers?'

'Harry and the men.'

'And did you sell any pictures?'

'Bert worked for the *Picture Post*.'

'And Harry would help you?'

'Harry was in the war. Same as you.'

The horizon was orange and the crowd at Blackpool was already on the promenade. He slowed the car and saw the dirty sea through the painted railings. He saw the North Pier, the new public art, the laughing men with their mates and their chips. A sudden feeling of excitement filled the air between them and Anne giggled before Luke turned right at a bookmaker's shop. It was late afternoon and the greyness of the town was expiring before their eyes. Kids had glow-sticks and coloured windmills made of light. 'In one hundred yards you have reached your destination,' the sat nav said. Anne sat up and craned her neck to see above the buildings.

'Tower,' she said.

He parked in York Street and Sheila answered the door. 'Ee, Mrs Blake!' she said. 'Lord Jesus, Mrs Blake, come in.' The paint was peeling on the door and the hall was filled with orange light as Anne stepped inside. Luke wasn't sure if she had any proper memory of Sheila, or her sister, who was standing in the hall with a tea towel and a glass of beer. But she certainly recognised the house and was beaming into the carpet and the stairs. It was as if they'd walked in on a family celebration. 'You'll see some changes, Mrs Blake,' said Sheila. 'Tony's a builder. He's renovated, God, a dozen times since Mam died. Did you know Mam died, Mrs Blake?'

Anne just smiled. She saw the lady talking and then wiping her nose. 'Don't mind me, I get emotional,' Sheila said.

'I know your mum,' Anne said.

'Of course you did. Of course. And she spoke fondly of you all her life, Mrs Blake.' The woman looked at her sister and bit her lip and took the towel to dab her eyes. 'Look, I'm away again!'

Anne stared contentedly down the hall, as if seeing a great deal there, her own life and the lives of other people, and when she turned to the old hall mirror she remembered Harry. She asked herself if the bed upstairs would still be the one they bought.

Luke went out to get the bags and stopped to look up. It seemed for a minute that everything around him was available, and he knew, just there, standing at the open boot of the car, that this was a night he would always remember. Years on, perhaps, when it happened he was sixty or seventy, he would remember York Street and the look of the promenade and would still see Anne in the lighted hall with those women. The house was tall and it looked like an old B&B with lace curtains. Before he went back in he thought about Harry's letters. They were full of advice about how she could develop her photographs, about how to work with contrast not only to get at life but to enhance it. Luke saw their past with Harry's voice in his head, and realised he could hear a conversation between them. When he brought the bags into the hall he could see Anne standing apart from the women, contented but lost, and he returned Harry's words to her without opening his mouth. *I love you darling for your promise and the things I never had. It takes courage to be a true artist and I don't even have enough to catch the train.*

Don't talk to me about what's true, Harry. No more, do you hear me? No more about the truth. Life isn't a photograph.

Isn't it, darling?

Anne reached over and touched some scarves that were hanging on the pegs, a few coloured scarves, one of them with mittens sewn in at each end. She took off her glove and gently put her hand into one of the mittens, and smiled.

'Will she be okay with the stairs?' Sheila asked.

'No bother,' Luke said. 'Thank you.' She reached up and kissed his cheek, then turned to Anne.

'I'm leaving you to get settled in,' she said. 'But I'll be here, Mrs Blake, if there's anything you need. If there's anything at all you want you just tell me, okay?'

Anne moved with surprising steadiness up the stairs and Luke came behind with the bags. At one point, on a high landing, she stopped and he waited a few steps behind. When he looked at her face he saw a trace of something young, as if the landing light knew and liked her. For a moment he imagined a young woman contemplating a fresh start, coming up the stairs with a vision of work and the man she loved. Did he ever come? Framed drawings of seabirds were hung around the landing.

It was warm inside, curiously warm, as if the heating had only recently been turned on again in the room. When they stepped inside Anne just walked to the middle and stopped. 'Don't put the light on,' she said. He closed the door and stood with his back against it and watched her step around the bed and put her hands on the window. The sky outside seemed blue in the way time itself can be blue, a perfect dusk with Blackpool framed in the windows. Anne looked out as if the scene was something she had always known. She didn't move. And after a moment she turned.

'Is that you, Harry?'

A MIND OF WINTER

The truth would keep for another day. Anne was sitting by the window with a cup of tea in her lap and Luke was unpacking the bags and placing things in the bathroom. On the keyring there were smaller keys, which Sheila said were for cupboards above the sink. She said they were full of old things belonging to Anne. 'Mostly papers, I think. My mother warned the whole family not to interfere with Mrs Blake's privacy.' Luke asked her why her mother was so strict about it. 'I'll tell you when we sit down and have a drink, love. Your grandmother was good to us. She was good to us and we don't forget.'

He'd never seen one before, a bedsitter. That's what it was, a fine old bedsitter in Blackpool. The bed was under the windows and was made up with a fresh white eiderdown. There was a table with two chairs and a vase of roses Sheila had placed there. Anne bent down to sniff the flowers and she said how nice and warm it was in the room. Along the wall on the other side was a bed settee that Sheila had made up for Luke. The light was dim and perfect, Anne thought: just enough to make you concentrate on the view, because that's what you came for. 'I'll tell you,' Anne said. 'We got a lot of things wrong but we got a lot of things right.'

'Oh, yes?'

'Because we knew what to look for, just like you.'

'Why do you say that, Gran? I'm not a photographer and I never did any of the things you did.'

'Yes, but you've got the spirit.'

'That's nice to hear.'

'Some of them said there was . . . that's right . . . justice in it.'

'Justice? That's a big word.'

'That's what it was,' she said. 'Making it real.'

She rocked a little in the chair. She rocked and the movement gave something to her words and to the evening light that came from the window and made a pattern on the bed.

'Are you all right, Gran?'

[253]

'I could just sit here.'

Luke pulled a bottle of Talisker from his rucksack and poured himself a decent measure. Sometimes whisky is just right for finding and knowing the heart. Across from the bed, two large photographs hung in simple frames. One of them had a label saying '*Winter, Fifth Avenue*. Alfred Stieglitz' and the second showed the old Wills cigarette factory in Glasgow, a flyover and a motorway in the foreground. He knew it from walks his gran took him on when he was a child.

Two full bottles of bleach stood in the sink. Luke didn't know for sure that other people often stayed here, but the feeling was confirmed when he found some loose Argos bags in the wardrobe and a Zippo in a cereal bowl. It was a guesthouse and the landlady had said rooms could be scarce in Blackpool in the summer months. What Luke found harder to understand was why Sheila and her family would've kept faith with 'Mrs Blake' through twenty-odd years of her hardly ever being here. Had she phoned them regularly when her mind was right? Had she come on trips without saying anything to anyone back home?

He bent down to see the books. Roger Mayne: *London Photographs*. Mark MacDonald: *The American Still Life*. *Darkroom Handbook and Formulary* by Morris Germain. On the bottom shelf, he found another series and he put down the glass. They were his university books. Here they were, all the stuff he had studied for his degree, the novels, the textbooks, set out next to each other. Good God. *The Trumpet Major*. Seeing them together gave solidity to some part of himself that he'd never considered defined. Here it was: personal history. He had met the world with these books, and seeing them together made him nostalgic for a person who was once keen to be transformed. Long before he became a soldier, the mystery of life was all in the mind, and now his books were physical evidence of what Anne once called 'your itinerary'.

He looked over to where she sat. She had preserved what she could of his young mind's entanglements. Up to a certain point she had kept pace with what he was learning and she must have known he would travel into other worlds, as she had, into fresh landscapes with their own souvenirs. She had taken steps to know him in the real time of his experience, not because she knew better but because she loved him.

'You're something else,' he said. And when she turned it was as if the holiday spirit rested with her.

'It's a nice night. Can we go down?'

You could hear voices on the street. You could hear the crowd gathering and the car horns. He picked out one of the books and it fell open at a place held by a Glasgow train ticket. It was something he'd loved when he was eighteen, 'The Snow Man', a poem by Wallace Stevens that he'd never forgotten. 'One must have a mind of winter,' it said, 'To regard the frost and the boughs of the pine-trees crusted with snow.'

THE ILLUMINATIONS

They weren't in a hurry to cross the road. They let people pass in front of them, moving faster, girls with buggies, men with beer. Anne was actually laughing: she pointed to a cockles-and-mussels van as if wonders would never cease. She said the Tower Ballroom was once on fire and if you wanted to know a nice shop in Blackpool it was the Camera Corner. She moved in and out of lucidity, in and out of herself. They strolled along the dark street and she appeared completely unbothered by the darting children and the girls in cowboy hats.

'Mods and rockers,' she said. He didn't know why she said it but it didn't matter. The tower soared above them. The crowd poured into the road and the kids were excited. Luke found a bench on the promenade with a good view of the bandstand, the compère and his teeth and the microphone up to his chin. 'Quiet, everybody!' he shouted and you could hear the bleeps of the coin machines behind the sudden hush. 'Welcome to the world-famous Blackpool Illuminations. With one switch, ladies and gentleman, we will light the city from Squires Gate to Redbank Road, over one million individual bulbs and strips of neon!'

Luke had once seen a lit-up Ferris wheel on the cover of a book, the yellow lights revealing a face in the dark blue magic of the sky, and he thought of it again on the prom at Blackpool. He was sure that the lights were made to reveal them all. Waiting for the switch-on, the crowd grew nostalgic and swayed as one, seeming to sense an unknown social purpose in the loveliness of the spectacle. The everyday street lamps of Blackpool appeared in those final minutes to concede their own dullness in the face of what was coming, and they dimmed. 'Have a wee drink, missus,' said a drunk young man behind them. Anne smiled up at him and took the cup and stared at it.

'Is this mine?' she said.

'Pear cider. Top gear. Get it down ye, missus.' Anne put the cup to her mouth and the man seemed pleased and Luke just shook his head and laughed. A blonde pop singer jumped up and down on the stage and blew a kiss to the cheering crowd. Luke put his hand down to take Anne's when the countdown got low, squeezing it gently. The crowd was familiar with this annual spectacle, the Illuminations, yet the sense of anticipation seemed palpable, as if it was happening for the very first time. The pop singer hit the button and light travelled up the tower and spread from there like a beautiful, endless halo over the whole city. Anne stood up. The bulbs going towards the sea were perfect dots of red and they swung above the crowd. Luke's stomach lurched to see them, the red dots going into the dark, but when he looked in other directions he only saw people laughing and hoisting their kids. Gold light was falling from all the buildings and it fell on Anne, too: he could see it reflected in the wet surface of her eyes. Her face showed not only the happy time she was having but all the happy times she had ever had. He leaned over and put his arms around her. 'I'm so glad you came with me. So glad.'

'It's nice here, isn't it?'

The sky was something else. As they walked on to see the illuminations beyond the North Pier, Luke thought of how the sky had looked above Kajaki the night they finished. He'd heard the last of the grenades and the fighting was over and when he looked up, he felt there was nothing but cold stars.

They went through the crowd and Anne put both hands on his arm and they walked slowly. Children darted past them and around them and the movement seemed to please her, as if this was what children should do on a night like this. They came onto the North Pier and he felt the heat of the many bulbs. They walked among the old slot machines, peep shows, one-armed bandits. How to Choose a Sweetheart. What the Butler Saw. Ghost Story. She touched each of the booths as if she knew them. And the one called The Gypsy she especially liked: a lady with a headscarf of coins dispensing predictions from behind glass.

Look at the sunset, Harry. And she says, she says . . . You don't need a camera for that.

Some things you just remember.

Life isn't a photograph, Harry.

Isn't it, darling?

They walked further down the pier and stopped to look back at the tower and the lights. Luke could see blue reflected light on the ridges of the sea. A man was playing a tin guitar next to one of the sweet kiosks and Anne pointed to him as they passed and squeezed Luke's arm. 'We used to go and see all the groups that played,' she said. 'Those four boys with the haircuts. The drummer was nothing to look at.'

'Did you go to the pubs?'

'Harry loved the bars,' she said. 'One of them used to put a monkey on the counter and you'd feed it nuts.'

They sat quietly, watching the lights.

'Do you want chips?' Luke said.

She nodded.

He brought them back and they sat down on one of the white iron benches. Up on the promenade a tram was passing encased in neon and it was playing the kind of tune you used to hear on the radio. She didn't look up and Luke could see she was all about the chips. With the colours around them and bulbs lit for miles up the coast, Luke wondered if Blackpool could be seen that night from the moon. A minute later the fireworks burst over the Irish Sea. She looked up, laughed again. Luke felt himself melting away, a snowman on the bench, sitting in for someone else. There was nothing beside her but the essence of Harry.

He breathed out. She would never know. But he'd learned from the letters that they weren't married and that she had spent many of her holidays waiting for him. Harry Blake was married to another woman and they had three children and he lived with them in a house in Manchester. All the stories she built around him came from a hope she had, a dream she made, but it was really an affair that proved impossible. He only came to the bed-sit when it suited him. It then occurred to Luke, sitting on the bench amid the lights and the smell of vinegar, that the letters had stopped when Anne was pregnant with his mother. Harry Blake, his grandfather, the great Harry, had left her in the lurch, and that was the thing she could never say.

BOSSA NOVA

Anne wanted to remain in the bar downstairs with Sheila's family. She wanted to ask Luke if that would be all right, but instead she just smiled at the mirror and walked down the hall while he was hanging up the coats. They were about to go upstairs when Sheila emerged and took Anne's hand and said she was having none of it. 'We're a long time dead, aren't we, Mrs Blake? Come into the lounge and have a glass with the girls.'

Anne sat with a vodka and tonic. The bubbles were nice and she liked the voices of the people. Sheila's family were all good at laughing and they sat at a round table, balloons taped to the wallpaper, while a man played an electronic keyboard. Anne said: 'Bossa Nova.' Then she stared at the beer mats, wondering if Harry would know where to find her. Behind the bar was a popular print of a crying boy and Anne fixed her eyes on it and felt it was a cold winter painting like ones of New York. Luke asked Sheila whether she'd mind if he went out for a couple of hours.

'Of course, love! Away you go and enjoy yourself.' She gave him a shove and took a gulp from her glass. 'A young man like you should be out causing a rumpus on a night like this.'

'Are you sure?'

'Away!' she said. 'I'll make up your bed in the darkroom and you can just climb in later. Away and do your thing. You don't have to pass the evening with blob-mouths like us! We'll look after Mrs Blake and get her up to bed.' He looked at Anne and actually saw her contentment, her sweet attention, float in the air of the room without quite landing anywhere.

'It's nice here, isn't it?' she said.

SPROGS

Flannigan was standing in the Washington. He's one of those guys who knows how to be good-looking as he waits at a bar. It's the stance, the confidence, the all-round readiness with the glad eye and the lip. Luke stood at the door and shook his head at the whole performance. 'Is that an AK-47 in your pocket or are you just pleased to see me?'

'Hey, dickwad,' Flannigan said, going for the shoulder hug. 'You're even uglier than you were in the sandpit, Captain. How's it shakin'? And I thought you only went to the classy places.'

'I do. This is old school.'

'It might be old school but it's full of losers. Look at the state of that fucken disaster over there.' He pointed into the corner of the pub, where Private Dooley stood grinning by the jukebox.

'Of all the chairborne motherfuckers in the history of the British army, if it isn't our own Captain Campbell.'

Luke walked up to him. 'Fuck sake, Doosh,' he said. 'I didn't know you were coming.'

'No. We kept it on the down low. I only emerge from the chatroom when I know the real Neanderthals are coming out. So when he told me it was Blackpool, I said "What! Awesome. This boy's getting on the first Ryanair out of here." So what you drinking, you lightweight?'

He ordered three pints. Three whiskies.

'I'm insisting on Irish,' Dooley said at the bar. 'None of your fucken sheep-shagging Highland cheeky water tonight.'

'Listen, dude,' Luke said. 'I know you live on the other side of refinement, but everybody knows Scotch whisky is unsurpassed, so suck it up, bitch.'

Flannigan laughed and nodded to Dooley. 'Oh, we've missed the old brain-box, haven't we, Doosh?'

'Fucken A,' Dooley said. 'You've left us with the fucken horror-pigs, man. I'm talking shite-hawks.'

'The other side of refinement!' Flannigan said. 'You crack me up, Jimmy-Jimmy. It's all tossers in the platoon now. We left all the education in a pool of piss in Kajaki. Fucken lady-boys giving it Super Mario on their da's old mobile. I'm telling you. Boys about thirteen they're sending us. Miserable as fuck at the base since you and the major fucked off to join Destiny's Child or wherever the fuck you've been.'

Luke noticed Flannigan was now wearing a fancy watch, the same as Dooley. They clinked pints. 'Get your big fat gypsy lips around that, Dooley,' Flannigan said. Dooley drank, then rolled up his sleeve and revealed a new tattoo. He said he and Flannigan and Lennox got them in Dubai on the way back and it was the most painful one he ever got. Luke leaned in and Flannigan also rolled up his sleeve. It wasn't a very typical tattoo, but it was identical on each of them: a short ridge of mountains and a bird above the summit with extended wings, the bird showering down heavenly light and the words 'Free Afghanistan'. Luke wondered if everything in life was about the image you were left with. Nothing might change on the ground but the movie could be made and the pics could whizz into cyberspace. The turbines at Kajaki would never leave their wrappings but these young men would carry these pictures to their graves.

'Very nice,' he said.

'Here's to it,' Flannigan said, lifting his glass. 'And good riddance to all the bullshit.' They battered through several rounds, talking about the regiment and what they'd been doing since the tour. They all avoided it for a while and then the business of Scullion came up.

'I think he was a mess going into it,' Flannigan said. 'Like, fucken totalled in the brain. He gave Rashid the baton and that guy was one turncoat motherfucker from the off. You could see it in his one good eye: ANA my arse, he was Terry, bitch, and riding hard for the biff, bang, pow. Remember? Remember his face, all kissy to the major, but underneath, man, he was plotting the whole time to fuck us right up. Rashid, man: to him it was open mic night at the Hotel Taliban. It was, as well. And he threw the whole fucken section into the mosh pit.'

'Not just us,' Dooley said.

'He had them watching us for miles.'

'The boy from the Caledonian . . .'

'Miles, man.'

'The boy he shot.'

'Fucken radioed ahead, didn't he, Rashid?'

'It was a day out, man,' Flannigan said. 'The fucken white rovers and the heavy metal. It was a day out. You could never have known it was going to be an ambush.'

'Stop,' Luke said. He was still nodding after he said the word and put down his whisky. 'It was a massive fucken error. A massive fucken error, do you hear? I knew the major wasn't stable. And I knew I wasn't fucken doing that well, either. And we were your superior officers. And the whole day and the whole fucken next day was bad shit from beginning to end. The boy's dead and those kids in the orchard are fucken dead, too.'

'Captain . . .'

'We can't fix it.'

Dooley waited a moment and then the all-nonsense version of his life kicked in and he smiled. 'I just want to clean my gun, Captain,' he said.

'Good on you, Doosh.'

'I'll never forget it,' Flannigan said. 'Remember the way the major shot him through the eye?'

'He was dead by then,' Luke said.

Dooley spun his empty glass on the table with a finger. 'Was it the good eye or the bad eye he shot?'

'They were both bad,' Flannigan said.

'I'm not so sure,' said Luke. 'He saw plenty we couldn't see.'

The privates were young enough to allow every military event to embolden their spirit. That was all. To them, the captain was a defeated man, but they wouldn't show it: they loved Jimmy-Jimmy. More than any test at home, more than any big event in their own lives, the events on the way to Kajaki would define for them what it means to have your courage measured and tested against other men. They had grown sure in their hearts that they knew more about real life. The captain was now adrift in the civvies' lightweight world, so the night was about nostalgia, and that was fine. It was what the two soldiers had expected. 'He's never coming back,' Flannigan said when Luke went off for a minute.

'What, from the bogs?' Dooley said.

'No, you dickwad. To the army. He's moved on, lad. He's not coming back and that's it.'

'Wish it was me,' Dooley said.

'No, you don't.'

Three pints. Three rums.

'Christ on a bike, Jimmy-Jimmy. Rum! Have you gone and bought your sailor whites and joined the fucken Andrew?'

'Bite my todger, Flannigan.'

'They will, man,' Dooley said. 'The Andrew, the British navy. They'll chomp off your birthday sausage and spit it into the English Channel.' He leaned over to clink glasses again. 'Come on,' he said. 'Let's get debaucherous.'

'Debauched,' Luke said.

'Whatever.'

They drank in silence for a moment and then Dooley stuck his hand in his pocket and produced a bag. 'E, anyone?'

'Shocking behaviour,' Flannigan said. Then he poked his fingers into the bag and took out two pills. He swallowed one immediately with a mouthful of rum and the other he slid into the breast pocket of his jacket.

'Later,' said Luke.

He wouldn't have said no point-blank. Easier, and less judge-mental, to drink your share and subtly dodge the pills. Most of his years in uniform had been spent artificially high or falsely tranquil, states that appeared, with hindsight, to mirror the campaigns themselves. He was the old dog now and in his mind he was easing towards the door. People would say it was all part of the general disorder to have smoked pot with the privates, but such people don't know the British army.

Another few drinks, then up to the darkroom. That was his plan. He didn't want to bail too early but he knew as he sat there that his compass was set for the off. Listening to himself banter about the army and its characters, its duties and compensations, he saw again how much he had once wished to live like a good, sensible machine. But he'd failed at that. He wanted them to know the failure was his. There was no such thing as an ordinary life. He'd learned that from Anne and he learned it from himself. You can only live a life proportionate to your nature. And he was calm. He was getting there. He could imagine a future less taken up with loss.

'With a drink in you, Flannigan, you're an absolute pest to all people of the female persuasion.' Luke said it as they walked down the promenade and Dooley joined in.

'He's even worse on E.'

There was scarcely a group of girls on the prom that Flannigan didn't stop and ask for a light or the way to another bar, allowing Dooley to bring up the rear with his shorter presence, ogling away. A posse of lip-glossed girls in dangerous heels told them to shut up a minute and listen. What they wanted was the Metropole

Hotel, down at the end of the prom, open late, where they had a great karaoke bar and a disco.

'Are you the shy, sexy one?' said a girl wearing something debatably more than a bikini, tottering up to walk next to Luke, offering him the dregs of a Bacardi Breezer.

'I'm their dad,' Luke said.

'Hey, slappers!' she shouted at the group in front. 'Wait for me and Dumbledore. We going up the Metropole?'

'Yo, bitch,' a girl in front shouted. 'Get your skinny arse in gear.'

'Is the place still open?' Luke asked.

'The Metropole never shuts.'

'But isn't it old people there?'

'Oh, aye. Like wheelchairs. You'll love it.'

'And why would you want to go there?' he asked.

'Three answers: cheap drink, cheap drink, and cheap drink. Plus the oldies go to bed and there's a fuck-off dance floor.'

'Can I ask you a question?' he said.

'Go for it, soldier.'

'Are those eyelashes real?'

'Definitely,' she said. Luke saw the waves rolling up and flattening on the beach, reflecting the lights, the hotel. 'You don't seem like a squaddie,' she said. 'They do.'

It was foldaway tables in a smelly ballroom. It was a handful of pensioners and a compère with a microphone, a tanned man in a nylon suit that came from another era. He was Scottish and he seemed delighted that 'the young team' had arrived and that the girls were already dancing. Luke went to the bar and came back with a tray of drinks. The Scouser was complete. 'All I want is a big juicy pint.' We're on a big night out, he thought, the music inside him, and these girls are definitely with us. 'Give it here,' he said, taking the pint and tanking half of it down. 'I love beer, me,' he said, putting down the glass and wiping his mouth. 'I love beer and I love Blackpool and I could drink a barrel.'

'Check him out,' Dooley said. 'He's having it.'

'I'm having it large,' he said.

The bass was loud and it filled the room. They settled round the table and the girls came back and forth to have swigs from their bottles and to open and close their handbags and fix their make-up. Other groups of young people arrived and the wallpaper began to gleam. 'It's just bollocks,' Dooley said. 'They have a trial and these three NCOs get off.'

'Who?' Flannigan said.

'The two sergeants and the corporal. Budgies.'

'What?' Luke said.

'The Royal Welsh. These three guys get acquitted the other month. They were beasting a young lad and he died.'

'It was a normal beasting,' Flannigan said. 'The boy was a tit. He was undergoing a reprimand.'

'Fuck off, Flange. The guy was twenty-three.'

'So what?'

'So everything, you twat. The guy was twenty-three and got a bit pissed at a party in the mess. He fucked about with some office equipment and he got smashed for it. But it was too much. They marched him out the next day, it was thirty degrees Centigrade, and they beasted the kid until he had a heart attack. That is totally fucked up, man.'

'If you don't want a good rifting, don't be an arsehole,' Flannigan said.

'This was on the news?' Luke asked.

'Yeah,' Dooley said. 'On the news. The adjutant captain told the three fucking bears, these feather-heads, the NCOs, to melt the kid out on the parade ground.'

'Where?'

'Lucknow Barracks.'

'Right.'

'It was over the top.'

'Oh, fuck off,' Flannigan said. 'How many times have you been trashed up and down the mudflats, Sponge Bob?'

'Not for hours in that heat. Not when it's boiling outside and I'm still dehydrated from the night before.'

'Dry your eyes.'

'No, seriously, Flange. That's fucked. The main guy who did it was the most hated dude in the battalion. A real fucken drill-pig with a hard-on for sprogs.'

'He wasn't a sprog.'

'He was twenty-three.'

'So what, our kid? That's old. You do shit, you get beasted. My dad told me they once beasted him from arsehole to breakfast-time just for dropping his stick. So stop fucking moaning, and bring on the rums.'

'The kid had traces of ecstasy in his bloodstream,' Dooley said, turning to Luke. 'He was off his tits when they were beasting him out there. Fucken animals. And the guys who did it get off because everybody thinks they're a bunch of hard-asses who can do what they like.'

Flannigan was looking at the girls. 'You can't have a military without militarism,' he said.

Luke put his drink down. 'And you think they deserve the Victoria Cross for that, do you, Flange?'

The two just stopped in each other's eyes, the younger man's pupils so large and so ready for action, engulfed by the moment. Luke paused to see just how far he would go, but Flannigan was biting his cheek and he came back with nothing. 'The boy was about the same age as the guy we lost,' Luke said. 'Remember him? The kid we lost in that stupid ambush? That's a fucken life, mate. And when you don't do the right thing and you rub out a life you've lost your decency.'

'Captain.'

'Just saying. That shit happens: you've lost your decency.'

'All right, sir.'

'Do you get me?'

They went quiet. 'I'm just messing,' Flannigan said. Then after a moment one of the girls came up to the table and pulled him by the arm. He looked up at the other men with a grin, and said, 'I'm off my face.'

'Go and dance, Flange,' Luke said. Flannigan saluted and was never so much himself as then. It would be a long road for him, thought Luke. He was vulnerable, his friend, a veteran of bad dreams, made for toughness, inclined to ruin. 'Away and dance, ya big daft bastard.'

'We're okay, aren't we, Captain?'

Luke smiled. 'Of course we are. Go and enjoy yourself.' Flannigan shrugged and turned out his hands.

'I get better-looking every day,' he said. 'I can't wait for tomorrow.'

Ten minutes later, Dooley was dancing so much in his seat that it seemed he could just take off. He got some water and then high-fived the captain. 'I miss my wife,' he said. 'You know she's a registered nurse, Jimmy-Jimmy?'

'A staff nurse, eh. She's qualified.'

'I'm going to make her proud, Captain. I want to become sergeant and then we'll buy a wee house.'

'That's a goal, Doosh.'

'Awesome.'

Luke sensed he wanted to say more. More perhaps about life in general and whether the captain had somebody special and would he like to settle down with her someday and buy a house? It was all on Dooley's face but he was too shy of the captain's privacy. Dooley wished he could summarise their friendship, and his emotions were rushing into the moment. But he wasn't easy like the Scouser when it came to feelings, so he just put his arm around the captain and said it was a great night. 'I feel fucken magic,' he said as he got up and joined the others on the dance floor. Luke watched his comrades-in-arms and thought them the best young men in the world. He realised how young they were and put two twenties under Flange's glass.

As he walked home, he looked out and saw a hill of deck-chairs stacked at the end of the pier. He looked over the sea and wondered if it might be one long dream, his family, his friends, the lives they tried to live. It was strange, but the dark water seemed experienced and alive, as if conscious of the people on the shore, as if it could see to the heart of things. The Ferris wheel was still but the lights blinked as he walked down the Golden Mile. There was no sound but the sound of the waves. This was Blackpool. The lights were part of the town but the moon was simple and white up there, and he loved how it shone without frailty over the sea and the coast.

Sheila stood on the second-floor landing with a mug of Lucozade in her hand and a cigarette going. You could smell bacon all the way up the stairs and it was a fine morning if you believed the sunlight. 'Oops,' Sheila said, spilling a drop, her hands busy as she spoke, wreathing the air with smoke and fizz. 'This carpet needs doing. Happen it's only three years old. Would you believe that? It's these young ones coming up and down in their boots. My mother ran it old-fashioned, you know, kippers for breakfast, two to a bed but she'd want to see the wedding ring.'

'She was strict, then?'

'Always wore a pinny, me mam. But good to the guests. She put a wireless in every room.'

'Who did the bird drawings?' asked Luke.

'That's Father. He loved birds. All his books are still in the cabinet down in the lounge. He was like Mrs Blake, an artist at heart, really. When she pointed a camera at something you really knew it was captured.'

Luke was pleased as he listened. According to Sheila's mother, who didn't have kids at the time, Mrs Blake was famous one summer for haunting the cafes of Blackpool. It must have been the summer of 1962, she said. 'The town was full of teenagers, they were always fighting and some of them drove their scooters up and down the front, and Mrs Blake was making a study of them.' Apparently, the darkroom was like an art gallery at the time, rows of photos pinned up around the walls and the smell of chemicals, good God, Sheila's mother thought she might have to say something. 'But Mam knew it was important for Mrs Blake to get on with her work,' Sheila said. 'She photographed all these youngsters and their hair.'

You couldn't resist Sheila. She said her mother spoke of all the places where Mrs Blake used to take pictures. Putting down the mug, she began to count them off on her fingers. 'The Shangri La Cafe on Central Drive. The Hawaiian Eye Cafe in Topping Street. Redman's Cafe in Bank Hey Street. The Regal Cafe on Lytham Road.'

'Wow,' Luke said. 'You've some memory.'

'And Jenks Cafe in Talbot Square.'

He took care to close the door. He put down the newspaper and the groceries and turned to see Anne sitting up. He made tea with lots of milk and he buttered the rolls and put ham inside them. Anne liked them, chewing quite happily, introducing sips of tea after every bite. She saw the day when she would run down to get the breakfast for Harry. And when she came back carrying the sausages or the bacon wrapped in paper, the bread, the brown sauce in a bottle, she would hesitate at the top, knowing he was inside the darkroom waiting for her. She could picture it: how she stood there, how she kissed the door before going in.

'Did you black out the windows?' she said to Luke.

'To let you sleep?'

'For processing. Harry and the blankets. Just like they did in the war. Harry was in the war, you know.'

'So I gather.'

'He flew planes.'

Luke tried to imagine the darkroom as it used to be, when it was invested with all the ambition in the world. He tried to see it: a studio, a love nest, a place of light music and waiting.

Anne had spent time with the women. You could tell. She seemed restored a little to her old self, less agitated after an evening of vodkas and songs down in the lounge. She spoke more that morning. It was as if her spirit had been encouraged by like-minded souls, the sort of people who take the elderly at their own estimation. The women loved memories of every kind and they weren't minded to frisk them for accuracy. 'Harry had medals,' she said to Luke. 'Because of the war.' She paused to have another sip of tea. 'And you're in the war, aren't you?'

'The war's over now,' Luke said. 'For me, anyway.'

He took her cup and plate. She began to doze and before long she was snoring into the pillow. He stood in the room and felt odd to be at the centre of Anne's lost horizons. The night before, on the way back to the guesthouse, he imagined the sea must be conscious, and now the room had memory. These thoughts were strange expansions of an old faith, like ghosts returning to their rightful place and living now with him, part of the person he'd become. He felt watched in the room as he cast his eyes up to the ceiling, just as he felt watched when he walked along the prom. Looking up, he saw the shape of dead moths in the frosted bowl of the ceiling light. They had flown too close and been there for years. His phone was buzzing in his pocket but he assumed it was the boys and didn't answer. He felt he had said goodbye, so when he took out the phone and saw texts and missed calls, he just pressed the button and turned off the phone.

He opened the cupboards. The files were dusty, the labels peeling. One cupboard was full of glass beakers and chemicals, droppers, lengths of tubing and packs of Ilford paper. His gran once told him that Harry mixed chemicals the way people in films did cocktails. Sheila knocked on the door at one point and suggested he go downstairs and have a coffee. Her sister was with her and they carried fresh towels. It was another aspect of Sheila's character: the no-nonsense approach to difficult necessities. They wanted to wash Mrs Blake and take her into the toilet. 'Go and have a cuppa,' she said. His gran woke up and stared at them. 'We're due to throw a good old Pippa Dee party in here, aren't we, Mrs B?'

Anne slept again that evening with the bed freshly made and the radio turned up a little. He'd arranged with Sheila to stop down for a chat. When he turned up in the hall at seven o'clock she already had her coat on and announced that her sister would go up and sit with Anne. 'I need a touch of fresh air,' she said. 'You don't mind, love?'

'No, let's go,' he said.

Walking along the prom, Sheila said Anne was still lagging from last night's festivities. 'The lounge got lively after you left,' she said. 'She'd a few drinks, Mrs Blake. A dark horse, that one. Confused, though, eh? Doesn't really remember anything in order. Gets mixed up. She kept thinking I was my mother and in the end I just said fine.'

'It's got worse.'

'Mind you. She still comes out wi' things. And you'll be like, "Lord Jesus, where did that come from?" Then she goes back into herself.'

'That's the pattern.'

'Bless her.'

They walked to the Pleasure Beach. Sheila was telling him how a popular ride called the Derby Racer had been scrapped a few years back. 'That was something in its day,' she said. 'You could hear the squeals for miles.' The lights still amazed Luke but there was nothing harsh in them any more, no reminders of tracer fire. It was just life repeating itself in a northern town and he was glad to be part of a million bulbs.

[274]

'Sheila,' he said. 'Why does she have that room?'

'It's like I told you,' she said. 'Your grandmother actually owns that bit of the house.'

'You didn't say that.'

'Well, she does. She rented it at first. Just a bedsit, you know, when she first started coming to Blackpool. But then my mother and father hit rough times. Mrs Blake's aunts died one by one up in Glasgow and eventually she got some money and one of the things she did . . . she bought that part of the house. It wasn't a lot of money. But my mother was in a lather at the time and your gran has always helped with the bills coming in. Off-season we used to sit and wait for Mrs Blake's cheque. And it would always come until it stopped about a year ago.'

'I always suspected something. My mother knew. She wouldn't really talk about it.'

'We're going back forty-odd years,' Sheila said. 'I was only a baby when the arrangement started.'

They sat down on a bench. He could tell Sheila wasn't sure how much he wanted to know. More revellers went past and she sent a smile after them, girls in pink safety helmets.

'Tell me about Harry.'

'Oh, Christ. Where do I start?'

'I know he's my grandfather. I know they were never married. It's nice of you to call her Mrs Blake.'

'My mother always insisted on that.'

'I know he was married to somebody else. Before coming here, I read some letters she kept. Letters from him. He was married to somebody in Manchester. Not Anne. Did he let her down?'

'It was awful.'

[275]

'Maybe I shouldn't have brought her here.'

'Never think it was wrong,' she said. 'In spite of everything she always loved it here.'

'That's what I hoped.'

'That man Harry,' she said. 'He were bloody deluded. That's the word, isn't it? Deluded. My mother always said so. She got the full story about that man, and, one time, she and my dad went over to Manchester to give him a piece of their mind. They went to his office.'

'He made things up?'

'All those stories about the war. My dad was a lot older than my mother and he did fight in the war, so he couldn't stand all that stuff that came out of Harry Blake's mouth.'

'About flying spy planes?'

'Oh. Spy planes. He'd worked in a chemist's shop in London processing film. That was his war. A dodgy ear is what he had. The marvellous Harry with all the medals. And then, according to my dad, he got himself into Guildford College, didn't he? A course in photography. The first, I think. I don't know how he got in. Night school, I suppose. Guys who had flown in the war went there because it were near the base. That's where Harry got all his stories – from those men.'

'And Anne knew?'

'She always knew. But she loved him. And when you love somebody that much, well, you need to believe them, don't you? She wanted to protect him, or something like that.'

'And he met Anne here? It said in the letters.'

'That's right. He was teaching photography at the college in Manchester. The end of the 1950s this was.'

'She came to a lecture of his.'

'I think that's right. Dad had all the facts.'

Luke leaned back on the bench. He told her it looked like Anne's life had been one long bid for freedom. From her own family in Canada to the career in New York. Then from the big house in Glasgow to Blackpool. She was always trying to rescue her youth from her family, trying to rescue her talent. 'It sounds like he was her last chance,' he said.

'Maybe,' Sheila said.

She lit a cigarette and blew out the smoke, narrowing her eyes at the sea as if it helped her remember. 'Three children he had,' she repeated. 'And my mother said he courted Anne, you know, here in Blackpool, taking her out and that, introducing her to people. And you can imagine what it must've been like for Anne to have someone just then. It was all domestic stuff in Glasgow. She couldn't leave.'

'But why not?'

'The old dears were bedridden.'

'But that wasn't her problem.'

'Apparently, it was. She'd promised her father. There was nobody else. Her family was all gone by then.'

'So Harry was a godsend? He knew about photographs.'

'Exactly. A godsend. He believed in her. My mother said she'd a lovely Canadian voice back then.'

'You can still hear it faintly. It's nearly seventy years since she lived in Ontario.'

'The accent's strong in Scotland. You're going to lose your accent if you stay there too long.'

'She still has traces.'

'I can hear it.'

'She got pregnant,' Luke said.

'She did, yeah. And you know what? I was telling you this morning about her haunting the cafes, taking pictures and doing work for a big magazine. My mother said she'd never seen her so happy as she was that summer. She'd got herself back. She was doing new things. It was looking great. Then she fell pregnant and he scarpered.'

'He just left?'

'He came back, but not much. There would be these long gaps. Me dad went looking for him. Harry was married, of course. He had the wife and the kids in Salford, as you say. I think my dad felt sorry for him, in a way. It happened to a lot of couples back then. Harry got Anne pregnant and then went back to his wife. I remember my dad saying that Harry was one of those people who live their lives through other people. All those lies about his war service and everything.'

'But he got her back to photography,' Luke said.

'That's true. He wasn't all bad.'

'And he loved her.'

'He filled her head full of dreams. But I'll tell you something: in all the years, she never spoke a word against him.'

'She was faithful to him.'

'Yes, she was.'

'When you read his letters,' Luke said. 'You see he wanted great things for her, things he couldn't get for himself. That's love, isn't it?'

'She had the talent.'

'He helped her become herself.'

'If you say so. He's your grandfather. And you're bound to want to see the good in him, just like she did. It's only natural.'

'Your own father—'

'He understood that people can get lost. To him, Harry was a smart fellow who just got lost in his own circumstances. He didn't like what he did – or the lies he told – but he believed that Harry was a victim of everything that happened at the time, just as Anne was.' She paused. 'It's not always the right people who take hold of your life. Half the women I know had men like that, but they got over them, and she didn't.'

'Well, she did,' Luke said. 'By turning him into something good.'

'Something better. She was an artist, after all.'

Luke considered it. 'The great Harry,' he said. 'She speaks about him with such reverence.'

'Well, that's the way she felt about him. He had a gift for making connections between people. People say he was a good teacher. He opened up something in her and if that happens, well—'

'It can last for your whole life.'

'In some cases, yes.' Sheila sniffed and pushed back her hair. 'Maybe Dad was right: you have to try to understand people like that, people who can't have the life they want and are always making it up instead or running away.'

'Yes,' Luke said.

'After a year or two, after she'd had the twins, they tried to make it work. They went on a few holidays together, him going up to Scotland in secret, you know, behind the wife's back. The twins were very small. And it was on one of those holidays—'

'Wait a minute,' he said. 'You said "twins". My mother had a twin?'

'You didn't know, love?'

'What?'

'Mrs Blake had twins.'

'That can't be true,' he said. 'Are you sure?' Sheila dropped her cigarette and leaned forward to step on it.

'Yes,' she said. 'Mrs Blake had twins to Harry Blake. A boy and a girl. The girl was your mother and the boy died in an accident.'

Luke just stared into space. He felt he'd arrived at a familiar place of which he had no knowledge whatsoever. 'Holy fuck,' he said.

Sheila felt it was getting cold so they went for a drink in the bar of the Seabank Hotel. There was a screen on the wall which advertised the bus-runs coming from Scotland. Pick-ups in Partick, Airdrie, Motherwell, Dundee, Irvine and Ayr. The hotel was full of elderly people. 'It leaves me not knowing who I am,' he said.

'What?'

'The information about the boy. About my mother having had a brother.' He took a sip of his beer and looked up at the screen and then back at the table, and when he sighed it seemed to include everything. 'When you think of it, Blackpool's really a suburb of Scotland, isn't it?' he said.

'It's a suburb of a lot of places.'

He waited. 'What happened after the boy died?'

Sheila's mother and father had tried to help Anne because she couldn't cope. The aunts weren't fit enough to help her with the child and it was after they died that Anne bought the room. 'Your mother was left with the neighbours in Glasgow half the time. Poor girl. I think Mrs Blake paid them to look after her. Lord Jesus. It's all me mam and dad spoke about for years. Mrs Blake felt it was her fault, but it was nobody's fault. Never really got over it. She stopped taking pictures.'

'That was the cause?'

'That was it. She turned away. And for years she would come down here. She was always by herself.'

'In the darkroom?'

'Stopping there for weeks at a time.'

'And he didn't come much, did he?' Luke said. 'That was plain from the letters, too.'

'Once in a blue moon,' she said. 'And it always made her happy. And that's why you can't really judge: people come up with all kinds of arrangements to make sense of what happens to them. You can't judge. I think the poor fellow didn't know what to do. I can picture him then myself. The 1970s it was. I looked out one night and saw him chipping stones up at her window. His lies had gone all the way into her life, but he really made something of her and she wanted him. So she was Mrs Blake and he was a war hero and the boy was never mentioned.'

'I see.'

'And your mam was hardly mentioned either.'

'But how did he die, the boy?'

She sat quiet for a moment. 'Weird, isn't it, how life turns out?' she said. 'My father died the same year as Harry, 1976. You find people are just people, after all. And we all have stories.' She took out a balled-up napkin from her sleeve. 'I remember Dad telling me the story about what happened to the boy. It was on one of those holidays up in Scotland. Harry was trying to spend some time with Anne and the twins. His second family. And he drove them out to some place. My dad said it had been snowing and they were on this particular road up there, this famous place, where, if you stop the car and take off the brake, you get the illusion of rolling uphill.'

'The Electric Brae.'

'That's the one. An optical illusion; you're supposed to see it in the daytime but it was dark by the time they arrived. Anne told my father they could see a bonny white rabbit on the road. Harry was driving or I think my dad said they were just rolling with the handbrake off. Harry told the children to look at how the rabbit's eyes were shining. He turned the headlamps off, you know, so they could see it better. But then a car came out of nowhere and they were in the middle of the road with no lights on and the other car went straight into them. And that was that.'

'Oh my God. That's horrific.'

'The boy died. His name was Thomas.'

Luke shook his head and stared at the table. 'That was the end of it.'

'For Mrs Blake, yes. And for your mum. My dad said Harry was like a bird, actually hollow inside, you know, hollow in his bones. He wasn't a bad man. He just wasn't there. Wasn't solid. And she found a purpose in covering for him and was happy in her own way.'

'It's hard to imagine,' Luke said. 'I knew they had their own secrets, but . . .'

'It's what they're made of.'

'All of us,' he said. 'We were all made of it. They never said anything.'

'Never once?'

'No,' he said. 'Not in so many words. When she got ill, she started to talk about a rabbit, and . . . well, maybe that's the rabbit in the story. For the last year, so much of her talk has been about Harry and her past.'

'Happens his wife had known about it for years,' Sheila said. 'Knew about his affair. Put up with it. But when he died she wouldn't have Anne at the funeral. She just came down from Glasgow and sat in the room with all her things. I remember that week, seeing her on the front steps. She was on her way onto the prom and she tied her headscarf and tried to smile. Gave me fifty pence. Her eyes were so sad.'

Luke was sorry and was lost for a moment. He knew it was monumental, what Sheila had told him, he knew it explained the people he loved. All his life his family had been moving, perhaps invisibly, perhaps unknowingly, around this terrible event that happened years ago and that was never mentioned. His hand shook when he reached for his pint, as if this secret about Anne had suddenly recast the story of his childhood and his mother's childhood too, changing everything.

'In Canada they want to put her into a show,' Luke said. 'The best of her photographs.'

'Do they?'

'Aye. They've got some pictures she did when she was young and they say she's one of the pioneers.'

'Lord Jesus,' Sheila said. 'That was the life she wanted. My mam and dad would be so proud of her.'

IF

Life had been rearranged, and always is.

If Luke had opened the newspaper he bought that morning, if he had listened to Anne's radio or turned his phone back on, he would have learned that Major Scullion had taken his own life the day before. When he did see the news, he was shocked, though it didn't really surprise him. He believed that Scullion knew he would never make it to India. If he hadn't seen him on that hill above Kajaki, if he hadn't seen how he rushed into the mortars in one last gasp of the old soldier, he might have been unable to believe it. Scullion loved poetry and he made others love that thing in themselves. Luke tried to calm down and salute him. He wrote a text and sent it to each of the boys:

Remember Charlie at his best. He wanted intelligence back in the game.

Flannigan texted back the regimental motto.

Veritas vos liberabit.

25 AUGUST 1962

In one of the locked cupboards, Luke found a stack of Airfix models of World War II planes. He opened one of them, a Lysander, that was half-built inside the box, a small tube of glue partly squeezed out and gummed around the cap. A betting slip from Ladbrokes was wrapped around the cockpit; it had something written on it in faded blue ink, a few notes about the closing of the Hawker factory at Squires Gate. Luke supposed it was Harry's hand and the remains of Harry's hobby.

The ladies had been in that morning. Anne was sitting up in the chair dressed and washed, listening to the radio, wearing a clasp in her hair and some carpet slippers Luke had found at the back of the wardrobe. Sheila was right: she looked beautiful and seemed content, just listening, occasionally looking over and saying something odd. The girls wanted to take Anne to the Regal Cafe and soon they arrived carrying shoes and winter coats. Anne wanted the scarf with the gloves sewn in and soon they were off down the stairs. 'Are you all right, Gran?' Luke said from the door. And when she looked up she was smiling like a gala queen.

'Shake a leg, Mrs Blake,' Sheila said. 'There's nowt in the world between us and a peach Melba.'

He placed the folders and boxes on the sink unit and then he spread them on the floor. He first opened a green, cloth-covered album labelled 'Menier Camp, 1948'. He got lost there, a pier with boats at an angle, *Light through the trees, Clifton Falls*. The album was filled halfway and ended with a group photograph, showing some young women lined up against a boathouse with linked arms. *Monica Eames, Reva Brooks, Ruth Silverstein, Diane Arbus, Anne Tully, Anne Quirk*. Her teenage face was so bright and he stared at the picture and wondered about the others, those young women. He wondered if their lives had gone elsewhere, too.

He didn't open any cans or the backs of any cameras. He didn't know about photography but he understood that new light isn't good for old film. The contact sheets were filed and so were many of the actual photos, some of them yellow or dark or only half-developed, with smears. One of the prints, labelled *Jane Street, New York City*, showed a box of soap powder sitting on top of an old washing machine. He'd never seen anything like it, so real and yet so imagined, in a realm of its own. He began to set some of her photos aside but he kept getting caught up in one of her new ventures, a make-up counter in Harlem, a row of prams in the Gorbals, a carpet factory in 1956, and, finally, what he'd been looking for, 'Teenagers, 1962'. He also found an old copy of a woman's magazine, fresh as the morning. It had a knitting pattern attached, but on the cover, above the title, he read five words written in pencil. 'I was his spiritual wife.'

'Teenagers, 1962' was thick with prints. There were contact sheets and in a number of round tins he imagined there must be negatives. The photos showed groups of young people with slick hair and cigarettes. A girl wearing lipstick was kissing a boy with lazy eyes. Luke noticed the slim ties on the boys and the way the girls laughed and he noticed their hands and the light coming off a vinegar bottle. Each print was described on the back and some of them had been taken in dark alleyways or out on the pier during the day. And then, towards the back of the folder, there was a group of twenty-four colour prints, sharp and clear as anything, labelled '25 August 1962, The Beatles, Fleetwood Marine'.

'These are edited. More on rolls. See contacts.' This was the folded note acting as a clip. In one of the photographs the group was smoking as they leaned from the tower; in another they ate in a seedy canteen. Here they were, the four boys in the back of a van, huddled round a newspaper, as if the words really mattered. In the nicest of them all, John Lennon lay on a sofa writing a postcard. Anne had caught the mischief in his eyes as he glanced at the camera. Luke had to stand up, astonished at the scale and the mystery of what she'd done. He lifted them again. He wanted to race down the stairs or throw open the window and shout, but he just paced the room. He just stood in silence. For all her mistakes and her bad luck, she had managed this. She had taken these pictures and kept quiet.

The boy died and the gift was gone. Harry was away, and maybe her talent departed along with her belief in herself as a mother. Luke couldn't say, and, for all he knew, Anne had simply set out to preserve an ideal version of herself, someone the world couldn't spoil, or recognise, or celebrate, or even know. She left herself behind in a room, and that way survived her own potential, until her mind began to fray. He cried into his hands and an hour passed when he had nothing to add. He just sat in the gloaming of these facts and wished he had known a way to rescue her from her secrets. When he returned the prints, he stood over the boxes, and he lifted a single photograph from the side of one of them. It showed the shadow of a woman and her camera against a grey pavement. *Self-portrait*, it said in Anne's hand, the same hand, he knew, that once wrote the names of the talented girls at the Menier Camp.

On his way down the stairs, Luke phoned his mother and was glad to hear her voice. 'At last,' she said. 'We were beginning to wonder what happened to you. Do you never answer your phone, Luke?'

'I switched it off. Sorry.'

'What's the weather like?'

He looked out and felt time was nothing at all. They were all young. A feeling of optimism fell from the deep past. There was a way to work out how to pity his mother and not blame her for needing it. He felt the impulse to move on, to improve things, to put what strength he had at the service of his family, without pausing for explanations or statements or reckonings.

'Clear today,' he said, 'but really windy.'

'Did you see the lights?'

'Aye. It was fantastic. All the way down the front. I think she's having a nice time. No stress, you know? Just peaceful.'

'Well,' Alice said. 'It's her place.' He waited. 'You know she's spent a fortune on it, don't you?'

'I suppose she must have, over the years.'

'A fortune. And she didn't have a fortune. But that's what she wanted to do and she did it. You could buy a house for the money she's spent on that flat. But she's never wanted my opinion. The bills alone . . .'

He realised he was listening to her for the first time. She rattled on, and she would always rattle on but Luke wanted to listen, just as he wanted to think the best of Charles Scullion. It wasn't justice and it wasn't quite understanding, but Luke was glad he had come to Blackpool. He wasn't sure if he'd ever mention what he'd found out. He could see her as a small girl with a dead brother, a boy she perhaps knew little about but who took up all the love, and Luke could see – even as Alice's old defences rose to meet him – that her mother's investment in her own life had left Alice out in the cold. It had shaped her life, and of course she couldn't bear to think of Harry or to admire her mother's talent, or to talk about the boy.

'I never liked Blackpool,' she said. 'And those people down there never had anything to do with me.'

'I'm sorry,' Luke said.

'Don't know what you're sorry about. It's her money to waste any way she wants. I've long since given up. And I bet you she's not even getting a rebate on her council tax. I mean, it's a second home, isn't it? That means she should be getting something off and it's always been a mystery, that flat. She's helped that family out, you know.'

'They're nice people.'

'They're *lovely* people,' she said.

'And they kept her room together.'

'She paid their bills.'

'It doesn't matter, Mum. They kept it together for her. Two generations of that family did that.'

'They probably had lodgers in.'

'It doesn't matter. Honestly, it doesn't. Her stuff was locked away. And they weren't interested in it.'

'What stuff? Her camera stuff?'

'Everything she had.'

She went quiet and he could hear the years over the phone and all the dismay of her unspoken life. 'Maybe sometime we can sit down and talk,' he said. 'Just you and me, Mum. It's going to be just us when this is all over.'

'I'd like that,' she said.

'And we're going to be fine.'

She cried very quietly into the phone and he just let her cry and said there was all the time in the world. When she stopped crying some of the old hardness came back and he saw her as a person who had always been bullied by the powerful stories that surrounded her and diminished her. 'I suppose you've been treated to my mother and father's great love story,' she said.

'It's not just about them,' he said. 'They've had their turn. And we'll see my gran through this time, but we'll do it together, okay?'

'Did something happen to you in the army, Luke?'

'We all have bad things to answer for. I've seen some evil and I might have done some, too. But you learn to forgive. You can even learn to forgive yourself. And I believe Gran would say that if she could.'

'I'm no angel,' she said. 'None of us is.'

'We're a family,' Luke said. 'Just a family. Sheila's people are a family but so are we. Let's do what we can.'

They just breathed for a moment into their phones and then Alice sighed, as if the practical world called to her.

'We put Mum's furniture in storage,' she said. 'The boxes too and the suitcases from the bathroom. The lady next door's been really great. She did it all with us.'

'How is Maureen?' he asked.

'Oh, she's fine,' Alice said. 'Has all her Christmas cards ready to post. Already! She said you can't be too early with things like that. Christmas, would you credit it? The presents all wrapped and sitting in a bag by the front door. She loves it. She loves all the drama. "Families!" she says. "Families!" One minute she's looking forward to seeing them at Christmas, getting the train, and the next minute she can't wait until it's all over. Oh, but she makes me laugh. I was just saying to Gordon: You can't keep up with people. You may as well not even try, because it's different every day and you never know about people's lives, do you?'

'I'm glad she helped, though.'

'Oh, she was brilliant.'

'That's good.'

'The warden, too. They all pitched in.'

'You could run a war, Mum.'

'That'll be the day. They wouldn't want the likes of me running up and down the place.'

'I've seen worse.'

Neither spoke for a moment and it was easy to wait and to think and let things settle. Alice sighed.

'Do you think she senses what's happening?'

'No,' he said, 'but I'll tell her eventually. I just want to give her this time. A bit of time down here. A day or two.'

'Blackpool was always her favourite,' Alice said, and Luke's heart went out to her. He could hear the hurt, the nervousness, fading into relief. It was somehow easier now for her to talk and he knew she wanted to say more. 'She never really wanted children. Her life had been held back enough. She wanted him. And Blackpool was the place where she hoped it would all come together.'

'I'm sorry, mum.'

'Ah well, Luke. It's over now. And I'm glad you're there with her.

'You're here.'

Luke drove to the Regal Cafe and found Anne sitting at a corner table with the women. He hadn't known it before, but his gran obviously liked women's company and had missed it – the girls at the Menier Camp, her aunts in Glasgow, the neighbour Maureen. She was laughing with Sheila and her sister when he came in and she touched the clip in her hair when she saw him and she looked up at the coffee machine. 'We were just on about Woolworth's,' Sheila said. 'Your gran mentioned it and we were just saying there was nothing left of Woolworth's nowadays. Harriet used to have a Saturday job there, didn't you, Hats?'

'I got fat on the Pick 'n' Mix,' she said.

Luke paid the bill. He turned to smile at Anne and the two sisters. 'I want you all to come in the car,' he said.

'Fab,' said Sheila. 'Are you taking us for a drive or something?'

'I want to take you to the Fleetwood Marine.'

'Is there something on?'

Luke said it was just a wee outing – nice for Anne and it wasn't far. And so they drove up the coast and passed the factory for Fisherman's Friends. 'That's very nice,' Anne said. 'The sweeties.'

'I could never stomach them,' Sheila said. Then she pointed

out the changes, new houses and spots where things had been demolished or done up. They came to a place close to the beach, an art deco building that seemed brilliant and white against the green hill behind. They got out and Anne took Luke's arm as they walked over the car park.

'I know it here,' she said.

Luke smiled. 'Do you now?'

They walked into the foyer. Luke didn't know why he felt as if a season was over. There was something new about her, and he admired how confidently she walked on the blue carpet, the look on her face and the feeling of her arm inside his.

'I danced here,' she said.

The print gets perfect with dodging and burning. Conceal this part to make it lighter if you like, and this corner, this bright place in the picture, expose it for longer, my love, and after it goes dark we can go to bed. All will be well. Come here, Harry. I waited up. This is your home tonight.

The girls looked around. They didn't know about Anne's pictures taken here once upon a time. They just thought it was a treat to see the place in the daytime like this. 'I could tell you a few stories,' Sheila said with her give-all laugh. 'We used to come here to raves in the 1980s and the building would be packed to the rafters. Don't get me started.' There were posters up for dance shows and comedians.

'Palm trees,' Anne said.

This is your home tonight.

She touched a pillar on their way along and was delighted with it, and when her grandson leaned over and kissed her cheek she felt sure they'd spent years together. There was nothing left to be afraid of and the sky was blue as they came outside and put down their bags by a signpost. The arrow pointed to Cleveleys and Blackpool, the sand was dark brown and the sun took them by surprise. Sheila lifted Anne's hand and then her sister took the other one and they led her all the way down to the water. Luke hung back by the wall and looked down at Anne and the women together in the wind. Their scarves were billowing around them and they shouted out when Anne's came off and blew into the air, the scarf going higher, the girls laughing as it stretched up and a hand reached out for the sun.